THE DEVIL'S ARTIST

A gripping crime thriller, burning with suspense

IAIN HENN

Published by The Book Folks

London, 2024

ISBN 978-1-80462-235-3

www.thebookfolks.com

*THE DEVIL'S ARTIST is the fourth standalone book in
a series by Iain Henn about a special FBI unit set up to
investigate seemingly unsolvable mysteries.
The full list of titles, all FREE with Kindle Unlimited and
available in paperback, is as follows:*

THE PIPER'S CHILDREN
THE WHISTLER'S OMEN
THE STORM KILLINGS
THE DEVIL'S ARTIST

*Details about these and Iain's other novels, the mystery
DEAD SET ON MURDER and the romantic thriller
THE GREATEST BETRAYAL, can be found at the
back of this book.*

"Can only have been painted by a madman."

(words etched in *The Scream* by Edvard Munch)

Prologue

The Artist

The young girl could never forget the sight of the boy falling through the air. Sometimes she would wake with a start in the middle of the night, sweat on her brow, a scream caught in her throat, a shriek that was silent in the waking world but ear-splitting in her nightmare.

She thought back to how she'd sat cross-legged on the forest floor, transfixed, frozen in shock. A wail had erupted from the boy as he'd plummeted, hitting the water, not with a splash, but a thud, as though he'd smashed onto solid ground. There were cries and screams from the others on the bridge.

She watched but the boy didn't surface and the ripples on the water, spreading like tentacles from where he'd hit, dissipated quickly as the current flowed.

Had he drowned? She looked across at the boys on the bridge but what could they do from up there? She squinted at the slope that ran down to the river from where the span of the bridge met the clifftop, wondering if anyone was rushing down to look for the boy but the sun distorted her vision and she wasn't sure.

She trembled and looked along the shoreline to where her friend sat nearby. Her neighbor. Earlier, her neighbor had given her a folded sheet of art paper and told her not to look at it.

"Why?" she'd asked.

"You'll see."

She'd slipped it into her satchel and then they'd sat by the riverbed, sketching the waterway before them. Now her friend inched back closer to her, showing her the current sketch being worked on.

The girl's eyes opened wide in confusion. "You drew the boy falling?"

Her neighbor grinned and then nodded toward the folded drawing poking through the top of the satchel. "Open the one I gave you before."

The girl unfolded the paper and there, sketched in crayon, was the same drawing again, of the boy tumbling from the bridge. "You'd already drawn this... before...?" Her mouth fell open. She looked at her friend in amazement. "How?"

"I knew it was going to happen," the other child said.

Twenty-two years later

I can see the fear in your eyes, and I can hear the scream rising from inside. Same as the cry from the man in the classic painting. The moment when you realize that all the beauty in the world around you is collapsing. Descending into chaos and there's nothing you can do because you're not in control. You never were. The realization that this is the future that was always patiently waiting, the dark side of fate, pointing its long, bony finger right at you.

Your destiny – unchangeable, preordained – meeting you face to face.

The fragmented images seem out of place in the corners of my mind. There are just twenty-four to forty-eight hours before it all plays out.

I could link the images – the whole picture is taking shape – but it's the individual pieces of the puzzle that fascinate me. How one step leads to the next. How every action has a consequence.

I make sense of these impressions by painting them. Not with a brush. Not on canvas or parchment. Not anymore. I need to feel unrestricted. Anything and everything is my canvas.

I paint the terrors as I see them unfolding.

PART ONE

Chapter One

Marjorie Graham didn't imagine she had only five minutes to live when she stepped onto the bus for her early morning commute. Minutes later, the 7.20 a.m. to Seattle, running ten minutes late, was on the Interstate 5 and Marjorie was on her phone, chatting with her sister, as she did every morning. It was their ritual, trading banter as they had since their childhood when they'd grown up, further north, in the wide-open spaces of Skagit County.

The traffic was heavy and the bus was approaching the point where an overpass crossed the highway. High above the Interstate, a gravel truck turned onto that overpass. Careering out of control, the truck crashed through the overpass's side barrier at over 100 mph and nose-dived onto the highway below, shattering and sliding across two lanes. Several vehicles on the highway crashed into it. The thunderous thud of metal clanging against metal filled the air, followed by the grinding screech of dozens of tires as successive cars squealed to a stop, many colliding with one another.

Marjorie, like all the other passengers, shot forward in her seat as the bus driver slammed on his brakes. The bus skidded and swayed but unavoidably it plowed into the ruined truck. The impact sent the bus rolling onto its side. It cut across the adjacent lanes, as another three cars slammed into it.

Marjorie barely had time to register her shock as the bus flipped and slid. She was thrown from her seat, her head cracking against one of the windows.

Marjorie's sister was stunned by the chaotic sounds she heard coming across the phone line. She cried out, "Marj? What's happening? Marj?" She pressed her phone anxiously against her ear, hearing only a strange, distorted cacophony of distant sounds coming over the line.

Trooper McCall was one of the first to arrive at the scene. Weaving his way on foot through the morass of vehicles that were now queued back for miles in all lanes, he was faced with a tableau that would be burned into his memory for the rest of his life. Sedans and SUVs were twisted out of shape, strewn across the highway, and in the center of it all, the misshapen hulk of the truck, with its gravel load spilled around it like a moat.

Minutes later, ambulance crews arrived and the first of the medevac choppers flew in to airlift the injured to Seattle's Harborview Medical Center.

Marjorie Graham was one of seven people on the bus who could not be resuscitated by the first responders. She was declared dead at the scene.

Chapter Two

Three days later

Day One

A painting can reveal the hidden depths of its artist's soul. And if that is the case, then something about the style of this piece revealed a conflicted spirit. A psyche that was sorrowful but also filled with rage. Intimate while at the same time out of reach. The painting was of a series of fragmented images, blending in a montage of warped lines, its colors the dark hues of sunsets and nightscapes.

I had never seen anything like the work of this graffiti artist, sprayed on the brick surface of a building in a Seattle alleyway. Conveying a sense of something chilling.

A photo of the mural was on the large screen in our main ops room. Nothing like the kind of thing I was usually called on to look at with the Unsolvable Crimes Unit. So visually arresting, it was hard to draw my eyes away from it.

I stood with my three colleagues around the horseshoe-shaped main console which housed the cutting-edge supercomputer Zoe Marshall had named Themis that was ringed with keyboards and monitors, the larger screen positioned higher on the wall directly above.

"What are we looking at here, Zoe?" I asked.

"Focus on the five images in this mural, Ilona," Zoe said, the fingers of her right hand doing their familiar dance across the keyboard as her left hand flicked through her thick, dark curls.

There was always a hyperactive energy coursing through Zoe but it was an energy I knew she'd learned to harness, as she was now, directing it to unraveling the different threads of information that were unfolding, courtesy of Themis's data.

At the center of these interwoven images was the cab of a truck smashing through the barrier of a bridge. We now knew that bridge was an I-5 overpass. Beneath this, two images – one of the crumpled front part of a bus and, alongside this, that of a single, lifeless outstretched hand. Protruding haphazardly from the right side of those two images was a partial, fractured piece of a license plate. And fused into the images from the left side, as though looking on in horror, a screaming man with his hands raised, cupping the sides of his face, covering his ears. His eyes open wide in torment. An image we had all seen before, the subject of a famous, classic painting.

"We all saw the news coverage of the accident," Zoe continued. "All the major elements of the accident are depicted in this painting."

She zeroed in and enlarged the battered piece of the license plate.

"What's more, the three numbers we see there are the last three numbers of the truck's license."

"All of which the artist could have got from the news," Marcia Kendall said.

"Yes, but not two days before the accident occurred, which is when this mural was seen and photographed."

"What? How did we come across this?" Marcia tilted her head, peering over the top of her spectacles.

Marcia Kendall was an FBI translator and analyst, who also worked with the UCU as a backup to Zoe in operating Themis. A calm and warm presence, the mother of three now-grown boys, Marcia had also been a wise and welcoming friend when I'd most needed it.

"Our old friend, Aiden Sharpe," Zoe said. "He's planning a series of special podcasts about sub-cultures, starting with graffiti art around Seattle. Beginning with a kind of pilgrim's progress, walking from one side of the city to the other. Photographing and shooting videos of every piece of graffiti art, large and small – not the government-commissioned pieces, but the random works painted by the unknown graffitists out there. So, there is a time stamp on the photos taken with his phone cam, and this one was stamped approximately forty-eight hours before the overpass crash."

"And I understand it's not the only one," Will McCord said, drawing his gaze away from the mural on the screen, and glancing at me. "There's another."

Will was the supervisory special agent in charge of the UCU. I'd known Will a long time and we had been romantically involved when we'd worked together over two years ago, before we went our separate ways. Since joining him on the UCU team, our old camaraderie had quickly fallen into place but we'd kept our relationship professional.

"Let's take a look at the other mural," he said to Zoe.

A moment later, a different mural filled the screen.

This time, six images, all part of a montage. These drawings depicted a portion of a street sign, a fire, a hand clenched around a steering wheel, a section of what appeared to be a propane gas container, the corner of a document with the symbol of a crown and the letters *S* and *O*, and the same screaming man seen in the first mural.

"The time stamp on this photo is twenty-four hours after the first one," Zoe said.

"And?" I pressed. I could tell from the looks on Will's and Marcia's faces that I wasn't the only one who was impatient to know what this was all about.

"A day after that mural was photographed, a car crashed into a propane gas tank attached to a factory in Everett. Caused an explosion and the factory went up. The factory was evacuated, and the fire was contained, but not before one of the workers inside was overcome by fumes and died later in the hospital. The driver was also killed in the explosion."

"And I'm guessing the factory was in a street that matches the sign in the painting," I said.

"You got it."

"What about the crown insignia and the lettering?"

"The crown is the logo of Sovereign Insurance, which also explains the letters *S* and *O* we can see beside it. We're just seeing a small portion of a document but that is precisely how those elements are positioned on the company's letterheads. And it turns out that the factory's insurance is with Sovereign."

"Even if it's hit by a car, it's unusual for a propane container like that to catch alight," Marcia said.

"They believe it was because the driver was smoking," Zoe said, "combined with a fault in the tank which had been raised by the factory staff but hadn't been acted on by the management."

"A perfect storm," Marcia observed, adjusting her glasses on the bridge of her nose as she squinted at the screen. "But how could this graffiti artist have painted random elements like that, and before any of it happened?"

"The same goes for the overpass disaster," said Zoe. "The truck crash was caused by the driver's heart attack and no one could have known the bus would be on that part of the Interstate at that precise moment or that those events, both completely random, would intersect with one another."

"The murals seem too specific for this to be coincidence," Will said. "Maybe Aiden Sharpe is mistaken about when he took the photos, could it be that the time stamp on the phone is faulty? Or even that he doctored it?"

"Why would he do that?" Marcia asked.

"Sharpe's a canny operator, always looking for an angle to promote his podcasts."

Knowing what a stickler Will was for tying things up rationally, I couldn't resist a friendly jibe. "We can't have Will believing in coincidences."

"Not when it comes to criminal investigations, although even I have to admit there are exceptions. Regardless of that, there is no crime here, other than reckless driving."

"Never thought I'd hear you admit there could be coincidences," I needled him, suppressing a grin.

"Good to know there are still some ways I can surprise you." He suppressed a grin of his own.

I was reminded of the easy banter we'd shared when we'd been colleagues in a different division, before the change in both our professional and personal relationships.

Zoe shot both of us an inquisitive stare. "You two okay?"

Although she'd been working with us for several months, Zoe most likely hadn't seen us loosen up and engage in a light-hearted exchange to this extent. When Will and I were on the job, we could be intense. Certainly, we were always focused on the cases to the exclusion of all else. As was Zoe. Although we all knew she had a mischievous imp inside her that wasn't adverse to jumping out from time to time.

"This isn't the first time Themis has highlighted something that isn't a crime," I said.

"Graffiti on public or private sites *is* a crime," Zoe corrected me, although she knew what I meant. "As you know, once there's a report in the system, it's accessible by Themis. The algorithms are programmed to zero in on anomalies. Unusual details, no matter how small, that are similar across different cases."

Themis was programmed to analyze the details of every newly reported crime across all the states. It searched for similarities between the new cases and older ones, both open and closed. Themis's specially designed set of algorithms then predicted which of the new cases had the highest likelihood of remaining unsolved.

"You think this is something for the UCU to look into?" I asked.

Zoe swiveled in her seat, spreading her hands. "If the time stamp proves correct, then how could this artist possibly have painted these disasters before they happened? I've always been on the fence when it comes to people being psychic, but this doesn't make sense. But there's something else. These murals conveniently appeared just before Aiden Sharpe began documenting graffiti art, and they appeared in the very first places he covered. Which meant he would notice the connection to the accidents and report it. It's as though the artist wanted Sharpe to photograph the murals and notice the parallels."

"Why has Themis flagged it?" Will asked her.

"Themis sees the similarities in the two murals reported, and then the discrepancy in the times between the murals being sighted and the disasters. It isn't programmed to legitimize psychic abilities. It recognizes instead the lack of any evidence or theory as to how this is possible. It determines the possibility of criminal action and the likelihood of the known facts remaining unexplained."

I looked at one of the smaller monitors on the console, which displayed the police reports. "Aiden Sharpe reported this to the SPD and supplied them with copies of his photos," I said, scanning the details. "Detective Paul Radner filed a report but it's clear the SPD didn't know what to make of it."

"Radner would be cautious about something like this," Marcia said. "He doesn't know Sharpe well enough to rule it out as being a hoax, even if he can't fathom how it's been done."

"And I can't say we know Sharpe well enough, either," said Will. "It seems a hell of a lucky chance that as soon as he starts shooting graffiti, these murals, supposedly painted by some kind of Nostradamus, happen to show up. And the simple fact that both paintings have that well-known screaming man means the whole thing's likely to go viral on social media, helping to promote his podcast further."

Marcia nodded. "He couldn't buy that sort of publicity."

"No, he couldn't," Will said.

We had encountered Aiden Sharpe during a previous case. His podcast, *One Voice*, covered true-life crime stories. What made it stand out from the crowd was Sharpe's combative, activist stance on law-and-order issues. He encouraged people to call in anonymously with details of crimes that they couldn't report to the police because they feared for their safety or reputation. Sharpe would then report the details on their behalf as well as present them on his program.

Sharpe's charismatic flair was something Will, ever the pragmatist, was wary of. His gaze shifted in my direction. "There's no evidence of a crime or criminal intent."

"I agree," I said.

I was the second-in-charge of the UCU and Will and I made joint decisions on which cases the unit would take on. We needed to adopt significant cases as part of our remit to demonstrate the validity of the Themis AI program in lowering the unsolved crime rate. But at the same time, while some of this could be passed off as coincidental, the fact that the license plate and the street sign were eerily accurate to the incidents was like a red flag to me, as I could see it was to Zoe.

"However," I said, "before we dismiss this, you and I should talk to both Detective Radner and Aiden Sharpe. There's something strange about this, and..." I paused, choosing my words carefully, "I think we all want to be certain there isn't someone out there, psychic or otherwise, who has information that could help prevent further incidents like these."

I wanted to look Sharpe in the eye as I questioned him. My impression of the podcaster was that, regardless of how much of a showman he was, he would not stoop to perpetrate a stunt like this. He was genuine and deeply passionate about using his podcast to help combat crime.

From the expression on his face, I was expecting some serious blowback from Will. It didn't happen.

"Point taken, let's get some clarity," he said.

Chapter Three

"I had the same thought," Detective Paul Radner said. "Had to rule out the possibility that Sharpe himself, or someone else, was perpetrating a ruse of some kind." He was responding to Will's comment that a hoax had to be considered, with Will citing the example of crop circles and how some people went to elaborate lengths to fool others. "So, I sent the photos to the lab for analysis." Radner shifted in his chair. "But the photos are legit and there's been no tampering with the time stamp."

"Have you seen the murals?" I asked.

"No, but I sent a couple of my officers out there. They're real and, I'm told, the artworks are even more impressive than they appear in the photos."

Even as he spoke, I had to will myself not to let my gaze wander to the framed photograph of Radner's daughter, Sarah. It was a few years since the teenager had become involved with a daredevil group of urban climbers and fallen to her death from a great height. I knew Radner had wrestled with his grief and that he'd devoted more of his time than was healthy, both on and off the job, clamping down on urban climbers around Seattle.

"What do you make of these paintings, Detective?" Will asked.

Radner gave a frustrated sigh. "Damned if I know. I can't see how some of those details could have been as accurate as they are. Is there a graffitist out there who's also psychic?" He shrugged. "Got to wonder. And what's more, seems this person doesn't want any attention. Both of those murals were painted in spots with no CCTV."

"You believe in psychics?" I asked.

Radner bit down on the side of his mouth, scratching at his short-cropped, gray-flecked dark hair. "Over the years, Ilona, we've had occasions where self-professed psychics have come forward with information on crimes." He stretched, leaning back in his chair. "But the information didn't pan out in any of those cases. So…" He left the sentence hanging.

"It's the fact there isn't one, but two of these paintings," I said, "that's prompted us to ask a few questions."

"You can now make that three." Radner's response came as a surprise.

I leaned forward in my chair. "Three?"

"I'd instructed all officers to keep an eye out for any elaborate graffiti art, old or new." He swiveled his desktop screen so that Will and I could view it from an angle. "One of those officers on the beat saw a painting in the same style. This is the photo he sent through just a short while ago."

The mural depicted the silhouette of someone falling from a clifftop, the back of a pickup truck, a grove of trees, and the same unsettling image of a man, hands cupping his face, screaming in anguish.

"The officer asked the locals and verified the art had been on the corner wall of a café for over a week. And it wasn't hard to match those images to an incident from just a few days ago. A teenage boy, staying at his uncle's twenty-acre property near Mount Vernon, took his uncle's pickup truck and went for a joyride on the land."

"What happened?"

Radner raised his hands. "We don't know. The pickup truck was found parked with its front poking over the edge of a clifftop at the property. But the boy wasn't in it."

My eyes focused on one of the images. It wasn't hard to guess what came next. "The boy was in a gully at the base of the cliff."

"Yeah."

There was a brief silence and I did not doubt that the detective's thoughts had turned to his daughter's fall. The similarities would be gut-wrenching for anyone.

"The kid had a troubled background, he'd been in juvey before being released to his uncle's care. He was raised by a single parent and she'd since died. Even so, there was no indication of suicidal thoughts in the boy's past. We don't know if he jumped or if he was larking about and fell."

"You're certain he was alone in the pickup truck?" Will asked.

"Yes. His uncle saw him race off, then got one of his other vehicles and drove off to look for him."

I pushed a strand of hair back from my forehead and pressed my fingers to my temple. *Another random event.* "Not something a graffiti artist in the city could have known or even planned," I said.

Radner's tone betrayed his bewilderment. "No." Clearly, he was still processing the fact that he now had another of these anomalies on his desk. "What I can do is interview any kids who've been arrested for graffiti over the past six months or so. Ask if they recognize the artist's style and if they know who it is. Even if they know something, though, it won't be easy to get them to open up. Many of these graffitists are basically vandals. They're bored, frustrated, and hostile toward society. Especially toward cops."

"Keep us posted on anything you hear that's of interest," Will said.

"Your computer thingamy bring my report to your attention?" Radner knew that our unit drew on data collected by a specialized AI program but he didn't know any more than that.

"Yes," I said.

His gaze shifted between me and Will. "I gather you guys are going to look further into this."

Chapter Four

It was the discovery of this third mural, hot on the heels of the first two, that changed the nature of our inquiry. No longer possibly coincidental. So, what was it?

Like the first two murals, this third one had been painted in an area without CCTV. The graffitist didn't want to be seen.

Our next visit was to Aiden Sharpe, who recorded and transmitted his *One Voice* podcast from the studio-fitted garage alongside his home. He welcomed us with a wide grin, sporting his usual short growth of beard and receding hair close-cropped. He was dressed pretty much the same as the last time I'd seen him, in a GQ-inspired, patterned shirt and open jacket, with a loosely draped scarf. "Special Agents Farris and McCord. Come on in."

"You look like you're about to start recording your podcast," I said.

"No. But I'm always ready." He ushered us to pull up chairs but as we had on our last visit, Will and I remained standing.

"We won't take up much of your time," Will said. "We're here about the mural photos you took into the SPD."

"Not the sort of thing I thought you guys would be interested in. You know something I don't?"

Sharpe didn't know about the third mural, and we weren't about to tell him. He would find out soon enough. "Just an initial inquiry at this stage," I said. "If there's a hoax at play here, then that would be a serious matter." I watched Sharpe closely as I said the word 'hoax.' He didn't flinch or give anything away with his eye contact.

His shoulders relaxed as he leaned back in his chair. "Hoax? In what way is it a hoax? Those accidents happened and people died. How could anyone have known enough of the detail, before any of it happened, to paint those images?"

I let Will take the lead. "These murals began appearing just ahead of you undertaking this photo/video project of yours," he said. "The timing's curious. Had you announced this project on air?"

"No. Too early for that. I envisaged this side project taking several months before I reached a point where I was ready to produce a special podcast covering it."

"Who else knew about it?"

"Just two of my colleagues. Brooke, you guys know. She appears every week on my show and I told her what I was doing. And an old friend of mine, Astrid Karlsen, a painter and art teacher. I outlined the concept to her and asked if she'd give an artistic commentary on the graffiti that I was planning to reveal on the podcast. She loved the idea, and then, when I called her about those two murals, she was, of course, more intrigued than any of us."

"Why's that?" I asked.

"She's of Norwegian descent and she's something of an authority on the works of the painter, Edvard Munch."

"Munch is the artist who painted the famous image of the screaming man," I supposed.

"Yes. *The Scream of Nature*. Commonly known just as *The Scream*. And this graffitist has emulated his style."

"What's the concept behind you shooting the graffiti art around town?"

"A limited podcast series, separate from *One Voice*. A record of the stunning graffiti art that's sometimes in clear view, sometimes in out-of-the-way places." His voice rose in enthusiasm. "There's a whole subculture of artistic expression that's right before our eyes, that's not being collected, gallery-like, for posterity. People go to art galleries and view artworks, modern and classic, but many of these graffitists are not only equally talented, but their work is a reflection of what is going on right now in our society. Genuine commentary from the underdogs on social and political issues. My podcast is another method of giving the unheard a 'voice,' and doing it before those paintings are scrubbed off the walls."

"Have you come across any other murals with the same styling, but which don't have the screaming man in them?"

"No, nothing else remotely like these."

"Have Brooke Goodman and Astrid Karlsen seen these photos?" Will asked.

Brooke was a journalist who worked for Seattle's major newspaper. The moment she had an angle on a potential story, especially something like this, she'd be out to scoop every other media outlet in town.

"Brooke hasn't," Sharpe said. "But I sent the images to Astrid. I wanted to start getting her views, not just on the style, but also this artist's rendition of the screaming man."

Will and I exchanged eye contact. We were on the same page. If Astrid Karlsen was an authority on Edvard Munch and she taught art, then her roster of students could be of interest.

"Where would we be able to find Ms. Karlsen?" Will asked.

Chapter Five

Astrid Karlsen cut a striking figure with her short, spiky blond hair, and deep-set, luminous blue eyes that seemed to compel you to look into them. She was dressed in a button-down shirt, jeans, and boots, giving off an appearance that was both timeless and contemporary. Perfect, I guessed, for an artist.

"First time I've ever had a visit from federal agents but then my mother always said there's a first time for everything." There was an unexpected grit to her voice. "But not the first visit I've had this morning about those graffiti murals. Starting to cause a bit of a stir, I guess."

We were seated at the front of the spacious room where Astrid taught her classes at a local Arts College. "Who else has been in to talk to you about them?" Even before Astrid responded to my question, I knew what she was going to say.

"One of Aiden's other colleagues, the reporter, Brooke Goodman. She filled me in on what her podcaster colleague told her. I have to admit it's a fascinating angle for a news story."

Will flashed me a look of frustration. It seemed every case we looked into, Brooke was either there before us, delving deep, or shadowing us as we went about our own inquiries. It was something I'd warned her not to do. Not that she would know these murals were on the UCU's radar, so I couldn't accuse her of shadowing us on this occasion.

We'd encountered Brooke on the UCU's first case. She'd been instrumental in helping us, whilst at the same time suffering a personal loss, and she and I had formed an uneasy bond.

"We're concerned that the paintings predict real accidents," Will said. "And it seems like the artist has used the screaming man image as a kind of signature."

"It's confounding," Astrid said. "But I've been giving these murals some thought ever since Aiden sent me the photos. It's quite possible the artist didn't know precisely what was going to happen, just had visions that related to parts of it."

"You believe the artist has psychic visions?" I asked.

Astrid shrugged. "Not sure how else you'd explain it. Doesn't seem possible it's a mere coincidence, not with two such events." She raised her hands. "But it is not my field of expertise."

"We're here to ask you specifically about the style of the art and *The Scream*," Will said. "I understand you're an authority on Edvard Munch."

"He's one of Norway's most celebrated artists. I was raised here but my parents were from Norway and I've visited the country many times. Munch has certainly been an inspiration and I include his works in my teaching. Do you know much about his most famous work of art?"

"No," Will said.

Astrid rose and went to a bookshelf that lined part of the back wall. She returned, carrying a large book of classic art reproductions. She turned to a page that featured Munch's most well-known piece. The twisted shape of a man with a terrified, otherworldly face, his mouth curved into a scream, hands covering the sides of his head. The figure was on a wooden walkway, surrounded by dark swirls of color, set against a bright orange sky.

"Its original title is *Der Schrei der Natur. The Scream of Nature.* Most people are surprised to learn that Munch painted four versions of this over seventeen years, from 1893 to 1910." Astrid's eyes were fixed on the page as she spoke. "One of the exercises I give to my students, for learning different techniques, is to copy one of the works of three classic artists. Turner for his use of light, Constable for his rich landscapes, and Munch's *The Scream*, for its ethereal, expressionist rendition not just of this man's emotions, but of man's connection to the natural world." Her eyes rose from the page and settled on me and Will. "This graffitist hasn't just painted the same screaming man, he has captured the fragile essence of Munch's style. It seems this artist identifies closely with the same themes that consumed Edvard Munch."

"What were his themes?" I asked.

"In this painting, anxiety, depression, and loneliness. A preoccupation with death."

"Do any of your students paint in this style?" Will asked.

"We learn from the masters, but I teach all my students to develop a style that is unique to them. Their vision of the world. None of my students, though, has copied Munch's works with anywhere near the flair shown in those murals. Particularly when you consider those murals are spray-painted."

I spied a row of spray cans on a shelf along the side wall, among other art utensils and paints. I leaned forward. "Do you teach spray-painted art?"

"My advanced course covers oils, pastels, acrylics, watercolors, and yes, spray-painting. A student will choose to specialize in one or two of these. The interest in spray-painting has increased in recent years, popular for painting on vehicles, and legal, government-sponsored graffiti projects. But none of my students seem anything like the type to be this mysterious graffitist."

"And casting your mind back, none have ever spoken to you about having psychic experiences of any kind?"

She gave it a moment's consideration. "No. Never." She smiled, gesturing to the line of easels that stood in the room. "Not the forum for it."

"We may want to talk to some of your students, Astrid," Will said, "so we would like a list of their names and addresses, both current and those you've taught here previously."

She raised an eyebrow. "May I ask why?"

"We need to ask them whether they know of someone, perhaps an artist friend that doesn't study here, who paints in a similar style. People sometimes have information that they don't think is of interest, but which helps us in our inquiries."

She nodded. "Of course." And then, scrunching up her face, she said, "Are there more than just the two murals?"

"What makes you ask that?" I said.

"Admittedly, two of these represent an oddity. But for the FBI to be sniffing around, there has to be more to it."

"Another one has come to light," I revealed.

It wouldn't be long before Brooke Goodman found out about the third mural and reported it, so it made sense to be upfront with Astrid Karlsen and keep her onside. Her knowledge of the art was likely to be useful.

"Surely you don't think this person poses a threat of some kind?"

"Not necessarily but we can't rule anything out at this point. If any more of these appear, then we need to know how and why this artist is doing this."

Chapter Six

In the car on the way back to the office, I said to Will, "A person skilled at using spray cans like this didn't just start doing it overnight."

"We'll get Marcia to contact local arts programs. Let's see if we can identify artists who exhibit the skills needed. We'll add those names to the ones we get from Astrid Karlsen."

I nodded. "We can also have Zoe use Themis to check for artworks online and in galleries with similar styling or references to Edvard Munch."

Convening with Zoe and Marcia back in the ops room, Will and I brought them up to speed.

"*Three* murals now," Zoe said. "Starting to sound more and more like something unnatural."

I knew she was having a dig because she knew Will didn't like that kind of thinking.

"The sort of thing that would be right up Zach's alley," Marcia commented. "He has a whole chapter in his book on psychics and how they've assisted police investigations over the years."

"None of that is proven," Will was quick to point out.

Professor Zach Silverstein had consulted with us on several cases. A university lecturer across criminology, history, and forensic science, he was known for his quest to uncover proof that the supernatural was real, and just a part of the natural order of things. He believed it simply represented a 'science' that humans hadn't discovered yet. His book covered many of these theories.

"Even so," Zoe said, "his insights on this would be interesting." She flashed her mischievous grin in my direction, with a side-eye to Will.

I hadn't seen Zach for a while but I knew he'd forged a close camaraderie with Zoe, who'd once been one of his students. The professor's slant on things, a full 180-degree turn from my own, nevertheless proved a useful devil's advocate for the cases he'd consulted on. Something that Will had reluctantly had to agree with.

"Why don't you text him," I said to Zoe, casting a roguish grin of my own at Will's unconvinced expression. "He'll be jumping out of his skin to give us his opinion on this."

"And Marcia," Will said, "get in contact with the coroner. Let's dig a little deeper into the details around the gravel truck smash." He shifted his gaze to Zoe. "The same goes for the other accident. Radner reported that the propane gas tank at the factory was faulty. See what you can find out about that."

Zoe gave him a thumbs-up.

Will's phone buzzed and he took the call. I noted a look of surprise on his face. Ending the call, he said, "Someone is waiting to see me." He directed that we were done with the briefing, as he headed to his office.

Minutes later, passing his office, I saw through the glassed portion of the door his ex-girlfriend from DC. I wondered what she was doing here and why Will, listening intently to her, had such a pained expression.

* * *

Four years earlier, Will McCord had been partnered on several cases with Special Agent Brett Rochester, and that was when he'd first met Brett's sister, Nadine. Also a special agent, Nadine was based in DC. When Will transferred to DC for a promotion, and after he and Ilona had called time on their romantic relationship, Will hooked up with Nadine. Looking back now, he could see that they'd never gelled, not in that deeply close way that defined long-term couples. Twelve months on, they'd broken off their relationship, a few months before Will's return to Seattle to head up the UCU.

Nadine smiled broadly and embraced him, and then took a chair opposite as Will sat at his desk. "I'll come straight to the point," she said, sweeping her hand nervously through her long blonde hair. "This isn't strictly a social visit. It's about Brett."

"How is he?" Will asked.

"Not in a good place. Have you heard about the OIG's investigation?"

Will put his hands on the desk, shifting forward in his chair. "No."

"They're investigating Brett for unprofessional off-duty conduct."

"What kind of conduct?"

"Misuse of position."

The OIG, or Office of the Inspector General, was the Attorney General's division for oversight of the FBI.

"Damn," said Will. "What the hell's this all about?"

Nadine exhaled, calming her nerves in the process. "It's Leo Vasquez. He made a formal complaint to the Attorney General that Brett had been going to his home and threatening him with an FBI-issued firearm. Will, Brett's going to need a lot of support. He needs you to step forward to the OIG and vouch for his character. You know him. And you were there, back when Vasquez originally approached Brett in that parking station."

Nadine's words were enough to summon a cinematic memory, immersing Will briefly in the past. Will and Brett were on the open-air top level of a parking station, heading for Brett's car when they were confronted by Leo Vasquez and another man.

Leo was the brother of Olivia Vasquez, just twenty-eight years old when she'd been an innocent bystander, accidentally killed when caught in the crossfire of a shootout involving the FBI and a drug gang.

Will and Brett had been part of an FBI team, watching and waiting for the members of a drug gang to exit the community hall where they were taking possession of a haul in one of the back rooms. The gang were heavily armed and when they realized the FBI was there, they panicked and opened fire.

Olivia, Leo, and a group of their friends were returning to their cars after a night at a concert. Olivia had playfully run on ahead of them, and for some reason turned into the alley instead of the street at the next corner.

Brett had fired the fatal shot. He and the rest of his team had been cleared of any wrongdoing or culpability in the death by an internal Bureau investigation.

But Leo Vasquez could not – *would not* – accept that.

Leo had been there at the time. That was how he knew Brett's identity, as he'd heard the agent identifying himself to the police who'd rushed to the scene.

Leo and his father had attempted to sue Brett, only to find that FBI agents have immunity from civil cases being brought against them. The Vasquezes then took their complaint to a higher court but during the process, Leo's father died of a heart attack, and the courts dismissed the claims, causing Leo to spiral further into grief-stricken anger.

On the parking station roof, Leo had said to Brett, "I'm going to ask you, man to man, to admit you saw my sister run into that alley but you went ahead and fired on those drug traffickers, anyway."

"That's not what happened," Brett said.

Leo had moved toward Brett, chest heaving. "You had to be the big shot, bringing down the bad guys–"

Will stepped between them. "That's enough, Leo."

"You were one of the others on that team."

"You're out of line confronting federal agents," Will said. "The matter was dealt with."

Leo's nostrils flared. "That investigation was bullshit."

Will remained calm but his voice was firm. "I'm instructing you to leave before you do something you regret."

The man who was with Leo took his friend by the arm. "Leo, they're not listening. Let's go."

Will fixed his attention on the man. Lean, bushy-haired, intense-looking, but far more controlled than Leo Vasquez. Will had seen him before, accompanying Leo to the courts. "You are?"

"Gabriel Vaughn. I'm an old friend of the family."

Leo was stabbing his finger toward Brett. "Arrogant. Reckless. You thought you could play God and get away with it but *you killed my sister.*"

"Gabriel, you and Leo need to go," Will said.

Vaughn nodded, barely suppressing a sneer as he stared back at the two agents. "Leo, you've said your piece. These honchos don't care." He tugged at his friend, and Leo, eyes blazing at Brett and Will, reluctantly allowed himself to be led away.

Brett had been visibly shaken. Will knew that Brett didn't need anyone else condemning him over the girl's death. Brett already blamed himself more than anyone, even Leo, ever could.

Nadine reached out, her hand gracing Will's wrist and lingering there, drawing him back to the present. "I'm worried Brett's sinking back into depression."

"I'll go see him this evening. Are you staying with him while you're in town?"

"No. Too much chaos at his place with those two young kids of his. You know me, Will, I need my own space. I'm in a motel nearby."

"I can give you a call when I'm on my way if you want to join me."

"That would be great. And thanks for this, Will. Brett's always respected you."

"No need to thank me. I'd always be there for him."

Her expression was pensive. "I know that. But, well… a lot of his friends and colleagues were a little, let's say distant, after the shooting inquiry. He felt it and I saw that it changed him in subtle ways. His mood. His outlook. He became a lot more guarded. And I know you were incredibly busy, and you had that big move to DC–"

"I didn't maintain the same level of contact," Will realized with a tinge of regret.

"I'm his sister, Will, and I didn't either. I was busy as well, and also in DC, but still…" Her voice trailed off as she struggled to find the right words.

"You never told me any of this while we were together."

"It wasn't until after we'd split, and then you'd returned here to Seattle, that I became acutely aware of how much Brett had struggled. And then, of course, it became much more apparent when the Vasquez family started pushing for these court hearings, and now, as well, with these problems with our little brother."

Will remembered that Brett and Nadine's younger brother, a few years back and when still a teenager, had been hanging out with a bunch of troublesome youths. They'd been cautioned by the police on a couple of occasions. "Luke? What's happening with him, nowadays?"

"He's got involved with some car-racing gang, staging burnouts, stunts, and races late at night. Brett's been trying to talk sense to him, but I know he's incredibly worried about it; we both are."

Will sucked in a deep breath and exhaled. He couldn't imagine the stress of a law enforcement officer having a sibling who was pursuing illegal activities. "I'll remind Brett I'm in his corner. No question."

"It will mean a lot to him."

Her eyes stayed focused on his in an expression of gratitude, but also… Will sensed something more, left unspoken.

"I'll leave you to it," she said.

As she left, she cast one backward glance, smiling gently as she waved. It occurred to Will that this meeting had none of the tension that had darkened the last weeks of their relationship. Instead, it had been more like their earlier times together.

Chapter Seven

Spying me as she passed by in the corridor, Nadine poked her head through the doorway to my office. "Ilona Farris. Long time, no see."

I'd met Nadine Rochester only briefly on a couple of occasions, and the last time had been quite a while back.

"Hi, Nadine. You're a long way from DC. On vacation?"

"Family stuff."

I nodded but said nothing.

"You're looking better than ever, and every time I see you I'm reminded how much I love that chestnut hair of yours."

I raised an eyebrow in acknowledgment of the compliment but wondered at the same time why Nadine felt the need to be so praiseful. Trying to get on my good side? "I can thank my mother for that," I said.

"So, looks like you and Will have put it all back together."

I frowned. "Put what back together?"

She smiled and half-rolled her eyes. "I think you know what I mean. And it's fine, it really is."

"Will and I are colleagues on a new unit. So yes, I suppose it's the old team back together."

Nadine tilted her head. "Not my business, of course, but I thought, maybe..." She raised her eyebrow suggestively.

"No," I said. "Why would you assume that?"

"He never stopped mentioning you," Nadine said. "After a while, I realized he wasn't just reminiscing about the old cases you worked on together."

I thought on this, allowing a beat. "That's why you and Will parted?"

"Not entirely. We'd started to drift. Didn't talk as much, not even about our individual workdays, and we'd always done that. One minute you're comparing notes all the time and doing spontaneous stuff like heading out to dinner or getting away for a weekend. And then one day it hits you that you haven't done any of that for a while." She took a moment. "I think his head was in a different place. And I'm sure his heart was, as well."

"Will and I aren't together."

I wasn't sure why I shared that, perhaps because she seemed to be opening up so much. Even so, my personal life wasn't something I wanted to share with her. I barely knew this woman.

"Funny how some things," she indicated her head and her heart, "go full circle. I thought separating was the best thing for us, but now…"

"Oh." I wasn't certain what I could add. I was about to say that perhaps she should be having this conversation with Will. Not me. But I held my tongue.

Why? Didn't I want her to have a heart-to-heart with Will?

"My brother's having some issues and Will's right on board offering to help," she said.

"Of course he would be."

She held my gaze. "Maybe there's more than a few things I should be talking to him about. Not just Brett."

"Maybe there is…"

We were interrupted as Marcia walked in. "Sorry, but we've got the coroner on the line about the truck driver."

"I'll let you get on with it," Nadine said, and with a tilt of her head, she was gone.

Even as I went through to the office with Marcia, I was thinking about Nadine. She hadn't been subtle in checking up on whether Will and I were an item again and she'd made it clear she was having second thoughts about ending their relationship. I didn't want that to bother me. But it did.

* * *

The coroner, a burly, mustachioed man, was on the large screen via video link. "You guys want to know more about the driver of the truck that caused that Interstate disaster, I understand."

Will had entered the office just ahead of me and Marcia, and Zoe was at the console. "Just had a look at your initial findings," Will said. "Cardiac arrest."

"That's right."

"Did the driver have a history of heart problems?"

"He had a heart attack twelve months earlier; he was on night-time medication, only light, and he'd been cleared for driving. It appears he lost control of his vehicle when he suffered the episode and crashed through the overpass barrier. He suffered blunt-force head trauma in the crash so I've yet to determine whether it was the heart attack or the head injury that caused death."

"When will you finalize your findings on that?"

"Another day or so. What's got the Feds interested in an accident like this? Did the driver have a criminal history?"

"Nothing like that," Will said. He changed the subject. "I also want to ask about the teenage boy who died last week on his uncle's Mount Vernon property."

The coroner took a moment, bringing up the details on his PC. "Ty Jansen," he said. "Only nineteen. Incredibly sad."

"He died from a fall?"

"There's a gully at the edge of the property's northern side. Not deep, but it's at its deepest where the boy went over. Depending on how he landed, the fall itself needn't have killed him but he hit his head on the rocks at the base of the incline."

"Was there blood at the scene?"

"Yes."

"Did you test it?"

"No. Why?"

"Could you test the blood and DNA, and confirm it's the boy's?"

"Of course. You think this was more than just an accident?"

"We've reason to look into it. And thanks for clarifying those details."

The coroner acknowledged this with a nod as the link was disconnected.

"I've spoken with the CEO of the bus company," Marcia said, "and he stated that the bus was running ten minutes behind schedule due to an unexpected, last-minute maintenance issue."

"No one could have foreseen or planned a truck driver's heart attack causing a highway pileup with a bus running behind schedule," Zoe said. "Yet both images appear together in the mural."

"The CEO did say, however, that they have several buses on the Interstate at around that time," Marcia added.

"Anything further on the factory fire?" Will asked her.

"The factory manufactures refrigerators, for which it uses propane gas, stored in the tank on the exterior of the building," Zoe said. "These tanks have bleeder valves, which open and release gas if the pressure inside the tank reaches a specific point. The release of the gas stabilizes the tank. It's rare but if for any reason the valve is left open and it's exposed to heat or flame it can catch fire."

"And that's what happened?" I asked.

"Staff had reported a week earlier that there were problems with the valve but the management had yet to call for repairs, instructing the staff to keep a close eye on it. It seems the valve had been open for a while releasing enough gas that when the car hit it, a fire and then an explosion occurred."

"Why would the impact lead to that?" Marcia wondered.

"The driver was smoking, as mentioned before, and the car had an oil leak. He'd booked it into a mechanic for the following week. The car smashed into the tank at such a high speed that the impact, the oil, and the sparks from the cigarette caused it to ignite."

"Another perfect storm of unrelated events," Marcia said.

"What about the driver? Was he a staff member? Or associated in any way with the factory?" I asked.

"Neither," said Zoe. "He lived nearby but worked on the other side of town. Office worker. He was driving home late, after socializing in the city with workmates, and he was known to be a heavy drinker."

"So, he was drunk and he lost control of the car," Marcia said.

"Way over the limit, and it seems he'd taken a wrong turn, onto the factory premises, at high speed, and then, well… bam."

"Take a deeper dig into the factory and the driver and any connections, however slight, with the other mural disasters," Will instructed.

"Already on it," Zoe said. "Themis accessed Radner's new report, about the third mural. It's pinged another alert, predicting these reports as related to potential crimes, and increased its percentage on the likelihood of them remaining unsolved."

I glanced at Will. "I don't think we have to decide about choosing this as a case. It's chosen us."

Chapter Eight

Brett Rochester lived in a three-bedroom craftsman bungalow on a leafy street in the suburb of Ravenna.

"Good to see you." Brett met Will and Nadine at the front door and ushered them into his study at the front of the house. As they entered the room, Will caught a glimpse of Brett's wife and young children in the living room, further down the hallway, watching television. The house had a comfortable, lived-in family feel about it.

Brett closed the study door and led them to the sofa. The study was workmanlike, a contrast to the rest of the house, and exactly what Will would have expected of his colleague. There was a desk, computer and bookshelf; the sofa, walls, and window drapes were in muted colors.

Will motioned to Nadine. "I had a visitor today. She reminded me that I've been acting like a bit of a stranger to you lately."

Brett shrugged. "I'm busy. You're busy, even more so, heading up a new unit. A mysterious new unit, I might add." He attempted a smile, but it wasn't the easy-come, easy-go grin that Will remembered from his friend. It was a half-hearted attempt. Brett's countenance was just a shade away from intense, his body stiff. He was a big guy, bordering six feet, solid and muscular.

"Not so mysterious," Will countered.

"A specialized team, tackling cases that contain a lot of classified elements. And that's all the rest of us have been allowed to know."

Will changed the subject. "How about you, Brett? How're things at the CCRSB?" Working in the Criminal, Cyber, Response, and Services Branch was where the two men had bonded.

"I'm on light duties, a heartbeat away from suspension. Being internally investigated by the OIG for something I haven't done." His expression remained rigid. "Otherwise, everything's just peachy."

"It's a hell of a thing to be put through," Will said "but just hang in there, okay? Let the OIG investigation run its course. They'll rule that the accusation is unfounded."

"Will they?"

"There's no evidence, no history of you ever having this kind of behavior, and this guy, Leo Vasquez, has been gunning for you ever since, well…"

"You can say it, Will. Ever since I shot his sister dead."

"An accident," Nadine chimed in, shifting awkwardly on the sofa.

"Vasquez says I went round to his house, pointed a gun at him when he opened the door and threatened him if he didn't stop harassing me."

"He doesn't have any witnesses," Will said, "can't have, since it didn't happen. And I presume he doesn't have CCTV set up at this house?"

"I don't know what he's got, or what he's presented to the OIG. They're keeping me in the dark."

"I'll put myself forward to speak with the OIG. I'll remind them I was with you on that occasion when Leo Vasquez approached you, hostile, on that parking station roof."

"This whole damn thing has been going on too long. *Years.*"

Brett was on edge and Will could imagine steam rising off him. Brett had always had that edge, though it was rarely on display. He recalled Brett's heated exchange with him when he'd learned that Will and Nadine were breaking up. He'd accused Will of leading her on, and of betraying the trust Brett and the Rochester family had in him. Will understood that his old friend was being protective of his sister. Later, things between them returned to normal. Or had they? Their contact with each other had been infrequent and Will often sensed a distance that hadn't been there before.

"I understand you've got concerns about your little brother?" Will said.

"Damn kid's got involved with a bunch of street car racers. Can you believe it?"

Will squinted at him. "Adrenaline junkie. Sounds like someone I know."

"*Used* to know," Brett corrected. "That was a long time ago. I tried it once or twice, then realized it was crazy-ass stuff, and quit. Luke never knew about any of that."

"So why don't you tell him you tried that once, that you understand what it's all about, being young, looking for that next big thrill? If you can relate to him in that way, perhaps he'll listen and let you talk some sense into him."

"That's a mighty big perhaps."

"All of this will get sorted," Will said. "Open up to Luke, give it a chance. Now, why don't we have a beer and you can bring me up to speed on everything that's happening with those cute little tykes of yours out there?" He could see it was important to get Brett to loosen up.

Brett nodded.

"I'll get the drinks," Nadine said.

They didn't stay too long, conscious that Brett needed to rejoin his young family in the living room. Will could see that Brett was going to need a lot of emotional support. Brett, Will was surprised to learn, had gotten heavily into computers and was interested in joining one of the cyber-crime teams.

Outside, Will walked Nadine to her car, which was a little further than his down the street. It was a calm night, and there was a full moon.

"You know," Nadine said, gazing directly into his blue eyes, "seeing you this afternoon, and again tonight, despite the circumstances, it felt really relaxed between us, like it was when we first got together."

Will smiled warmly but remained silent.

She raised her hands and pushed her hair back behind her ears. "I've got a bit of a confession to make."

"Oh?"

Her voice lowered. "I've been missing you, Will. And thinking about, how maybe, I didn't try hard enough."

"That's not true, Nadine. We were simply heading in different directions."

"Maybe we could get on the same path again."

Will bit down on the side of his mouth. He hadn't been expecting this. He knew exactly what Nadine meant, he'd felt it himself that afternoon. But giving things another try? Since his return to Seattle, his thoughts had been focused on rekindling his relationship with Ilona. She'd been resistant to anything romantic, and both of them were conscious of the need to keep things professional as they focused on making a success of the UCU. Was he fooling himself into hoping that, down the line, he and Ilona could regain what *they'd* once had?

"Ilona told me nothing was going on between the two of you," Nadine confided.

Their eyes met. Caught off guard, Will rubbed his chin. "It's late. Maybe we could talk about this, as well as about Brett, another time."

Nadine's gentle smile was one of understanding. "Of course."

Back in his car, Will let his mind roam over the past few months of working alongside Ilona again, and this evening, walking Nadine back to her vehicle. He felt torn. Ilona was never far from his thoughts, and there were moments when he wanted to draw her into his arms, but he'd always held back, keeping things strictly professional, hoping that something much deeper would come about naturally, in time. Ilona had kept her distance. It surprised him that he'd felt something for Nadine tonight, but what was it, really? Merely a revival of the friendship that they'd had, going back years, from before they were a couple? He'd known the Rochesters since he and Brett had been at Quantico. At one point, they'd felt like a second family to him, but there hadn't been that same sense of closeness since his romantic split from Nadine.

It had been good to see Brett again, although Brett's stressed demeanor worried him. He remembered again how rankled Brett had been when he told him he and Nadine were no longer an item.

Brett could have a short fuse sometimes, and as he turned onto NE 65th Street, Will wondered whether that fuse might have burned down in Brett's dealings with Leo Vasquez.

On impulse, he decided to drive to Ilona's apartment. Yes, it was late, and out of character, but he wanted to stand in front of her, feel that flutter in his heart, and remind himself that it was the real deal, not the rekindled friendship he'd felt with Nadine. And he had the perfect excuse, despite the hour. He wanted to share with her his meeting with Brett, and the concerns that were troubling him. He and Ilona had always confided in matters like that, and he was interested in what she might have to say about it. Maybe he just wanted her to tell him that he was reading far too much into Brett's edginess.

Ilona lived close to the city center. As he approached her apartment block, Will saw her come out the front of the building and head further along the street. She was dressed in a casual top and jeans and there was a duffel bag slung over her shoulder. Where was she going at this time of night? And with a duffel bag? He watched as she turned into a narrow alley that ran between two of the high rises.

Will drove closer to the alley entrance, parked, and followed in her footsteps. It was a long alley and he walked to its opposite end, where it joined another street. He looked to the left and the right. A lone car, driven by an elderly couple, passed by. Two young men were standing, talking, on a corner a couple of streets along. But there was no sign of Ilona.

Will watched the street for a few minutes and then, mystified, he retraced his steps through the alley and back to his car. Ilona had been reprimanded for her reckless behavior in their first few UCU cases but she'd seemed far more prudent since then. So, what was this late-night trek, with a bag over her shoulder, all about? If she was going to an all-night gym at this time of the evening, then she would have driven. Or *should* have driven.

Is there something else going on, something she hasn't confided in me?

Chapter Nine

Day Two

"I have to admit it came as a surprise, even to me, to learn you guys are interested in art. Graffiti art that depicts Edvard Munch's *The Scream*, I believe." There was a smug expression on Zach Silverstein's face and a lilt in his voice. With his longish, dark curls and large glasses, his lanky frame drew attention, accentuated further by the unusual combo of a long, dark coat and white sports shoes.

The professor strode into the UCU office, looking as pleased as punch to be called on, as I expected he would. He was always keen to help the FBI and, of course, he had his own agenda to fill.

Zoe brought the three artworks up on the large monitor, dividing the screen so that each of the three was positioned alongside the next. "These are the photos of the murals."

Zach was uncharacteristically silent as his eyes roamed over each of the illustrations. "Those lines, and the tones, are remarkably accurate, close to the original." He moved in closer, examining the pictures.

"The images, and the partial license details, can be linked to fatal accidents," I told him.

He turned to me. "Zoe filled me in on the phone. The murals were there before these accidents occurred."

I nodded. "Yes. At first, two of these came to our attention, but before we'd had a chance to put them into any perspective, there was a third, and so close in time to the first two, it became clear something very strange is going on."

"You think this artist is a psychic?"

"No. But you included a chapter on psychic phenomena in your book," I said. "I'm interested in your take on this."

He grimaced but there was a smile in his eyes. "You still see me as your devil's advocate."

"In a good way, but then I've told you that before," I countered. "In your research, did you ever come across anything like this?"

"No. But psychics have approached police with visions of crimes many times, in many countries, over the years, and police have consulted with psychics—"

"None of those instances have ever been proven," Will stepped in, his stare harsh.

I knew he wasn't prepared to go down that rabbit hole. He seemed more intense than usual this morning, casting me a strange look when I'd come in, his chiseled jaw set more firmly than usual. I sensed he might be holding back on something he wanted to ask me but I figured he'd broach the subject whenever he was ready. I asked him how things had gone the night before with Brett. He'd been filling me in on that when Zach strode in.

"You might not think so, but there's a guy, Garrett Gainsford, whom I interviewed for my book, that you should have a word with—"

"What we want to ascertain, Professor," Will said, "is whether you have come across any accounts of paintings that appeared to depict future events."

"Ever the skeptic," Zach shot back with a brief grin. "No, not paintings or graffiti as such, but it's not unusual for a person who experiences visions to sketch what they've seen in those visions. And where it's the prediction of a crime of some kind, they've been known to approach police with that information." Zach blinked rapidly as his speech accelerated, a common trait once he was on a roll. "There's a whole body of information that police have solved cases with the help of a psychic, but" – he shrugged in his theatrical way — "the official reports have downplayed any such cooperation, leaving it vague and closed to any further consideration." He suppressed a breath in frustration.

"And yet," said Will, "this supposed psychic, rather than report these visions to the authorities, spray-paints a vague collection of images in alleyways. That doesn't make sense."

"Perhaps because this person knows they wouldn't be believed," Zach suggested, "but also, quite possibly, because the artist doesn't know what the disaster is, either. Maybe they're getting the visions in these fragments, just as they've painted them. Psychics don't always understand the meaning of the messages they receive, and there is a difference between psychics and psychic mediums. Some psychics believe it's their spirit guides feeding them information, but others believe there is a kind of universal energy they are tapping into. It's not an exact science."

"It's *not* a science, Professor," Will said.

"Not recognized as such. Yet. And you only call me 'professor' when you're irritated with me."

"If that was the case, I'd never be calling you anything but."

Zach gave a tip of an imaginary cap. "Touché."

"But, Zach, even if this artist believes they can foresee these events," Marcia said, "and isn't sure what it means or that they'll be believed, why not do something more than just spray-paint graffiti on walls?"

I saw Marcia's point. "It's like it's a tease."

Zach's attention was back on the murals, scanning the images. He glanced at Zoe. "Can you enlarge?"

"Sure."

He motioned to the mural depicting the truck crash. "In the top left of this one, there's a very small line of what could be letters, near the edge, blending with the imagery. I want to see what that is. Can you enlarge just that spot?"

Zoe highlighted the area and magnified it.

"See that?" Zach angled closer, his finger tracing the spot. "The mural contains the letters *k k v m a e g m.*"

I focused on the screen. Zach was right. Looked at closely and in larger proportion, the letters became apparent. Embedded within the image, hidden in plain sight.

"Edvard Munch painted eight words, in a tiny line of text, in the upper right corner of his *Scream* painting."

"You know a bit about Munch?" I said.

"A bit, yes, but when Zoe told me on the phone that the screaming man was in each of the murals you were looking at" – he held up his phone – "I decided to brush up, do some online research on the way over. I read about Munch's transcription, in Norwegian. *'Kan kun vaere malet af en gal Mand.'* The letters here represent the first letter to each of those words."

Will was staring hard at the letters in the image. "In English?"

"Could only have been painted by a madman," Zach said. He motioned to a similar spot on the mural sitting alongside the first. "If you enlarge this one, and the third mural, as well, I think we'll see the same."

Zoe highlighted the same position in the remaining two murals and the same lettering became visible in both.

"I think, with the same screaming man image and those same letters in each mural," Zach said, "the artist is trying to tell us something."

"Us?" Zoe questioned.

Zach pursed his lips. "Yes. Us. As in law enforcement, either the police or the FBI. They expected the links between the images and the accidents to be noticed, and the greatest likelihood of that was when Aiden Sharpe began photographing murals. I think the artist expected it would be brought to the police's attention."

Zoe met his gaze. "In which case, the artist had to know about Sharpe's project, and made those murals ready for discovery at just the right time."

"We've considered that," I told Zach. "We've spoken with Sharpe, and the only two people who knew about his project were Brooke Goodman and an art teacher named Astrid Karlsen, and neither had mentioned it to anyone else."

"Astrid?" Zach said.

"Yes. You know her?"

"She was part of some lectures on symbology I arranged at the university, a few years ago. Her contribution was about the symbology in art."

"Astrid told us about the symbology in *The Scream* painting. Man's connection to the natural world. And that there was a preoccupation with death through much of Edvard Munch's work."

"*The Scream* is a painting that's been known to scare children and make adults uneasy," Zach said. "That terrified, inhuman face. The ghostly sky behind it. Exactly how you might feel, surely, if you experienced powerful visions of disaster and death." Enlivened by the subject, Zach's speech sped up with each word. "Munch captured all of that by painting in an ethereal, unrealistic style. He was painting what was in his soul, a moment of what he perceived as an existential crisis. So, what does that symbology mean to us? Why has this graffiti artist used that to tie together all these images?"

"What do we know about Edvard Munch's life?" I asked.

"He lost his mother when he was very young and his father was a verbally abusive man. He grew up with that discord in his head. He suffered a lot of health problems as a child and missed a lot of schooling. *The Scream* represents man's connection to the chaos in nature, and it's believed is a reflection of the disorder that Munch grew up with."

"Okay, so this graffitist may identify with those same personality traits," said Zoe.

"Quite possibly." This was Zach's criminologist side coming to the fore. "And just as Munch expressed his anxiety and depression in his work, so this graffitist could be doing the same."

"So, whoever it is, they're a fan?" wondered Marcia.

Zach waved toward the murals on the monitor. "You don't mirror a famous artist's style this closely unless you both admire and feel a spiritual connection to them. But I wouldn't use the term, *fan*. I'd say this artist is something more akin to a disciple."

Will narrowed his eyes. "Or a fanatic."

My phone rang and I checked the display. It was Detective Radner and I felt a curious chill at the nape of my neck as I answered.

"We've come across another one of these murals," he said.

Chapter Ten

"One of my officers just called it in," Radner said. "I'm heading over there–"

"We'll join you. Where?"

It was three blocks north of our office, in an alley off the main street. One of Radner's beat cops had spotted it. As Will, Radner, and I, with Zach and Zoe, entered the alley, a black cat, looking for ways to scavenge the garbage bins lining one of the walls, scampered away. There was a stale aroma of fish and cooking oils, this alley being at the rear of cafés and restaurants that lined the next street.

Two of the SPD forensic officers were surveying the scene.

"I had to call in a favor to get forensics guys out here for something that isn't a violent crime scene," Radner told us.

The first thing that struck me was that this montage, on the higher brick wall opposite the bins, was larger than I'd expected, almost epic in its scale. There were three images entwined around a central illustration of sparks flying off railroad tracks as train wheels strained. A portion of the cabin above the wheels was showing. The surrounding images were of a partial body shape lying crumpled, its arms outstretched with the miniature shape of an anchor beside it; the crushed edge of a car's license plate showing just the last three numbers and end letter; and the screaming man.

The disparate images blended into one another in ripples and steep angles. Viewing the actual mural at its full size, not a photo of it, heightened the sense of unease that the images conveyed. The drawing of the screaming man was particularly mesmerizing in its curving lines and dissonant tones of dark orange, blood red, and yellow and blue-green hues. The other point of difference was the small, highly stylized sentence that was shaped around the points where the images fused. 'What lies ahead.'

"This time it's being made crystal clear," Radner said. "The Artist, which is the term we've been using here to identify this person of interest, is predicting a disaster."

"We've got company," Zoe said.

I turned to see Brooke Goodman and Aiden Sharpe approaching. It was no surprise that the two of them were staying close to the SPD reports. Sharpe acknowledged us with a wave but held back, getting into position to take photos and videotape the mural and the activity now surrounding it.

"It seems the frequency of these murals is increasing," Brooke said. With her center-parted, long dark hair, determined stance, stylish outfits, and shoulder cam and cell phone at the ready, she came across as every inch a Lois Lane for the digital age.

"You haven't filed any stories on these murals yet," I noted. It wasn't like Brooke to be constrained on something as unusual as this.

"I need facts, not theories, to make a splash. The last three murals were all sighted a week or more after they'd been spraypainted, and *after* the accidents they supposedly foretold. People will speculate that the timing was faked, or that it's a trick, or simply coincidental. *This* time" – her finger stabbed the air – "I'm here in person right after the mural's been painted. If the images can be matched to an accident in the next few days, then I can show that I observed the phenomena for myself, and with the evidence" – she indicated Sharpe and his equipment – "to prove it." Brooke's eyes wandered to the mural and as I expected, she picked up on the message straight away. "What lies ahead." She shuddered, her attention back on me. "So, Ilona, what do you guys make of all this?"

"We're making inquiries," I said, "on who is painting this graffiti, and the how and why behind the images. But it's early days. Like you, though, we'll now have an opportunity to see if this mural relates to anything yet to happen."

Radner had gone forward and was consulting with one of the forensics men. Will signaled to me, and he and I joined Radner.

"No traces of paint fragments or hairs or fibers," the forensics officer said. "Which is unusual, because the paint on the wall is only several hours old."

"You believe the spray-painting was done well after midnight, then?" Will supposed.

"That's right." The man shrugged. "No wind or rain overnight. Calm conditions, so you'd expect some trace evidence but there's zilch."

"It's as though it was painted by a phantom," the other forensics man said.

Radner turned to me and Will. "I'm having CCTV from the roads at either end of the alley checked for anyone entering or leaving."

"We did that for the roads surrounding the previous three murals," I said. I didn't need to remind him that those street cams had revealed nothing. "Let's get scrapings from the paints on the wall." It was important to match the paints used on this mural to those used on the others. There wasn't much doubt it was the same artist but matching the materials would help confirm it. And we'd continue checking that info against paint purchases made in local stores. "The time lapse between the other three murals appearing, and the accidents they envisioned, was less than forty-eight hours." My eyes were fixed on the images in this mural. "Which means we've got a very narrow window to figure out if there's another disaster looming."

* * *

Zoe and Zach walked back to the car ahead of the others.

"Will certainly shut down the whole idea, back at the office, that psychics have ever helped solve crimes," Zoe noted, shooting Zach a sympathetic look. "Maybe a tad harsh." Her expression morphed into an impish grin.

Zach responded with a smile and a shrug of acceptance. "The more the skeptics try to belittle the whole idea, the more determined I am to find evidentiary proof that the supernatural is real and that it's happening, in large and small ways, all around us, every day."

He averted his gaze for just a moment, navigating to a web page on his phone, and then he handed it to Zoe, his fingers indicating the archived news items on the screen.

"Back in the 1980s," he continued, "a woman named Rosemarie Kerr was the first person called as a witness in a murder trial in her capacity as a psychic. Kerr had held a photo of a missing man, Andre Daigle, and sensed that the man was dead and that his body was in a New Orleans swamp. When the police found the body in the swamp it led them, ultimately, to the murderers." He took back the phone scrolled to another news feature and held it aloft for her to see. "With all the research you've done on law enforcement, you might've heard of Dorothy Allison. The US Department of Justice's website doesn't endorse or validate the use of psychics, but it makes mention of Allison. She was a highly controversial psychic, believed by some to be a fraud, but it's stated she assisted police departments in over 4,000 cases back in the eighties and nineties. Those are just two random examples of psychics working with police. Yes, there are thousands of examples of a psychic's information proving useless, but there are also examples where that wasn't the case. It's not a perfect science, as I said to Chief Skeptic McCord." He beamed with a wide grin at this. "But people who experience psychic phenomena are often confused by it, not certain of its meaning, and that goes for the more experienced as well as the novices–"

"Slow down, tiger," Zoe said.

Zach nodded and slowed down, but only marginally.

"So, on the whole," he continued, "Will's comment that there's no definitive proof, even on those occasions a psychic does supply something that's shown to be right, is correct. But many instances suggest the opposite."

"It doesn't help your cause," Zoe said, "when there are so many frauds out there, using methods like retrofitting to facilitate their scam."

"I know all about retrofitting," Zach said. "Putting forward a whole bunch of diverse clues, and then if just some of those hit the mark, reinterpreting them to fit the facts that become known." He threw his hands up. "Muddies the waters."

"But," Zach added, glancing behind him at the murals, as he and Zoe exited the alley, "there is nothing in the murals so far to suggest the visual clues could be retrofitted. Every one of the images has been remarkably accurate."

"The real problem with this," Zoe pointed out, "is that this so-called psychic isn't using their visions to assist the police. Instead of approaching authorities, they're using their premonitions to tease us that there's a disaster imminent, almost as a dare to try and figure it out."

Chapter Eleven

Back in the UCU office, we grouped around the Themis console. Zoe hadn't taken her usual seat, she was standing, like the rest of us, too hyped up to settle. She'd brought up on the screen a photo of the fourth mural.

Will's expression was stony. He ran his fingers through his light brown hair, which I noticed was a little longer than he normally wore it. "Once again, Aiden Sharpe was on the scene, taking photos for this pet project of his. Only this time he had the SPD and the FBI on site, adding an element of drama to his visuals."

"You still think he could be manipulating all this?" Marcia asked.

"It's all publicity for his special podcast, so we're damn well going to keep an eye on him. I've asked Radner if he can appoint a couple of men to keep tabs on his movements. But at the same time, I can't rule out that the graffiti artist has engineered these accidents."

"I wondered the same thing," Marcia said, "but I can't see how, given the random events that led to each of the tragedies."

"You call me your devil's advocate," Zach said, his eyes flitting from me to Will, "but I think the whole team needs to assume devil's advocacy for this. Assume, despite what you believe is or isn't possible, that a psychic has foreseen this and that there is a disastrous event imminent."

"Which means we focus on figuring out what that disaster is and how to prevent it," I said, seeing his line of reasoning. I'd already figured that was the best way forward, for the next forty-eight hours at least, and I was sure Will would be on the same page despite any misgivings.

"We're all in agreement on that," Will said. "And in the meantime, with Themis looking for connections between the accidents, hopefully, we'll have a chance of identifying a trail to the artist at the same time."

I moved closer to the large monitor, the photo of the fourth mural filling the screen. "What these images represent to us, right now, are clues. There's the suggestion of a train pulling up suddenly. There is what appears to be a lifeless body. The obvious inference is someone is hit by a train."

"First clue," said Will, "is the exterior coloring on the train. We're seeing the edges of some letters on the cabin. White on blue. Unlikely to be freight, so most likely one of the commuter transits."

Zoe was furiously typing on her keyboard. "Here's a map of the commuter routes out of Seattle." The map appeared in a bordered section to the upper right of the screen.

"Could it be a derailment, mirroring perhaps the truck crash at the overpass?" Marcia wondered. "A train skipping the tracks on a bridge and going over the side?"

"God, I hope not," Zoe said. She reconfigured the screen, bringing up another map of a different kind. "Another possibility is that the images are depicting a railroad crossing incident. There are over three hundred of those crossings in the state, and 30% of all rail fatalities in the US occur at railroad crossings, many involving cars. It could explain the image of a distorted car license plate."

I was focused on that image. The twisted, stylized illustration meant it was uncertain what some of the numbers or the end letter might be. One of the numbers could have potentially been a three or an eight. The end digit was possibly one of three or four letters of the alphabet.

"Zoe, have Themis determine what each number and letter could be and produce all the configurations," I said. "I'm guessing we'll end up with hundreds of possibilities but it's better than thousands. Then run a search and list every Washington car license ending in our narrowed-down four digits. And then cross-reference those with addresses within, say, fifty miles of each of the railroad crossings on the commuter routes. The previous accidents occurred in the greater Seattle region, so for starters, we'll concentrate on the same region."

"Okay."

I wasn't sure I'd ever stop marveling at how our AI, used as a crime-focused search engine in addition to its predictive analytics mode, could accomplish in minutes what would take many weeks for hundreds of agents. Moving closer to the large screen, I indicated the tiny anchor shape alongside the outstretched hand. "This, I'm guessing, is another clue."

"The anchor is a symbol of hope," Zach said, "and of calmness and security."

"Hardly what we're seeing here," I said.

From her position at the other end of the console, Marcia gestured to Will and me. We grouped around her as she indicated the data on her screen. "I've had word back from all the galleries and art societies. No one has seen anything like the work our graffitist is doing. The one constant piece of feedback I got was that Astrid Karlsen was their go-to authority on anything to do with Norwegian artists and in particular Edvard Munch."

"Astrid is sending us a list of her students, past and present," Will said. "Could you chase her up for that?"

Marcia nodded. "Sure."

Hearing Astrid's name, Zach said, "You know, when Astrid was guest lecturing at the university, she and I created a special brain game, not of facts or figures, but instead, solely using imagery. It was a fun after-hours pastime for the students, and a learning tool as well. Astrid was brilliant at it, and it's given me an idea."

"I'll bite," I said.

"The names on Astrid's list, as such, mightn't mean much to us, or even to her. Students come and go over the years. But it's highly likely that somewhere among the students she's had, there's something, a piece of information about one of them, and about Edvard Munch's work, that could be linked. Creating a brain game using images from her classes might just spark a memory of someone or something buried away in her mind that could prove crucial."

Will frowned. "This sounds like a harebrained way to go about interviewing people who can assist us."

"Not really," Zach said, "and certainly not where Astrid is concerned. Generally, people play brain games for fun but they also sharpen our minds. Activities like puzzles and crosswords train our brains in cognitive functions, like problem-solving, planning, and *memory-jogging*. The game Astrid and I created for students used specific pictures to refresh their memories about the facts and figures they'd been studying. But to make certain nothing was confronting about it, we included plenty of comic images along the way, for laughs, so that it was a fun way to learn."

"I hadn't pegged you for fun-lover," Will said drily.

"Oh, there's plenty of whacky facts you don't know about me yet," Zach shot back.

"Maybe we should keep it that way."

Zach grinned from ear to ear. "Very droll, just the way we prefer our special agent in charge."

Refocusing everyone's attention, while casting a bemused expression at Will, I said to Zach, "I'm intrigued, and right now I think we're open to any course of action. I'll leave it to you to organize."

But Zach wasn't wasting time. As we watched, he touched the screen on his phone and then held it like you would a microphone. He had the call on loudspeaker, and when it was answered, he said, "Hello, Astrid? It's Zach Silverstein."

"Well, this is a blast from the past."

"I specialize in them." Adopting his serious voice, he continued, "I've got you on speaker and I'm with the federal agents who visited you yesterday."

Her response was tentative. "Okay…"

"I'm told you're sending over lists of all your students."

"That's right. I've just combined them and made a PDF."

"Have you looked over those lists?"

"Yes, I have."

"Any names jump out at you with regard to Munch's style?"

"No."

"You once told me," Zach said, "that you like to take photos, with each student's permission, of a sketch or a painting they've done at the time they join your class, and then another one at the end of one of your terms, to show the progress they've made."

"That's right."

"You liked to have a select few of these on the walls of your classroom, as inspiration for your new students, and as an endorsement of your teaching methods."

"You remember that?"

"Of course. You showed me a few of these once. I remember thinking, what a brilliant idea. Do you still do that?"

"Yes."

"So, you have an archive of before and after photos of each student's progress?"

"Yes." There was a brief pause. "Where are you going with this?" she asked.

"Remember the photographic brain game we constructed for our college students?"

"How could I forget? Great fun. And a great learning tool."

"Can you bring those before and after photos over? On a USB or a portable drive. I want to select a bunch and print out copies."

"Why?"

"I'll explain when you come in."

Zoe chimed in, "Zach, get those images to me, along with your ideas for this brain game. Themis can construct the whole thing for display on the screens."

Will rolled his eyes as he and I walked to the corridor that led to our adjoining offices.

"You were telling me, earlier, about your visit to Brett last night," I said. "He's got a lot on his plate."

"And then some." Will winced, stopping at the door to his office.

"The OIG shouldn't be investigating him. This man, Varquay—"

"Leo Vasquez."

"Right. He already had a history of confronting Brett and of trying to have criminal charges laid against him. Charges of which the FBI had already cleared him."

"I'm going to present myself to the OIG," Will said. "See if I can put in a good word for him."

I nodded, and as I turned toward my office, Will said, "I dropped by your place last night after I left Brett's but just missed you. It was late, I know, but I just wanted to sound you out about Brett's situation. He was holding it together but knowing the stress he was under, kind of rocked me. I saw you heading off somewhere with a duffel bag over your shoulder."

I bit down on my bottom lip but quickly deflected. "Sorry you missed me," I said, trying to sound casual. "I was just restless, out for a walk, took my bag in case I decided to hit the gym."

"There's a twenty-four-hour gym near you?"

"Yeah."

"The Bureau's got a gym right here in the building."

I shrugged. "Which I haven't been using as much as I should. Anyway, I wasn't planning to take that long a walk."

Will bopped his head, as though in understanding, and I hoped I'd convinced him.

"I work out a few times a week, early morning," he said. "You should join me."

"Maybe I will."

I headed into my office and I shuddered at the thought that Will could have, under different circumstances, followed me last night, to catch up with me.

I was unsettled and the feeling didn't lift as I took my seat and tapped my keyboard, bringing up the case file on the PC screen.

There was a distracting voice in my head, a voice that constantly reminded me that I should no longer be going out in the dead of night. A voice of reason that said I had to stop letting off steam in a way I knew wasn't just dangerous, it could also spell the end of my career. But it wasn't the only voice jostling for attention up there. There was that other, argumentative speaker, telling me I needed to release tension in the way that most suited me. And, after all, I was experienced at what I was doing, and I didn't take crazy chances. So, who exactly was I hurting?

Sometimes, when I had these thoughts, I imagined my mother watching from the corners, her face full of compassion. I remembered her voice. Gentle, caring, wise.

What do you make of all this, Mom?

A moment later, Marcia walked in and eased herself into my only visitor's chair. "There are three different paint colors used in the murals, which are mixed by the painter to create a range of colors," she said. "All in common usage and sold by literally hundreds of stores across the state. If our suspects have those same colors, we can match the paint scrapings from the walls."

"All we need now are suspects," I said.

Marcia grinned. "Always helpful." She leaned forward in a conspiratorial way. "Those three sons of mine, all young men now," she said, "are all sci-fi freaks. Aliens. Time travel. Future gadgetry. You name it, they're into it. Not my cup of tea. They would be fascinated by this case."

I returned the grin. "We should send Will over one night to hang out with them."

"Three geeks and a super skeptic." She gave a hearty laugh. "I'm thinking, like me, and most certainly like Will, you don't think this artist is seeing the future. There has to be some other explanation. And yet, what?" She sat back, smoothing down the bangs on her short blonde bob. "A lot of people believe that humans have psychic abilities. Do you really think there could be a train disaster about to happen?"

I spread my hands. "Having been presented with this mural, I can't ignore the possibility. If there's even a hint people could be in danger, I have to try and stop it."

"I think that's how we all feel."

I drew back my shoulders, relieving some of the anxiety I was feeling. "We follow the clues," I said. "And, most importantly, we find this artist. That's how we get an answer to how and why this is happening." I had prints of the mural photos positioned across my desk. I glanced over them for the umpteenth time. "Let's follow up and broaden Themis's search to include any common denominators between the people and the companies involved in each of these disasters. Any links between the staff of the different companies, and what about their clients and their external contractors? For example,

Sovereign Insurance is depicted in just one of the murals, but is it connected with any of the other incidents?"

"I'll get on it," said Marcia.

Zach appeared in my doorway. "Something was bothering me about this fourth mural," he said. "There was something different and, of course, it's so damn obvious, don't know why it didn't ring alarm bells straight away."

"Go on," I said.

"The previous three murals didn't have a worded message like this one. And this is the first one being examined by us *before* a supposed event." He entered the office, hyped up, practically pacing on the spot. "It's as though the Artist knew there would be an audience taking the art seriously. This time, as Detective Radner said, the graffitist was making it clear this was a vision of the future. *What lies ahead.* But what if it's more than that?"

"More?"

"What if it's a clue that ties in with the images?"

I thought back on Zoe's comment about railroad crossings. I shifted in my chair, leaning forward, placing the edge of my hand on my desk as though to indicate a specific point. "As in, *what lies ahead* on the tracks to an approaching train?"

"Yes."

"We'll regroup with Zoe in half an hour," I said, "and see what Themis has pulled together that matches the other criteria."

As Zach and Marcia moved out, I pulled up the photo of the mural on my PC. The images had a hypnotic quality, immersing you in their warped reality. But my focus froze on the tortured face of the screaming man.

What lies ahead.

Can only have been painted by a madman.

Chapter Twelve

Marcia signaled to me when I entered our comm center a little later. She directed my attention to one of the smaller PC monitors, where a page from today's edition of *The Seattle Chronicle* was displayed.

"Brooke's report," Marcia said.

I cast my eyes over the article's headline: 'Is graffiti artist a modern-day Nostradamus?' The spin was classic Brooke and would certainly capture the attention of even the most casual reader. The article went on to speculate that the graffiti art was eerily prescient of disasters that had occurred in the past week and that Brooke would be watching and reporting if that proved to be the case with the most recently sighted art with the same style.

"She didn't waste any time getting that posted to the paper's website," I noted.

"She wasn't alone in getting it out there," Marcia said. She navigated to Aiden Sharpe's *One Voice* podcast site. "His latest podcast, just loaded."

The now-familiar theme music played and the *One Voice* logo scrolled across the screen.

> *Today, I'm unveiling a special project that I'd intended to reveal when I was ready to premiere it as a one-off special. A little over a week ago I began a series of walks, intending to eventually cover this great city of ours from one end to the other, showcasing some of the incredible graffiti art...*

He went on to detail his experience thus far, introducing Brooke along the way, who appeared alongside him, referring to her news article.

"It seems that girl has a sixth sense when it comes to whatever cases the UCU is looking into," Marcia said.

"Perhaps she's in the wrong line of work," I teased.

Marcia gave me a disapproving stare. "You think she should be a psychic?"

"I think maybe she'd make a damn good special agent."

Zoe called to us and we headed across to the main console. I was struck, not for the first time, by how the console would look like it was missing a piece if Zoe wasn't seated there, tapping, scrolling, and scanning all of the monitors as she did so. Zoe brought us up to date. Themis had tabulated dozens of potential license-plate numbers and listed the accompanying addresses.

Those addresses and the owner of the vehicle garaged there filled the large monitor.

"I condensed these further to positions within fifty miles of a railroad crossing in the greater Seattle region," the AI informed us.

I'd listened to Themis's Greek-accented female voice so many times now it was almost as though it was just another human member of the team. *Almost.*

"There are fifteen possibilities that fit the parameters."

"Themis, run printouts of those," I instructed. Turning to Zoe, I said, "If you, Marcia, and I each take a few and phone them we can cover the lot in half an hour or so. We need to know whether the driver intends to travel anywhere near those crossings and whether the symbol of an anchor means anything to them."

Five of the drivers couldn't be contacted. Six of the others had retired and confirmed they rarely, if ever, drove over their nearest rail crossing, and the anchor held no significance to them.

Sally Corcoran was a different story. The contact number, a home landline, was answered by her father. Twenty-four-year-old Sally, a nurse, was out, and due back soon, but her father knew that there was a crossing on his daughter's route to her job. And he was surprised by the question about the anchor. His daughter wore a black cord bracelet with a silver-plated anchor charm, a recent purchase that meant a great deal to her. Frank Corcoran had given Marcia his daughter's cell phone number, but Marcia hadn't been able to raise her.

"The railroad crossing is only twenty minutes from Sally's home, but the good news," said Marcia, "is that Sally's dad said she's been on a break and isn't due back at the hospital until tomorrow."

I drew in a deep breath and exhaled, looking at Will. "An anchor bracelet isn't uncommon–"

"But your gut's telling you we should go and talk with this girl."

"How'd you know?"

He raised his eyebrows. "My gut's telling me the same."

I glanced at Zoe. "What can we find out about Sally Corcoran?"

"Already looking up her details." Zoe screwed up her face. "Hmm… Not what I expected."

"What is it?"

"Six years ago, before she was a nurse, she was admitted to the hospital where she now works. She'd attempted suicide."

"Suicide? How?"

"Overdose."

"Her father never mentioned that," Marcia said.

"No reason he would," said Will. "We weren't asking about his daughter's medical history."

"Sally recovered, got counseling for her depression, and decided to honor the medical community that helped her, by becoming one of them," Zoe said.

"Marcia, keep trying to contact Sally. In the meantime" – I started heading for the exit, signaling to Will – "we've got a house call to make."

* * *

Sally Corcoran sat by the lake, eyes on the bank opposite, watching the flock of European starlings that flittered about the shore and the grove of trees. With their short wings and spotted plumage, they were gorgeous creatures, comforting to watch as they cavorted among themselves. She could always rely on the birds, often in small numbers, to be somewhere in the vicinity. Not a care in the world. She wondered, as she had many times before, what that would be like.

Not a care.

She smoothed her fingers over the silver anchor that adorned her wrist bracelet. The symbol of hope. She knew it was always out there, something perennial – hope – and yet it could be hard to find. For her, anyway. At the hospital, she saw people helped and saved daily, their hopes realized, and yet she also saw the flip side. Not every story had a happy ending. She'd thought, as recently as just yesterday, that all her hopes and dreams were coming to fruition. She'd come a long way since 'the incident.' Hadn't she? And then, on a night she thought would be magical, it had become anything but, when her boyfriend, Jake, told her he'd accepted a job on the other side of the country. He'd decided to make a clean break with everything. Including her.

Just like that.

She watched the starlings for a little longer and then she drove the short distance back home.

She put on a happy face when she entered the house and her father called out, "Hi." She didn't want to burden him with her feelings.

"Had the oddest of calls," her father said, "from a federal agent, would you believe? Asking about that rail crossing on the way to the hospital. And the agent wanted to know whether anchors meant anything to you or me."

Sally fixed her father with a curious stare. "Why on earth would you get a call like that?"

"They said it was part of a general inquiry. Thanked me for my help."

Sally rolled her eyes. "Dad, it was probably a prank call."

"They said they'd been trying to call you but you didn't pick up."

"I haven't had any calls. As I said, they were pranking you."

He stared back at her, bemused, and he caught a glint of sorrow in her green eyes. "Everything okay, hon?"

"I'm fine."

Minutes later, the landline rang, and Sally answered.

* * *

The Corcoran home was in a semi-rural suburb a half-hour drive from the city. Frank Corcoran was broad-faced, with a genial expression and a down-to-earth manner. He was clearly surprised when he opened the door and we introduced ourselves.

"Guess it wasn't a prank, then," he said.

"What wasn't?" I asked.

"I told my daughter about your call and she thought it sounded like a prank."

"Sally's home, then?"

He shook his head. "No. She wasn't home for more than a few minutes. She had a call from the hospital, asking her if she could come back a day early and fill in at short notice for someone who'd called in sick. And of course, my Sally would never say no, now, would she?"

Will and I exchanged a hurried glance. "When did she leave, Mr. Corcoran?" Will asked.

"Not more than five minutes ago. You just missed her. If I'd known you were coming… but what's this about? Sally in some kind of trouble?"

"She may be able to assist us with an inquiry," Will said.

"You could try calling her but she wouldn't answer while driving, she's a good girl, does the right thing."

While Will was finishing up with Frank Corcoran, I stepped away, phoning the office. "Marcia, when is the next train due at the crossing near Sally Corcoran's home?"

I waited while she consulted the routes. I knew the crossing was twenty minutes from here and with Sally having left five minutes earlier, that meant she was just fifteen minutes away from reaching it.

Marcia came back on the line. "The train crosses that section of road in twenty minutes."

That meant Sally would pass the crossing five minutes earlier. I should have felt a sense of relief but instead, my mind scrolled over the details of Sally's background. Her depression and suicide attempt six years earlier.

I turned back to her father at the front door. "What was Sally's mood like, sir?"

"Well…" He cocked his head, considering this. "She did seem a little… distracted."

Will thanked Frank and we headed back to our car. I was aware that he was staring after us with a worried expression.

I filled Will in on what I'd learned about the train schedule.

"Then there's no reason to believe the girl's in any danger," Will said, as we stepped into the vehicle.

"We can't take any chances with this, Will. The girl once attempted suicide. The rail crossing, the anchor bracelet, there are too many similarities to the mural–"

"No one could have anticipated her being called in to cover for a sick colleague. Or even that she'd say yes." He fired up the ignition and pulled out from the curb. And then he put his foot down. "But we'll go as fast as we can to reach that crossing before the train passes."

The suburban streets quickly gave way to wide, open spaces. I looked out the window at the landscape racing past but all I could see, manifesting itself in my vision, was that tortured face, eyes wide, hands over ears, shrieking internally at the chaos that swirled all around. And against all reason, all logic, I feared for Sally Corcoran.

Chapter Thirteen

As Will drove, I phoned Sally's number, even though I knew Marcia was doing the same. If she heard her phone ringing multiple times, Sally might pull over to the side of the road and answer, thinking it was something urgent. Still no answer. I sent a text, as well.

> *Sally, this is special agent Ilona Farris. Please pull over and call me on this number urgently.*

I stared hard at my phone's display as though that might elicit a response.

It didn't.

Where the way was clear, Will pushed down harder on the accelerator.

I phoned Zoe. "Can you get in touch with the transit authorities? Can we get the train to stop before it passes over the crossing?"

"I'll see what can be done."

For a moment, I felt a sense of doubt. Were we acting like crazy people? Sally Corcoran was just a young woman on her way to her job. By all accounts, she was a careful, sensible driver who, according to her father, would never even answer her cell while driving. Her teenage depressive episode was in the past. The railroad crossing's gate would be down and the red light would flash when the train approached.

And yet it *could* have been her car's license plate in the mural, and the anchor bracelet had to be more than just a random coincidence. Was there a chance, however slim, this girl could be on the verge of suicide? And then another thought struck me.

I called Zoe again. "We need to make certain that the crossing's electronics aren't malfunctioning."

I glanced at my watch. We were less than five minutes away.

* * *

We rounded a bend, a straight line of road stretching ahead, the rail crossing in sight. Even from this distance, I could see the gate was down, the red light was flashing, and sitting stationary on this side of the gate, was Sally's Ford sedan. She should have already passed over the crossing but regardless, she was waiting safely. On the horizon, I saw the approaching train, speeding toward the crossing. I wondered if the transit authority had communicated with the driver about stopping.

"All seems okay," said Will.

As we came closer, it seemed the train was slowing, though I was aware that it could take an eight-car passenger train up to a mile to come to a stop, depending on the train's size, weight, speed, and condition of the track.

Will slowed our vehicle and we came to a stop behind the Ford. It was at that precise moment that, without warning, Sally's Ford revved and sprang forward, crashing through the barrier and then stopping suddenly on the track.

A suicide attempt?

"God, no…" I leaped from our car and ran forward.

A screech filled the air as the train's wheels skidded on the rails from the sudden application of its emergency brake. I reached the driver's door of the car and tried the handle but it was locked. Peering in I could only see the back of her head. She was unmoving, facing the direction from which the train was coming. Frozen in fear? I banged on the window but even as I did the front of the train loomed large in my vision, less than fifty feet away, the train's horn blaring, sparks coming off the wheels as they strained against the rails from the rapid braking, the stench of metal grinding on metal at high speed filling my nostrils. Sally's head turned suddenly to face me, her face etched with sheer horror, but instead of unlocking the door and leaping out, she banged her fists against the window as her eyes locked with mine. Had she changed her mind at the last minute but forgotten in her terror that she'd locked the door? In that instant, time seemed to stand still but my thoughts were racing. I knew, with a sickening, plummeting sensation in the pit of my stomach that Sally was lost, that I had mere seconds, if that, to save myself. I wrenched myself away from the car, turned to flee, and as I did Will grabbed hold of my arm and pulled me with him as he sprinted clear of the tracks.

The impact was deafening, and almost immediately a twisted, flying piece of the Ford's metal struck Will in the upper arm with such force that it knocked him off his feet. He hit the ground with a shriek of pain, rolled, and lay immobile on the road. I lost my footing at the same time. I scrambled to my feet, and in the corner of my vision as I reached for Will, I saw the crumpled wreck of the Ford, smashed against the front of the train, but rather than flashing by on the track, the entire front of the train derailed and toppled over onto its side. The front carriages slammed down onto the open field beside the road and slid to a stop, glass shattering, screams erupting from the passengers, and debris scattering through the air and across the ground.

Will groaned. I checked his irises and his pulse.

"Just hang in there," I whispered close to his ear.

I phoned 911 and then I phoned Marcia.

"I'll speak to the AD and get agents out there," she said.

Will tried to sit up.

"Just lay still," I said. "Emergency services are on the way."

"Hurts like hell." He sat up, despite my protests. "We've got to help…"

"You're in no shape to help."

He grimaced as he moved his arm. "A monster bruise, but nothing broken. I'll be fine."

"You stay there, Will. I'll see if there's anyone in need of desperate help."

I took a breath, and ran my fingers through my hair, pushing it back off my forehead. Then I looked down at my hands. They were shaking.

"I can't believe this has happened," I said. "Exactly like the mural…"

Will coughed. "Yeah…"

I glanced behind us, where the front of the train carriage lay on its side, the mangled remains of the Ford wrapped around it. "We couldn't save her. I thought we could get to her before… before anything like this…"

Will reached for my hand. Clasped it. "I know."

"Why would she kill herself like that? Driving in front of a train." My eyes searched Will's. I thought about the four murals and the four disasters foretold. "How can this be happening?"

I pushed myself to my feet and scanned the carnage. The carriages at the rear of the train were still on the rails. People were stepping out of those, disheveled, stunned, and they seemed to wander aimlessly, some of them approaching the derailed cabins and trying to see into them. As they did, a few people, covered in blood, crawled out through the shattered windows.

My eyes came to rest on a middle-aged man who'd become stuck scrambling through one of those windows. Blood seeped from a gash on his forehead. The overturned cabin was unstable, and beginning to tip. If it rolled over again the man would be crushed. I ran forward and grabbed his shoulders, yanking him but to no avail.

His voice was a croak. "Please. Help me…"

"Sir, I want you to suck in your belly and push forward as hard as you can."

At the same time, I braced myself and, grabbing hold of as much of his upper torso as I could, I pulled. He groaned in agony as his body came through, his hips scraping the broken glass of the window. There were cries from others inside the cabin as it began to keel over. Drawing on reserves of strength I didn't know were there, I dragged the man to the side as the carriage overturned, the window side slamming against the ground.

In the distance, I heard the sirens of the first responders.

"You'll be okay here until the paramedics arrive," I said to the man.

He stared back at me, pale and trembling, his mouth open, gasping for breath.

I looked across to where Will, back on his feet, was marshaling a group of people together in an area of the road that was clear of the wreckage. I was heading toward him when I saw him unexpectedly stagger, his legs unsteady, and then collapse, his head hitting the asphalt with a sickening thud.

Chapter Fourteen

Zoe, Marcia, and Zach joined me in the waiting room at the Harborview Medical Center. On the wall-mounted television screen, we watched the news coverage of the railroad crossing fatality and the resulting train derailment. Ambulances were lined up along the road as paramedics attended to the injured. One hundred firefighters and fifteen paramedic teams were at the scene, and six helicopters were being used to airlift the most seriously injured to nearby hospitals. As night fell, rescuers worked under arc lights to free those still trapped. The newsman at the scene reported the current toll as being eight dead and forty-seven injured.

I sat there, watching the screen, part of my brain taking it all in, another part disbelieving that this could have happened. Exactly as prophesized in the mural.

How could that be?

Zoe's phone pinged. Glancing at the display, she said, "I get an alert every time a new *One Voice* podcast drops."

She held the phone out so we could all see Aiden Sharpe on the screen. He began:

> *On my previous podcast, I explained how I was documenting the incredible graffiti art that goes largely unseen in our city. And just yesterday I documented a mural that begged the question: could there be a graffitist who is also a psychic, and who is receiving visions of the darker side of fate that awaits some of our citizens?*

The camera pulled back, revealing Brooke standing alongside him, and behind them, the mural in the alley that depicted the train disaster. Now Brooke spoke.

> *Yesterday, I announced that I was waiting to see if the images on the mural you see behind me did, in fact, occur. And as we now know, the images shown in this montage foreshadowed the horrific train crash that occurred earlier today, many hours after the painting was discovered. How has the artist been able to do this? And if this graffitist has such prophetic visions, why not alert the police rather than foretell the tragedy in such an obscure manner?*

The podcast had hundreds of thousands of listeners, and I could see from the livestream register in the bottom corner of the screen, together with the ream of responses in the comments box that it was going viral.

When the doctor approached us, I sprang to my feet, my attention diverted and my heart pumping.

"Agent McCord's collapse can be attributed to shock, pain, and severe bruising." He was brandishing a medical chart and looking at us over the top of his glasses. "All of which caused a sudden drop in blood pressure, making him lose consciousness."

"He'll be okay?" I pressed.

"He'll be fine. He's on painkillers for the bruise. The main thing to keep an eye out for is infection. We'll be keeping him in overnight for observation, but all being well he'll be released in the morning."

We moved into the private ward where Will was sitting up on the side of the bed. I'd expected he might be in a hospital gown, but he was still in his day clothes.

I gave him a gentle hug. "You had me worried there for a while."

"A momentary drop in blood pressure," he said. "I'm fine." He waved his right hand about. "This is overkill."

"It will not hurt you to take it easy tonight," Marcia chided him. "Doctor's orders. And I'll stay here and enforce them if I have to."

Zoe grinned at him. "You can't always be the one giving the orders."

He gave her a frustrated look. Then, changing tack, he said, "Have we learned anything further about what happened with Sally Corcoran?"

"Her father's in too much of a state of shock to be any help at the moment," Marcia said. "I've contacted some of her workmates and no one detected any behavior that suggested she was suicidal."

"There can't be the slightest doubt now, though," I said, "that the disasters being shown in these murals are happening soon after they're painted, and we need to take them deadly seriously. And urgently, because as we've now seen, they could happen, not just within days, but potentially within hours of being painted."

"Any more murals reported?" asked Will.

"I've checked in with both Aiden Sharpe and Detective Radner," said Marcia. "Nothing else as of this moment."

"There's another point, not something any of us want to consider, but we may need to," Zach said.

I looked at him, raising my eyebrow. "And that is?"

"If these are visions of the future, and I know you're still not convinced of that, *but still*… if these murals are the work of a psychic" – his delivery sped up and once again he was talking fast – "then it may very well be these events *can't* be changed. Think about the words entwined with the images in the last mural. What lies ahead. If the future is preordained, then what is going to happen is going to happen and no one can alter that–"

"Zach–" I began to interject but he was on a roll.

"The theory of predestination is that everything that happens has been predetermined by God, or the universe, or whatever. A master plan from which there is no deviating. Controversial in religious quarters as it negates the concept that man has free will, but the theory is that the creation of the universe – the Big Bang, the planets, the beginnings of life, the evolution of species, of man, right down to the individual everyday lives of every living thing, all mapped out, set in stone, and unwinding in a linear fashion, at least that's how we perceive it–"

"Zach," I raised my voice above his, "however, and whyever this is happening, there's no way I could ever accept people's deaths as a predetermined fate. If we know a disaster is imminent, we *have* to try and prevent it, and we have to find this artist."

Zach raised the palms of his hands. "Not saying we shouldn't. But you need, we all need, to be prepared that this is something way beyond any of your other investigations."

The others had been silent through this, and in particular Will, always the most resistant to any suggestion of the supernatural. When he did speak his words were quiet and considered.

"We are going to find out how and why this is happening," he said, "and we're going to put a stop to it."

"As I mentioned earlier, for my book's chapter on psychics," Zach said, "I interviewed a local man. A former military officer and at one time, a cop with the SPD. He worked with psychics who he says helped with solving cases. But he claims those details were redacted from his reports by his superiors."

"And does this guy claim to be psychic himself?" I asked.

"Yeah. These days he runs a meditation class and works as a healer and spiritual advisor."

Will's expression soured. "As in fortune teller?"

"Not the term he, or I, would use," Zach rebutted, "but despite all that you'll find this guy very down-to-earth, considered, even pragmatic, and he knows a lot of people who are part of the psychic community."

"And you're insistent this guy is worth us talking to," Will said.

"If you want insights into how the psychic mind works from someone who's part of a whole network of practitioners, who has a military and police mindset, I think he's worth a visit. What's more, he dabbles in art. The more I think about it, like Astrid, he might also recall someone whose interests would now seem suspicious."

Despite whatever misgivings Will might have had, I wanted to explore every angle. This approach was certainly different, and precisely the reason I considered Zach Silverstein a valuable consultant.

"Give him a call," I said to Zach, "let him know we want to pick his brain."

I was still there after Marcia, Zoe, and Zach had left. Will was restless, shifting his position.

"You might not have been physically injured out there today, Ilona," he said, "but just like everyone else, you got a hell of a shock. Even more so than some, I mean – hell – you were on the track seconds before impact. Looking in at Sally Corcoran–"

"She was facing away from me at first, not moving, so I didn't... there wasn't much chance to connect..."

"But she turned, you saw her face," Will said.

My hands were in my lap and Will gestured to them. "Just mentioning it... your hands are shaking. You need to go home and get plenty of rest. And you should be talking it all through with someone. Like Marcia."

I gave a wan smile. "I'll admit I'm tired."

A voice came from the doorway. "Some people can't stay out of trouble, can they?" Nadine's grin was wide and cheeky as she swept in. "So glad you're okay," she said, embracing Will. "I came as soon as I heard. Brett wanted to come with me but both of his kids have got the flu and–"

Will sat up a little. "It's okay, I'll speak with him later. And, really, this is no big deal. A big, bad bruise, left arm." He held it up, with only a slight grimace. "I'm fine."

Nadine shot a glance at me. "So sorry about what happened out there with that poor girl."

"We all are."

"Are you okay, Ilona?"

"I'm fine." I noticed that Nadine was cradling a plastic container.

"Home-made apple pie," she said, noticing my gaze. "I know Will well enough to know that relaxing isn't his thing, so hopefully this will help."

Glancing at me, Will repeated his previous comment, "Go home and get some rest."

I gave a nod of agreement. What's more, I wasn't sure I could handle too much of Nadine's bubbly, switched-on manner.

My eyes met hers. "Will needs rest, as well."

"As soon as he's had some of this pie with me, I'm leaving him to it."

I waved as I left. On the ground level, I exited the automatic double glass doors to find Marcia standing in the forecourt. "Were you waiting?"

"I figured you wouldn't be far behind me, and I wanted to get a private moment with you." She adjusted the glasses on the bridge of her nose and fixed me with a look of concern. "Everything's been going a million miles per minute this afternoon and we've all been worried about Will. But Ilona, you were a hair's breadth from that train hitting. I'm worried the shock is going to hit you once you have a quiet moment."

There was a croak in my voice. "I thought we'd get to speak with the girl before anything happened. Never expected…"

I took a deep breath and looked past her at the clouded night sky. I felt the first sprinkle of light rain.

"None of us could have anticipated that if there was a train crash, it would happen so soon."

"If these aren't psychic visions, Marcia, then what on earth are they?"

"You've already made it clear what we need to do," Marcia said calmly. "We find the answer by finding the artist. And we suss out any common denominators between the disasters."

We strolled back to our cars, and Marcia said, "I saw Nadine Rochester going in."

"She headed over when she heard what had happened." I sensed that Marcia was wondering about Nadine being back on the scene in Seattle. "Her brother, Brett, is having some issues, and Will's helping out."

Never one to shy away from being forthright, not with me, anyway, Marcia said, "I got the impression there could be more to it than that."

"I think you might be right."

"How do you feel about that?"

"I don't feel anything about it." I bit down lightly on my lip, aware I'd answered that a little too fast, a little too harshly.

Marcia pursed her lips. "Positive?"

This time I allowed a beat before answering. "Positive."

* * *

Driving back to my apartment, the voice of mischief in my head was questioning everything I'd said to Marcia.

I don't feel anything about it.

But I did.

Positive.

Liar.

I had felt as though my heart was going to explode when I'd watched Will collapse. There was an overwhelming sense of relief on discovering he was okay. For a few dark moments there I'd wondered what the world would be like without Will McCord in it and I'd held back tears, my stomach churning, as I'd waited with the others.

I enjoyed coming to the UCU every day and working alongside Will and the camaraderie that had been growing between us these past several months. Will had hinted on a couple of occasions that we might get together for some dinner, and catch up on what was going on in our lives outside of work. I hadn't ruled it out but I also hadn't given it a great deal more thought. And Will was not pushing for it in the short term. The status quo was something I enjoyed. There was that word again.

But Will's collapse and Nadine's appearance had prompted feelings I'd been keeping at bay, at least while Will and I were building the UCU.

My cell rang as I walked into my apartment.

"I've gone over last night's CCTV from either side of that alley," Zoe told me, "and there's absolutely no sign of anyone entering or leaving. I've double-checked with the shops that have back exits into the alley. There's only

75

three, and all confirm the doors were locked and there'd been no break-ins."

"We need to look at this with fresh eyes in the morning," I said.

* * *

I walked out onto my balcony and leaned against the railing, gazing out on the Seattle skyline. The light rain from earlier hadn't amounted to anything and there was a crispness to the air. Nightlights shimmered across the patchwork of urban and green spaces. I'd come to love Seattle since arriving here over four years earlier to join the Washington branch of the CCRSB, the Criminal, Cyber, Response, and Services Branch, long before the UCU had come into being. I'd grown up in DC, raised by my father, a former Assistant Director of the Bureau, and I often thought of how he'd beamed when I'd graduated from Quantico. It couldn't have been easy for him, after the death of my mother from cancer so many years ago, but he'd never let it show. Always calm, considered, and in control. But he'd broken protocol when he'd secretly negotiated with the men who kidnapped me for ransom when I was just fourteen. And rather than be demoted in disgrace he'd taken early retirement. It's one thing to have strict rules when it comes to negotiating with criminals, but quite another when you are faced with such a personal crisis. What would any of us do? My father had always been an inspiration to me, for his years of duty, and for the dignity with which he'd acted in his final years. I missed him dreadfully.

It had been early evening and I'd been walking to a friend's house on a quiet street, not far from my home, when a car pulled alongside me on the street. A man had stepped out, quickly covering my mouth from behind, with what I later learned was a cloth doused with chloroform. I'll never forget the sheer terror I felt when I awoke in a small box, my hands tied behind my back. A micro cam in the box sent a video feed of me to my father's home PC. At the same time, he'd received an email from my kidnapper, demanding he release classified documents to the media that incriminated another agent of corrupt behavior.

The video feed was on a recurring loop. My father had no way of knowing I'd freed my hands and managed to shift the heavy lid of the box, giving me air, and eventually enabling me to create enough of a gap to get out of the enclosure. Looking back even now, I remember hearing the voice of my mother, encouraging me, urging me to try harder to shift that lid. *You can do it, Ilona. Push. I'm here. I'm with you. I'm always with you. Keep pushing.* Had her spirit been there with me? Or was her spirit so strong in my memory that just thinking of her had the same result, embodying her strength and her love? Much later, those kidnappers were caught but I'd emerged from the ordeal a different person. Whatever steel I might have had inside me before the kidnap was magnified a thousandfold, and I was determined to follow in my father's footsteps as an agent.

In his enforced retirement, he had always been interested in the cases I was working on. As I did many times, I imagined him standing beside me at the railing, and I asked him, "Do you believe in psychics?"

He answered as he always did. "Depends on the evidence."

"And what do you do when all the evidence points to the impossible?"

He replied with his other stock-in-trade response. "Same as Sherlock."

I'd always laughed at that and couldn't resist a gentle smile now. That famous line: 'When you have eliminated all which is impossible, then whatever remains, however improbable, must be the truth.'

I'd told Will I was tired, and I was. But I was also wide awake and as restless as he was in that hospital ward. My mind turned over the facts as they stood. Murals were painted to tie in with Aiden Sharpe wandering the city and photographing graffiti art. Always in out-of-the-way spots where there was no CCTV. And another thought struck me. The murals were always on the sides of buildings that were six or so stories high. Not skyscrapers.

I needed to let off steam and felt the urge to go out into the night. At least I knew Will wouldn't be arriving for a late visit and see me heading off, duffel bag slung over my shoulder. I'd promised myself that I wasn't going to continue to pursue the one thing that was dangerous to me both personally and professionally. At the same time, I kept convincing myself that one last time wouldn't hurt. I looked out on the rooftops that outlined the cityscape against the heavens. I thought of that alley where the most recent mural had been discovered. And I had an idea.

Chapter Fifteen

I changed into my hoodie and sweatpants and drove to the street which was joined by the alley. It was after midnight and the area was deserted. Even so, I checked and double-checked the street for anyone lurking or following.

Nothing.

I took my infra-red binoculars from the duffel bag on the back seat, hung them around my neck, and made my way across the street to the alleyway. My heart fluttered and I felt the old familiar tingle of excitement.

The older-style brick, glass, and steel structure here was perfect for an urban climber. I took a running jump and grabbed hold of the piping and the upper ledge above a ground-level window, pulling myself up, my hands rapidly exploring and finding the foot and handholds in the ridges and the ironwork that enabled me to scale the expanse of wall. My blood pumped and my adrenaline rocketed as I made the ascent, and the exhilarating sense of freedom I felt was as strong as ever.

When I'd freed myself from that narrow, dark box during my kidnap, years before, I'd found that I was at the bottom of a deep shaft. A locked concrete and steel door meant the only way out, was up. The rough, rock-hewn shaft above me seemed to rise forever. Looking back, I'm not sure I'd ever know what possessed me to try and climb the wall of that shaft – naivety, anger, bravery, all of the above – but I'd made it more than a quarter of the way up when my rescuers located me and got me to the top before I fell. I'd been like a spider, clinging to the sides of the shaft, slowly scrabbling my way up.

Even at that young age, I'd taken control of my situation. The freedom I'd tasted when I emerged into the air above the shaft had changed me, emboldening me in ways I could never have imagined.

The impish voice inside my head constantly reminded me there was no greater release of tension for me than climbing the elevations of the city, rising above the chaos, and feeling the touch of the higher breezes against my face. Over and over. I've no doubt that if a psychologist was ever apprised of my obsession, they would analyze it as a constant attempt to relive that sense of freedom and exhilaration. I didn't care. I just knew what worked.

I clambered onto the roof and took in my bearings. It was a mildly sloping steel-reinforced roof. I moved to the spot directly above the space on the wall where the mural had been painted and examined the area. I found exactly what I was looking for straight away. Four tiny drill holes that could screw in a metal roof anchor. An anchor to which you could attach abseil ropes, used by workers to lower themselves in harnesses down the side of buildings, for window cleaning and repairs. That was why there was no sign of the graffitist on the CCTV and why there was no forensic trace evidence on the ground. The Artist had come across the roofs, abseiling most of the way down this building, and spray-painting from various positions, stabilized in a flexible full-body safety harness. Buildings of around six stories were perfect. Afterward, the metal anchor was unscrewed but of course, the tiny holes remained, unobserved.

Was the Artist out there somewhere again, tonight? This was an ideal time, allowing enough hours to complete a mural before early morning workers might pass in the alleys or back streets.

There was only a short gap between the buildings in this row. I moved with caution even though the roofs were no longer slippery from the earlier drizzle, stepping from one to another, and then, where there was a wider gap, I leaped across. I reached a place from which I had a wider view of the surroundings, and I scanned three-sixty degrees with my binoculars. It was a hell of a long shot but if the Artist was anywhere in the vicinity and I detected even the slightest movement then I would check it out.

Nothing.

I glanced at my watch. I felt energized enough to give my search another half hour. I thought of Sally Corcoran, crushed out of existence when the train smashed into her car. I thought of the eight people who lost their lives in the derailment. Who was this graffitist?

When I could go no further across the tops of this cluster of buildings, I climbed down into another back street and walked to another alley, a few blocks further south. I scaled the side of another building – this one four-stories high – and once again, walked across the roofscapes that were unseen and unknown by the world we inhabited below, stopping now and then and scanning the steel-topped terrain.

What on earth am I doing?

Tiredness overtook me and I knew it was time to stop. For now.

I was heading to the edge of the roof when I heard a soft, metallic scraping sound in the distance, coming from the very next building. I raised my infra-reds and at the far end of the nearby roof was a figure, obscured by a hoodie – a light folded harness strapped to the figure's back. This had to be the graffitist who, kneeling, had unscrewed a metal anchor and was packing it away with their ropes.

Looking up in my direction, the Artist immediately took off, sprinting along the roof and then leaping across to another building. I ran and jumped the narrow stretch between this roof and the next, keeping my eyes focused on my footing, but also trying to keep sight of the fleeing graffitist. I caught a glimpse of the figure kneeling momentarily on the edge of the adjacent building, a flurry of movement I couldn't discern, but it was for no more than mere seconds and then they were darting away again. But not fast enough. The Artist was hampered by the equipment while I knew how to move safely and rapidly across these rooftops.

I reached the edge – another short gap – and leaped across. But as I landed on the other side, I became aware, too late, that there was a fringe of color there. The Artist had sprayed a slick of paint while kneeling and my feet slipped out from under me. My body twisted as I fell backward, over the edge, and I plummeted toward the ground four stories below.

* * *

It takes less than four seconds to fall forty-eight feet, the approximate height of four stories – just a few seconds of sheer gravitational force, no time to react or plan before it's all over. But there was an alfresco sidewalk café directly below, with a broad canvas awning at a height of one story, and I hit it and rolled over the side of the canopy, hands flailing to grab hold of its edge, but missing. I smashed to the ground, dislocating my shoulder, the breath knocked out of me. I had just a moment of consciousness before I felt as though crushing pressure was closing in and everything went black.

Chapter Sixteen

The Artist

The young girl woke with a start, and she began coughing. It was a hot summer night and her bedroom window was open, the drapes streaming out from a strong breeze, but it wasn't just a breeze, there was smoke drifting in, and she saw through the window a fiery, flickering light strobing the sky. She leaped from her bed and rushed to the window, becoming aware now of the sharp snapping, crackling sounds. The house directly across the street was a sea of flames, the fire's glare blinding, the air heavy with billowing smoke. She coughed again, and as she did the door to her room was flung open and her mother raced in.

"Stay away from the window, darling," her mother said, slamming shut the windowpane. She clasped her daughter's hand and led her out of the room.

"What's happened, Mommy?"

"Just stay close to me, honey, we may need to evacuate."

"What's evacuate mean?"

But the girl didn't get an immediate answer. She stood by her mother's side on their front porch, looking across to the fire. Her father was at their front gate, talking with another man and woman who lived on the street.

The girl wondered where the people who lived in the burning house were. Did they get out or were they trapped inside? She wanted to cry but her eyes were smarting already from the smoke and her throat was dry. She needed a drink but didn't want to say anything. Then she saw that the house next to the burning home had also caught fire. Sirens filled the air and the first of the fire trucks rolled into the street.

She looked over to the front lawn of the house beside hers, and her neighbor was standing there, a sketch pad in hand. What was her friend doing with a drawing pad in the middle of the night? And then she remembered the page that had been taken from the pad and handed to her a couple of days earlier. "Don't show this to anyone," the other child had said. "Put it in one of your drawers and then take another look in a few days from now."

She remembered that it was a sketch of a burning house.

The scene she was gazing at now was almost exactly the same as that sketch, and she was reminded of the time when her neighbor had drawn the boy falling from the bridge a day before it had happened.

The next day she heard that one of the people across the street had perished in the fire. The man who lived there was a smoker and she heard that some people thought the fire had been caused by a cigarette that had been left burning.

The girl told her mother that her friend was able to draw the future.

"You really do have quite an imagination don't you, darling?" her mother said dismissively.

But the girl knew this wasn't something she'd imagined. Was that why her friend next door had said not to tell anyone? Because it wouldn't be believed. Even if she showed her parents the sketches she'd been given, there was nothing to suggest they'd been drawn before the boy on the bridge had fallen, or before the house across the street burned down.

She wondered if she could draw something that would then happen in the real world. She tried it a few times over the following week but nothing she sketched ever became a reality.

Perhaps her friend next door was the only one to have this strange ability and something about it scared her because the sketches were always of something frightening. Something horrific. She'd had nightmares after she'd seen the boy fall from the bridge into the river.

Now she began to have nightmares about being engulfed in flames.

Twenty-two years later

I sketch the black and white pictures in pencils and crayons, detailing the full scene, but when I have my spray paints and a great big sprawling natural canvas spread out before me, I concentrate on partial elements of those sketches. My creativity blooms with imagery, fragmented scenes, and impressions that depict the whole. All linked, of course. All part of the bigger picture that will play out. And when my mural is complete, anticipation builds, and I can hear the dreadful scream howling in my head and in my ears.

There are so many horrific things that can happen.

There is so much despair in the world.

I paint the terrors as I see them unfolding.

PART TWO

Chapter Seventeen

Day Three

I woke to the touch of a hand on my shoulder. I was on my side, my eyes level with the road, a shimmer of early morning light glinting off its surface. There was a dull ache throughout my whole body. I knew the awning, in breaking my fall, had saved my life. How long had I been unconscious?

There were a few cars on the street, not many, and a uniformed cop was diverting them around me. Someone was crouching alongside me. With a slight shift of my head, I saw the face of a black woman in a paramedic's outfit, and she checked my pulse, her persona a blend of compassion and authority.

"Can you tell me your name, hon?"

My voice was barely there. "Ilona…"

The woman checked over my arms and legs. "Are you in pain?"

"Yes."

"Can you tell me what happened, Ilona?"

I'd fallen four stories. What could I say that wouldn't expose my urban climbing addiction? I cleared my throat but remained silent.

"You've got some serious bruising and a few lacerations, but nothing's broken. Were you attacked, Ilona?"

She didn't know I'd fallen. Did anyone? "I was mugged…" I croaked, letting my voice fade.

"Well, your vitals are okay but we're getting you to the hospital for a thorough check. You must've put up quite a fight."

"I'm an FBI agent," I said.

Another paramedic joined the woman and they shifted me onto a stretcher and placed me in the back of an ambulance. A small crowd of onlookers had gathered and a few phones were raised, taking pictures. A comment that another agent had once made flashed into my thoughts. "The thing about these cell phones is, they've brought out all the ghouls."

They took me to the same hospital Will was in but as I was in Emergency, I hoped our paths wouldn't cross. I felt a confronting, confusing mix of emotions as a diligent young doctor examined me. I was incredibly fortunate, not just to be alive but to have not suffered life-threatening injuries or broken limbs. But this was all the result of my combining my penchant for climbing with the pursuit of a suspect. Dangerous, reckless behavior. Exactly the kind of action I'd sworn to myself I would never repeat.

My dislocated shoulder was manipulated back into place. I had a cut down the left side of my face, nothing serious, and the bruising down my left side was painful but could have been worse. My thoughts swirled, memories resurfacing and I was in the past, reliving my first-ever urban climb. And my first fall.

* * *

I'd been unsettled for the next few months after my kidnap and rescue. Strangely, I found that the best way *not* to think about that dark, dank shaft was to imagine the open air, the blue sky, and the soaring skyscrapers of the capital that seemed to reach for the heavens.

I decided I wanted to climb one so that the shaft wouldn't be my one and only memory of having climbed. I needed a memory of climbing that could erase that earlier one. Something I was in control of. Something that represented freedom. And then I read a news article about a young daredevil who climbed one of the buildings in the business district in broad daylight, shocking and scaring the onlookers below.

I was still in high school but wanted to know more. I scoured the internet, eventually finding a series of blogs written by urban climbers and urban explorers, adrenaline junkies who shared their experiences and invited like-minded others to join them. I private-messaged one of the main bloggers and after a few exchanges over several weeks, he gave me the location of an upcoming climb. It was a seven-story brownstone on the outskirts of the city, in the early evening. I snuck out and went to the address, where I met the young climber and two others, and they invited me to follow them.

It was my first urban climb. And my first fall.

Fortunately, I was only at the level of the second story when I lost my grip and fell, grazing my arm and leg against the brick wall and crashing onto the sidewalk, spraining my ankle. The other climbers didn't even climb back down to check on me, they were lost in their own worlds. Laying there, I realized how exposed I was, and how much trouble I'd be in if I was seen and arrested. And how devastating that would be for my father, who'd already lost so much in the aftermath of my kidnap.

I realized I hadn't given this climb the same measured, methodical focus I had when climbing that shaft during my kidnap.

I got myself home and in the days that followed, I hid my scrapes and bruises and came up with an excuse for my damaged foot. But I was determined to learn from my mistake. I went back to that same building in the evening a month later. This time, I wore a sports suit with a hoodie to disguise my appearance and gloves with open fingertips and traction-designed sneakers to assist both hands and feet with grip. This time I wasn't trying to follow or impress a reckless group of thrill-seekers. This time I took it slowly, assessing each move.

Last night was the only occasion I'd fallen since then. And like that first time, my focus had lapsed.

* * *

I was sitting on the side of a bed in the hospital, lost in those thoughts, awaiting clearance for a discharge when I had an unexpected visitor.

Will.

"Ilona, are you okay?"

"All clear, apparently." I made an effort to keep my face expressionless, desperate not to give anything away.

"I was being discharged when I heard an FBI agent had been brought into Emergency." He placed his hand gently on my good shoulder. "They said it was a mugging."

"Yeah. Some random street guy. But there was nothing to mug, I didn't have my purse with me. An early morning worker saw me on the road and called 911."

Confusion passed across Will's eyes. "What were you doing out so early, in that part of town?"

I shrugged. "Woke before dawn and couldn't get back to sleep. I decided to go take another look at that mural, and maybe see if I could spot another one anywhere in the vicinity." I was making this up as I went along, and an opportunity presented itself to me. "And I did."

"What? Another mural?"

"Yes. We need to get the team out there. And forensics."

"Where was it?"

I told him the location but Will held himself very still, watching me closely, the confusion still etched into his features.

"But that's several blocks from where you were mugged."

"I wanted to scout the area as quickly as I could, hoping the Artist might've only just finished that work and not be far off."

I didn't like Will's questioning stare but there was nothing about my story that wasn't credible, and I was certain I sounded convincing while at the same time still shaken up by my ordeal.

"What were the images in this new mural?"

"I didn't stop long enough to get a good look at the detail," I said. "I figured if the Artist had only just left that I couldn't waste any time scanning the area."

Will's voice took on a dark tone. "Ilona, this isn't the first time you've put yourself in danger, off on your own looking for a perp."

"I couldn't have anticipated being mugged, Will."

He rubbed his chin. "We'll talk about it later."

"There's nothing to talk about," I said, my voice steely.

He ignored this and changed the subject. "Nadine is coming to pick me up. We'll wait for you outside and she can drive us straight over to where the mural is."

I raised an eyebrow. "Nadine?"

"She phoned earlier to check on my discharge and said she'd pick me up and drive me home."

She wasn't wasting any time getting back in Will's good books, but I held my tongue, what the hell did I care? I nodded as he headed out of the emergency ward.

* * *

This time there was no Aiden Sharpe, Brooke Goodman, or Detective Paul Radner. Just Will and me, with Nadine, and a couple of FBI forensic officers. I knew they wouldn't find any trace evidence on the ground but they'd be able to take photos, and an idea of how to reveal more of what I knew about the Artist was germinating in my mind.

Gesturing toward the forensic team, Will said, "Looks like they're coming up empty-handed again."

"And I think we know the street cams near the alley will be the same," I said.

Will frowned but said nothing.

"How's this graffiti artist doing this?" Nadine wondered out loud. Will had filled her in on some of the details of the case on the way over.

Seeing an opportunity, I glanced skyward, and said to Will, "You'll have noticed that with each mural, the buildings they're painted on are no more than six stories."

He processed the thought. "Okay."

"If the Artist isn't going into the alleys via the back exits of the buildings, and it seems that isn't the case, then that leaves" – I pointed – "up there."

Will and Nadine looked upward.

"What do you mean?" Nadine asked.

"They could be scaling down the sides of the buildings, the same as window cleaners and maintenance workers do."

Nadine wasn't convinced. "Why would the Artist go to such extreme lengths just to avoid street cams?"

"Why would they do any of this?" I countered.

"We'll get the roofs above the murals checked," Will said.

We moved closer to the wall, surveying different areas of these newly painted images. The terrified face of a child submerged in water. An empty schoolyard. Another partial license plate. A portion of a sign with the letters $N\ S\ S\ C$. And the screaming man.

My eyes were fixed on the drawing of the empty schoolyard. "No." My voice was hoarse. "Not children…"

Chapter Eighteen

Nadine dropped Will and me off at the front of the FBI building.

Zach, Zoe, and Marcia were in the UCU command center when we walked in. The photo of the new mural had been sent through and was up on the main Themis screen.

"This one's extremely distressing," Marcia said, her face drawn, "a child's face, submerged in water." She took a breath. "We've listed any place in which a child could be in the water, a river, a lake, the Puget Sound, and not necessarily even in deep water, it could be a pool or a bathtub."

"And Themis is running all the state license plates that contain those partial numbers or letters," Zoe told us, "and condensing the result to the greater Seattle area, as we did with the last mural. We'll then look for the closest schools in those areas and, of course, the waterways."

"The empty schoolyard suggests that all the schoolchildren are gone," I pointed out. "Which means we could be talking about not just one, but several children underwater." I shuddered at the thought.

A young woman from the front desk came in and told Will he had a visitor from the OIG, and he left us to it, heading to his office down the hall.

Zach whirled toward me. "Oh, and I've been in touch with Garrett."

"Who's Garrett?" I was distracted, my mind still ticking off all the avenues of investigation that we needed to cover.

"The ex-military guy and former policeman I mentioned last night, the guy who's now a psychic."

I raised my head slightly. "Right."

"You wanted to pick his brain. He's fine if we call on him at any time."

I bit down on my lip, considering this. "Probably as good a time as any to have a word with him. We'll head over to see him, as soon as Will is free."

"And when we get back, Astrid will be here. She's already sent over her students' art before-and-after photos for the brain game."

"Except it's not a game," I said.

* * *

The OIG man had a face like granite that immediately gave the impression he wasn't someone you could slip anything by. He introduced himself as Special Agent Ronson, he shook Will's hand, and both men seated themselves.

"I understand you wanted to talk to me about Special Agent Rochester," Ronson said, "and I'm on my way out but have a few minutes to spare."

"Thanks for agreeing to meet," Will said.

"I'm aware, of course, that you worked alongside Agent Rochester at the CCRSB, and that you were present when Rochester encountered Leo Vasquez at a parking station a while back. We have all the details from that report on hand."

"I know," said Will, "that you're also aware Vasquez has made attempts to sue Agent Rochester. I simply wanted to make it known that I would like to act as a referee for Brett Rochester and state that it would be totally out of character for him to threaten Vasquez or anyone else."

"Noted," Ronson said, and then, after a pause he added, "I can advise you that we have testimony from other agents who've worked with Rochester that he can be quick to anger and that he has a stubborn streak. Would you agree?"

Will didn't allow a beat to pass. "No."

"No instances whatsoever of overly aggressive behavior?"

"Nothing that I would label that way."

Ronson's gaze was direct. "That's rather vague, Agent McCord."

"As you're aware, CCRSB agents encounter a wide range of situations, some of which may necessitate a strong response. Agent Rochester's actions were appropriate in all the instances I observed."

"Very well."

There was a moment's silence and Will had the distinct impression that Ronson was sizing him up.

Rising to leave, Ronson said, "We have our investigation in hand, so we won't be requiring anything further from you. But thank you for your input."

Will rose also, feeling a stab of anxiety as he felt the communication between Ronson and himself was stilted.

"I understand that matters relating to the investigation are confidential," he said, "but let me ask, is there any hard evidence to suggest Agent Rochester threatened and harassed this man? The agent is a close colleague, he's already suffered a great deal over the accidental shooting of the young woman, and I'm concerned about how this is affecting him and his family."

Ronson didn't answer the question, but simply replied, "We're conscious of that, it's the case with all of the internal investigations we undertake, and I can assure you the matter will be processed as quickly as possible." He shook hands with Will, and then headed for the door.

Will sat rigid, staring into space, lost in thought. He felt as though Ronson had paid him the brief visit simply to tick a box. He wondered if the OIG had something in hand that cast a different light on Vasquez's complaint.

And he knew, deep down, that he hadn't been totally honest with Ronson.

His reverie was broken when Ilona strode in. "How did you go with the OIG guy?"

Will shared his misgivings with her. And then he opened up about one particular incident.

"This isn't something that I reported," he said, "or that the OIG man brought up, but there was one time when Brett and I were involved in an apprehension that turned violent. Brett threw more punches than needed and I had to pull him away after the other man had gone down." He took a moment and frowned. "I didn't think any more of it at the time. Agents are under a lot of stress when confronted by violence in the field, and I never witnessed any behavior like that from him on any other occasion."

"It doesn't mean Brett's been stalking and menacing Vasquez," Ilona pointed out.

Will acknowledged the comment with a tilt of his head but wondered if there was in fact more to Brett's recent behavior than he had been prepared to consider. And if anxiety was getting the better of Brett, what else might he be capable of?

Chapter Nineteen

"Are you right to join Zach and me visiting the psychic Zach suggested?" I asked Will.

He was on his feet before I finished the sentence, welcoming the distraction.

"Let's do it," he said, grabbing his jacket.

It was a twenty-five-minute dive via the I-5 N to the suburb of Bitter Lake, where we pulled up outside a rustic stone and wooden cottage on a leafy, winding street.

Garrett Gainsford was not what I was expecting. He looked more like an aging hippie than an ex-military man and former SPD cop. His long, graying hair was pulled into a ponytail that corkscrewed its way around to his left side and trailed over his shoulder. He looked to be fiftyish and was fit and toned, the energy emanating from him like a coiled spring ready to snap. He looked us over with inquisitive eyes after he opened the windowed cedar door and then he ushered us through into a large, sprawling room that was as ramshackle in appearance as the exterior of his cottage. A thick, patterned rug sectioned off part of the original hardwood floor, and a wide, deep window looked out on a porch in need of a coat of paint. The waters of the lake could be glimpsed in the distance.

Zach introduced us all. Glancing around the room, my gaze settled on a wall adorned with a series of misty, atmospheric paintings of the lake.

"How's that book of yours doing?" Garrett asked Zach, as he sank into his sofa and gestured for us to do the same.

Zach smiled. "Provoked a lot of thought which is exactly what I wanted."

"I reckon that chapter on psychics, where you quoted from your interview with me, was what got people interested," Garrett said with a wry grin.

Zach laughed. "No doubt."

"I'll tell you what I think of your harebrained ideas about proving the existence of the supernatural." Garrett shifted on the sofa, getting comfortable – his long, jean-clad legs stretched out. "Even if you presented hard physical, irrefutable proof of something otherworldly, a large percentage of the population wouldn't believe you anyway, or would remain skeptical. Why? Because it's all a part of our conditioning. We grow up in a world of lies and scams, of whackos with weird ideas, of politicians who can't be trusted, and of claims, scientific or otherwise, that we aren't sure about, or which are sometimes later revealed as just plain wrong. When it all boils down, we tend to believe in what we can see right in front of our noses, and we're hard to convince of anything else. But hey, keep writing those books and giving those lectures and chasing your rainbow, I commend you for it, anyhow."

Zach made a face. "When are you going to tell me what you really think?"

Garrett shook his head in mock dismay. His gaze then took in Will and me. "So, from what Zach told me on the phone, you wanted to sound me out about the psychic community, in relation to a case you're working on."

"Zach tells us you worked with psychics when you were with the SPD," I said. "Given your background, we'd be interested in what you can tell us about people who claim those abilities, what their motivations are, and why, in fact, they often don't lead anywhere."

"People who have psychic visions are often as much in the dark about it as those around them," Garrett said. "They don't know where the visions are coming from, or why. A higher power? Sure. But what, exactly, is that? Why do some folk get visions and not others? And what's more, they may be seeing the future, but if they are seeing it in fragmented scenes, they won't necessarily understand what it means."

"Does a person experiencing these kinds of visions always try to do the right thing with the knowledge?"

"Not sure I know what you mean."

Will stepped in. "Are there psychics who might deliberately withhold vital information that could save lives?"

"It's not something I've come across in my interaction with others. If anything, it's the opposite. That's not to say there might not be a psychic who would act in that way. Anything is possible, after all." The question had piqued his curiosity. "You think someone is letting bad things happen without intervention?"

"It's a line of inquiry we're pursuing," I said.

I was surprised when Will, usually more circumspect than me, offered more. "There seem to be painted images that point to tragic incidents. Incidents which then occur within a very short time frame."

"How short?"

"One to two days."

Garrett mulled this over. "Never heard of anything remotely like this. I'm guessing you think the artist wants someone to see this esoteric painting and decipher its meaning. Knowing all the while it will be too slow a process for them to prevent the outcome."

Will nodded slowly but didn't interrupt Garrett's thought process.

"Something like this is bound to attract the attention of law enforcement." Garrett gestured. "Which clearly it has. Probably just what this person wants. I'll tell you what's coming to mind; this is both the ex-military man and the spiritualist speaking, and those two don't always come together up here" – he tapped his forehead – "but it sounds like this psychic doesn't just get dark visions, seems like they actually like it, and then love it even more when the tragedies play out. He or she craves the excitement but more than that, they hold a deep-seated grudge, likely against everyone and everything, but perhaps mostly against law enforcers."

I raised an eyebrow. "And what makes you discern all that?"

"The psychics I dealt with during my SPD days weren't predicting future crimes, they were pointing us in the direction of crimes already committed. They meant well. If this psychic you're alluding to had a good soul, they'd be working with you guys or the cops or the media, desperate to do whatever they could to avert these tragedies. They're doing the opposite. Painting pictures with cryptic clues just a day or so ahead. And who better to play this cat-and-mouse game with, for an adrenaline hit, than the F-B-oh-so-glorious-I." He gave a mock salute and for a moment I wasn't sure whether he was someone who would be on our side or not. "I'd say you've got yourselves facing off against a very clever, totally deranged Machiavellian type of character."

It was an odd and rambling response. Almost as though Garrett was enjoying the concept as much as he believed the mysterious graffitist was.

My attention was drawn once again to the paintings on the far wall. Through a gap in the slightly ajar door further to the back, I glimpsed what appeared to be an easel. "Are those your paintings?"

He nodded, pursing his lips. "I think that painting is the most spiritual of all the arts. Complements my meditations. A calming influence on the soul of this old soldier." He gave an expansive gesture. "And I sculpt. Lately, I've been writing a book. All tied-in. My life journey from military madness to spiritual wonders. But then the Prof knows all about that from when he interviewed me for his book." He fixed his gaze on Zach. "Your quest to prove the truth of the supernatural all around us."

Zach acknowledged this with a gesture of his own. "I have to confess, though, that I've always considered psychic phenomena as man's connection to something… grand. All-seeing, all-knowing. A force for good."

"A benevolent creator."

"Perhaps. A gift that psychics, like the ones who approached you at the SPD, wanted to use to help others. But I hadn't figured on there being a darker side, enabling psychic visions for darker purposes. This artist is more like an instrument of the devil."

"Where there's light, there's dark, Prof. Even in the psychic world."

I knew Will wasn't buying into any of this, but he didn't interject. He was watching Garrett closely.

"Have you encountered anyone, either in the spiritual or the arts community or one of the psychics who approached you when you were policing, who strikes you as having a hidden side like that?" I ventured.

Garrett shook his head. "No. But then, the operative word there, Agent Farris, is 'hidden.' Is it not?"

I couldn't help but note a twitch at the corners of his mouth, as though he was suppressing a grin.

"Could you direct us to others in the psychic community who might be worth speaking to?" I asked.

"No one specifically comes to mind," he said. "So, what is it you're hoping to achieve?"

"I would have thought that's obvious," Will said. "We need to track the artist down and find out how they're doing this. *Are* these premonitions, or are the disasters being orchestrated somehow?"

"There's now been more than a few of these predictive murals," I added, "so we're looking at it from every angle in order to get to the truth."

"Truth?" Garrett raised his eyes. "Is there such a thing?"

"What do you mean by that?" I asked.

Garrett took a moment to collect his thoughts. "If Person A tells the truth, and Person B tells a different truth about the same matter, and Person C's account is somewhere in between, then each of these accounts cancels out the others. These days, people speak of 'his truth,' 'her truth,' or 'their truth.' But there can be only one. So, if we can't know which is *the* truth, perhaps that means there isn't one, and everything is just personal perception."

"I see your point," I said, "but our job is to navigate through all of that to find answers."

He grinned. "Spoken like a true law enforcement officer. But it doesn't solve the conundrum of what is real and what isn't. It's still someone's perception."

It was the kind of thinking that could cause a person to seem a little odd, and Garrett was nothing if not a little on the unusual side.

"If you do think of an artist or a psychic you've encountered, particularly if it relates in any way to the works of the Norwegian artist, Munch, then please get in touch with us," Will said. "Even a detail you might've considered insignificant could prove vital to us."

"Edvard Munch, eh?" His eyes lit up as though in appreciation. "I gather you've spoken with Astrid Karlsen?"

"Yes," Will said. "Do you know Astrid?"

"She and I have sat together on a couple of art competition judging panels. Great lady. Interesting character. If there's an artist that fits the Munch profile, Astrid's your best bet in finding them. And if anything does come to mind that might relate to this case of yours, I'll be in touch. No matter what else I might be doing in this life, I'll let you in on a little secret" – he made a fist and gently struck his chest – "there's always a bit of the copper still inside."

Chapter Twenty

When we returned to the UCU, Astrid was there with Zoe and Marcia. Zoe had brought up photos of all the murals we'd discovered so far, and Astrid was looking over them. One of the monitors displayed a photo of Munch's original painting, *Der Schrei der Natur.*

Zach moved in alongside Astrid and Zoe, while Marcia stepped away and gestured for Will and me to join her. "We're still searching for common denominators between the people and companies involved in the accidents," she said, "but what we have established so far, is that the overpass truck, the car that hit the factory, and the Corcoran vehicle, were all insured with Sovereign, the same insurer that covered the Everett factory, *and* Sovereign is also the insurer for the state train network."

"Not so unusual, though," Will pointed out, "given Sovereign's one of the largest insurance firms in the state."

"Still, a line of inquiry I'd want to pursue," I stated. To Marcia, I added, "Keep scanning for links between all those accidents."

We moved toward the others.

"What do you make of the graffitist's work?" I asked Astrid.

Astrid turned to me. "It captures the essence of Munch's work. A very good copyist. It's particularly interesting to me how the screaming man connects to all of the fragmented images. It tells me something about the soul of this artist."

"What is it telling you?"

Astrid turned back to the murals, staring hard at them. "*The Scream* has been an internationally famous work of art for over a century, not because it reflects the specific mental health issues that Edvard Munch suffered but because of its timeless quality. It represents how all of us feel about the chaos, the loneliness, the disasters, and the death that we all fear, that we're all confronted by either in person or by observation of the world around us. It is like a collective mental illness infecting the entire human race, and Munch captures it in that pallid, ghostly, screaming face."

She paused, gathering her thoughts, and then she raised her right arm and made a sweeping gesture. "Look at what has been going on in this country over the past few years. Mass shootings. Riots. Political and social unrest. Viruses. The threats posed by other nations. And then look further afield at other countries. Whether it's military invasions, war, or natural disasters like earthquakes or tsunamis, it doesn't end. This artist feels the weight of it, as we all sometimes do. The Artist, like Munch, is expressing the sheer enormity of it all. And what is more, the act of graffiti like this, which is an act of anonymous vandalism, is known for expressions of resentment, despair, and misdirected energy."

"I think it's more than that," Will offered. "I think this artist is getting off on this and wants these tragedies to occur."

"Have you had any further thoughts on a student who might know something about all of this?" I asked.

Astrid pursed her lips and shook her head, clearly disappointed that she couldn't offer something more.

"Which is the reason it won't hurt to play my little brain game." Zach moved toward the console and glanced at Zoe. "All set up?"

"Ready to rock," Zoe said, but despite the lighthearted response, her expression was businesslike.

Her fingers flew effortlessly across the keyboard and the first of Astrid's before-and-after photos of her students' art – showing their progress from the beginning of a teaching semester to the end – appeared on the large monitor. The first painting was very simple, with farmyard animals in a rustic setting; the second painting, its craftsmanship much more developed, was of a lone horse running wild in a vast expanse of greenery. "I don't recall these paintings or who painted them," Astrid remarked.

The program constructed by Themis simultaneously ran a series of photos unrelated to Astrid's classes, all panoramic bird's eye views of the countryside.

"Any thoughts at all coming to mind?" Zach asked.

"It's put me in mind, not of a student, but another art teacher I had for a while when I was older. He always told us how he'd grown up in the country and all of his art was influenced by that. But he'd moved to the city and discovered that deep inside he was a real city slicker. And every time he told us that it got a laugh." She smiled gently at the memory.

"Pictures can trigger buried memories," Zach reminded us, "causing us to recall precise moments in time.

Something neuroscientists have known for more than half a century and which they've used in countless areas of research."

"That was the purpose of the college brain game Zach and I created," Astrid elaborated. "It showed students that if they got stuck on a question in an exam, then picturing in their mind a raft of images relating to the subject could spark their memory of the specific information they'd studied."

Zach continued, his already rapid speech accelerating even further as he became more and more impassioned. "When we see words, they're encoded in our brains. But pictures are encoded twice, once for the image, and once for the word we associate with that image. For example, looking at a picture of the sky, both the image and the word are cataloged in the brain's archive. It's called the picture superiority effect and put simply, it means pictures are more effective in bringing forth forgotten memories than words, such as names, are. And I'm assuming that with someone like Astrid, who is a highly visual person, that effect will be magnified."

"We'll keep going," Zoe said, "and if there's a particular image you want me to freeze, just say so."

Themis ran a few more of the sets of before-and-after artworks, accompanied by a short gallery of similar photos gleaned from photo libraries.

One of the 'before' sketches was of a high-tech vehicle in a futuristic metro setting. It was good but it lacked depth and its proportions were awkward. The corresponding 'after' of that artist, from many months later, was a striking, atmospheric painting, of sleek, visionary car designs.

"Oh, I remember this guy," said Astrid, "quite the sci-fi geek. Terrific illustrator, inspired by movies, he just needed a few hints on craftmanship."

"When was the last time you even thought about him?" Zach asked.

She shrugged. "Couldn't say. But not for a long time."

"Do you think he might've got involved in movie design work himself? Do you remember anything else about him?"

Astrid shook her head. "No…" but then she stopped short, tilting her head to the side, squinting her eyes as a memory resurfaced. "Actually, I am remembering something."

"What is it?" Zach pressed.

She thought on it for a moment longer. "I remember another student, maybe a friend of his, sometime later, telling me that my futurist art student had gone to work for a TV production company. I'd completely forgotten that–"

"But these photos, used as a brain game, are jogging memories you didn't know you had." Zach shot a triumphant glance at Will. "Which is the whole idea of the exercise."

"Let's keep going, then," I said.

"The next step," said Zach, "is to explore whether any of your other students painted something in a similar expressionistic style."

Themis's slide show continued with Zach pressing Astrid on anything those artworks brought to mind. One of the student art pieces was of seascapes and boats, and Astrid recalled that she'd once had another student whose day job was working on the Puget Sound ferries, another memory from the distant past that she'd all but forgotten until now.

Astrid seemed to be enjoying the varied recollections the images ignited but, as they went along, she began to screw her face up, wrinkles rippling across her forehead.

"You look like you've got something else on your mind," I said to her.

"I keep thinking back on that sci-fi movie-inspired student, and there's something else… not about him, not about futuristic drawings, but… something else… nagging…"

Zach offered a few prompts. "Another student, maybe something they drew, or something they shared with you, or maybe this is about a group discussion in class? Something about the future?" Zach turned to Will, Marcia, Zoe, and me. "Drawing out all these memories of different people and past times, it can have a Pandora's box-type effect, releasing a whole host of related memories."

Astrid rose from her seat, stretched her legs, and then moved away from the screen. She sat in one of the other chairs, away from the console, staring at the wall. She seemed almost physically shaken.

"Astrid, are you okay?" I said, approaching her.

"I can see her face."

"Whose face?"

"There was a girl, younger than me. I remember her saying she loved to paint beautiful things, hopeful things. I said that's a lovely gift to share and she said she needed to do it, to make up for all the bad things. And I asked her, 'Have you seen bad things?' and she said she used to draw with her neighbor when she was very young and that this other person, who was older than she was, knew of horrible things that were going to happen and liked to sketch them."

"Okay," said Zach, "let's run through the names again, of all the students you've had over the years and see if—"

"It wasn't one of my students," she said. "This was a long time before I began teaching. I was very young, and of course, I didn't believe her, and neither did the others she told. We thought it was just one of those childhood fantasies, a kid with a wild imagination." She rubbed her chin, digging deeper into her thoughts. "It was so long ago, that I'd forgotten all about it. But I can picture it now. There was a small group of us, and we were chatting, and we were sitting at our easels."

"This was when *you* were a student?" Will said.

"Yes."

"Who was your teacher?"

"A well-known Norwegian art teacher. I studied with him for several years, in my teens and early twenties. But I barely recall this girl, so she can't have been a student for long. There were always quite a few students who weren't stayers. They came to classes for a while and then dropped out."

"Is the teacher still alive?" I asked.

"Yes. Retired now. Lars Andersson."

"We need to have a word with him," I said. "Will you come along with us?"

She gave an animated gesture of support. "Of course. Anything I can do to help."

Chapter Twenty-One

Will drove with Astrid alongside him and I was in the back seat. "We met with an old friend of yours this morning," I said to her. "Garrett Gainsford."

"Now there's a man with a very interesting background." She peered at me in the rearview mirror and I could tell by the faraway look in her eyes that I'd caused her to cast her mind back on a different set of memories. "A very talented but also very troubled artist," she added.

"Why do you say that?" Will asked.

"He didn't tell you about his military days? He was on a tour of Afghanistan when the jeep he was in ran over a landmine. The other three soldiers in the jeep were killed. Garrett survived, badly injured, but he made a full recovery. Physically, anyway. Not sure you can ever escape the trauma of something like that mentally."

"We know he was ex-military and ex-SPD. But he didn't mention any of that to us."

"I don't suppose there's any reason he would have," she said. "He tends to keep those thoughts to himself, especially with people he doesn't know. And he seems to have his own ways of dealing with it. Every now and then he just ups and disappears for a few days, maybe weeks, goes walkabout. I think that's one of his coping mechanisms."

"We were there to talk to him about people in the psychic community," I said.

"Picking his brains the same as you picked mine about my students over the years?"

"Yes. He wasn't able to help us identify anyone who might be of interest. But as you say, he's certainly an interesting character."

"We were on the same judging panels in a few art comps," Astrid said. "I got to know him quite well. There was a lingering bitterness there, he felt his military superiors had let his unit down, that they should have known about the landmines on that particular track. I gather the intel was flawed. He was in the SPD when I met him but he seemed to regard the police chiefs the same as he did the defense commanders. Always at loggerheads with them; at least, that's what he confided in me. I think that leaving that whole scene and involving himself in spiritual endeavors – art, meditation, and psychic medium studies, should have been good for him, good for his soul."

"You knew him around the time he made that decision?"

Astrid nodded slowly. "I'm not sure if it was his decision, or if it was made for him. He had a lot of run-ins with his boss, some senior detective who Garrett said spent too much time obsessing about some maverick group… something about dangerous climbers…?"

"Urban climbers," I said. "The detective would have been Paul Radner."

There was a spark of recognition in Astrid's eyes. "That was the name."

It didn't take us long to reach the suburb of Hunts Point, on the shores of Lake Washington. Lars Andersson lived in a double-story, European-style residence with a driveway that swept past a three-car garage to a patio that featured stately French doors for the entrance. Astrid told us on the drive over that in addition to his long years of holding sought-after art classes, Lars was the owner of an exclusive art gallery in Bellevue. It had obviously all been very lucrative. "Not a starving artist, then," I quipped as Will pulled over outside the front entrance.

Astrid responded with a grin. "Lars likes his food."

Lars met us at the door and, after introductions, he motioned for us to follow him through to a spacious drawing room with a bay window. It provided a view of the narrow channel that ran alongside the residence before opening into the wider expanse of water a little further north.

Lars was an elderly man who moved slowly and carefully and spoke in measured tones, but there was an unmistakable glint in his eyes, a reminder that the spirit of the artist and the entrepreneur was still very much in attendance.

"I must say, I'm very intrigued," he said. "When Astrid phoned to say the FBI wanted to talk with me about a graffitist who's been emulating the style of Edvard Munch's *The Scream*, I was… well, curious is hardly the word." He clasped his hands together as he sat on one end of a long sofa. "I was somewhat fascinated, anxious to know more."

I proceeded to outline what we'd encountered so far with the graffiti art and the resulting accidents. Lars listened intently, his gaze never wavering as I spoke. I asked whether he'd ever come across anyone who might fit the profile of this artist.

"No," he said, almost apologetically. "Of course, there have been students over the years with styles that I would term as ethereal, but no one specifically Munch-like comes to mind." He looked at Astrid and smiled. It was obvious he was pleased to see her regardless of the circumstances. Refocusing on me, he asked, "Has this graffitist committed a crime – apart, of course, from defacing private property with his paintings?"

"Not that we're aware of," I said. "At this point, we want to find this person and ask how they're visualizing these events."

"I'm sensing" – Lars's gaze flicked over me and Will – "that you don't believe this person is psychic. Surely you don't think the artist is perpetrating these events in some way?"

"We can't rule it out," Will offered.

"Although," I added, "given the completely random nature of the events leading to the accidents, it's hard to see how that could be the case. But more to the point of our visit here, Astrid remembered something about one of your students." I recounted Astrid's recollection of the girl whose neighbor painted events that occurred soon after. "I appreciate we're talking about a girl who would have been in some of your classes over twenty years ago but are you by any chance able to recall anything like that?"

Lars's expression was one of surprise. He took a moment, deep in thought, and then his face softened again. "I certainly do remember that girl." He tapped his forehead with his right forefinger. "It's coming back to me. The lass who told the others she knew someone who could paint the future. Such a long time ago. Not normally an incident or a moment that I would have stored away up here" – he tapped his forehead again – "but I remember sitting down with my granddaughter and chatting about this girl's claim. It led to a great big conversation about whether people could have visions and about all the mysteries of life and the universe. We had a wonderful evening talking about it all."

"Your granddaughter?" I queried.

"Yes." He smiled gently at the memory. "I don't remember the other girl's name, or very much about her, only that she was my granddaughter's best friend from school. Or as the young ones would say today, her BFF." He chuckled.

"Is that the reason this other girl attended your lessons?" Will asked.

Lars nodded. "My granddaughter, Danielle, loved coming along to my special after-school children's art classes. I ran them for a few years back in the day. I didn't charge very much for those classes, and people could pay me on the day. There was no commitment to attend, so unfortunately for you, I didn't keep a roster of the children's names. It was all very casual. Danielle brought her friend along. Her friend loved to draw and was pretty good at it as I recall, but she only came for a short while. I'm not sure what became of her after that, or even if Danielle remained in contact with her." He shifted his gaze to Astrid. "And you were in those classes and remembered the kids talking about it?"

"Yes," said Astrid. "Though I didn't know who the girl was and didn't remember that your granddaughter was in those same classes."

"You more than likely didn't know," Lars said. "There was no reason for me to announce that one of the other children was my granddaughter. But for you to have remembered any of that from so far back... well done."

Astrid shrugged. "The memory was prompted by a brain game."

Lars gave a bemused expression. "What on earth?"

"That's a story for another time," Astrid said.

"Do you think your granddaughter might remember her friend's name after all this time?" I asked.

"I'm sure she would. But you'll have to wait a few hours until she's up and about before you try phoning her."

"Why's that?"

"Danielle married an English boffin. She's been living in London for several years now."

Chapter Twenty-Two

Marcia, Zach, and Zoe were huddled around Zoe's main monitor when Will and I returned. Zach slid his chair back to give us space. Marcia was on a call and had her phone pressed to her ear. Zoe glanced briefly at Will and me, just as quickly returning her attention to the map on her screen.

"Themis configured the license plate numbers based on what the digits in the mural seemed to be. There weren't too many but the one that stuck out belonged to a bus that's leased out to various community groups, as well as schools. It's owned by a company called Easy Transit. We've obtained a list of the schools that use the company's services and we've whittled it down to this one – St Martins School." Zoe tapped her keyboard and a cutaway on the screen showed us the sign in the mural. "It's the only school with the letters $N\,S$ and $S\,C$ as they appear in the portion of signage that was drawn."

"Great work," said Will.

"I'm on a call with the principal over there," Marcia added, "and they have that bus booked every week to take most of their students to the nearby field for the weekly sports day."

"Which day?" I asked.

Marcia winced. "Today, would you believe? The bus is due to return now and I've asked the principal to get in touch with the bus company and have them contact their driver to stop the kids getting on the bus. He's got me on hold while he makes the call."

"That's why we've got the local map up on the screen," Zach said.

Zoe shot me a concerned look. "The principal told Marcia the bus's route includes a part of Lake Washington Boulevard South."

Will and I moved in closer. Zoe had set a red line to show the route. There was one stretch, near South Horton Street, where the road ran alongside the lake with just strips of grass and an embankment between the road and the water.

"Can we get a visual on that?" Will asked.

A moment later the screen was filled with a close-view aerial shot. It was a place I'd driven past on a few occasions. A sloped embankment to the water. Trees skirted the green spaces.

The photo of the full mural was on the larger monitor. I glanced at it, taking in the submerged face of a child, and the empty schoolyard. Like each of the murals, the images were strong, the style eerie and atmospheric, but as with the other paintings, it was the looming figure of the screaming man that magnified the sense of dread.

Marcia motioned for silence as the school principal came back on the line. Her face tightened as she listened to him and then she turned to us, her eyes widening in alarm. "The bus is ahead of schedule. The kids are already onboard and they've left the field."

"Have the principal get the bus company back on the line," I instructed. "We need them to tell that bus driver to pull over to the side of the road."

I exchanged a hurried glance with Will. It didn't matter right at that moment what we believed or didn't believe, whether the graffitist was psychic or whether something else was going on. We had all the evidence we needed that the disasters depicted in the murals were occurring. And it was happening faster and faster. All that mattered now was stopping those children from somehow ending up in that lake.

"There's something else," Marcia said, looking at Will and me. "The guys you sent to check out the roof of the building where this mural was painted. They found drill holes for a metal anchor that you'd use to attach abseil ropes."

"Your hunch played out," Will said to me. "This is how the Artist is avoiding CCTV and why there's no trace evidence on the ground."

Marcia got off the line from the school. "The principal's contacting the bus company to relay the message to their driver."

"Did you get the bus company's number?" I asked.

"Yes."

"You speak to them as well, make certain they understand the urgency," I said.

My heart was beating rapidly, a dark sense of foreboding gripping me as my mind flashed on the horrific scene of the passenger train smashing into Sally Corcoran's car. We'd been unable to stop it. Zach's earlier words echoed in my brain. *Predestination… the everyday lives of every living thing, all mapped out, set in stone…*

"Let's get out to the lake," I said to Will.

Chapter Twenty-Three

Bill Morrow had been driving for the Easy Transit company for fifteen years, and for the past few he'd been rostered to the sporting day transports for the local schools. He was particularly pleased that this gave him the chance to drive one of the newer model, electric-powered buses that were easy to handle, quiet, and gave a smooth ride. He thought today, as he did on each of these occasions, how lucky these kids were to be traveling in such comfort, with plush, roomy seats, and AC. A far cry from his days as a schoolboy.

He watched as the kids packed up their sports bags and were shepherded into the bus by the two teachers on duty. Around thirty boys and girls, all sweaty and talkative, still brimming with adrenaline from their games. Once all were on board, Bill climbed back into the driver's seat and minutes later they were on the road heading back to the school.

The day had started sunny but now it was overcast and a light rain drizzled. It didn't spoil Bill's enjoyment of the boats bobbing on the calm waters of the lake at the marina as they drove past. The kids were all too busy chatting excitedly amongst themselves to appreciate the beauty of their surroundings and Bill felt a stab in his heart remembering his carefree student days, juxtaposed in his mind at that moment with the separation he was going through with his wife and its effect on his two young girls.

There was a voice message coming through the communicator, but it was faint and garbled. That confused him as all the other systems were fine. Keeping one hand firmly on the steering wheel, he tapped the keyboard on the console to see if he could correct the sound of the message.

* * *

Penny Samaz had been a resident of the area all her life. These days she enjoyed nothing more than taking her two small Jack Russell Terriers for their walks along the shoreline of Lake Washington. The light rain wasn't bothering her, she'd be home soon. The problem was that the two little terrors – the term Terrier suited them down to a T – had much more energy than she did. They were straining against the double leash, Penny telling them to slow down in the firm tone she knew they'd learned to understand. That was when she heard the screech of tires. At the same time, the dogs began barking and jumping. She caught sight of the bus as it failed to make the turn at the bend in the road and sped across the green strip right toward where she was walking. Penny froze, losing her grip on the double leash, and the Jack Russells darted away. The bus clipped the side of one of the cherry trees that lined the strip as it careered forward, missing her, and then hurtling down the dirt slope. Dazed and shaking, Penny glimpsed the frightened faces of schoolchildren through the windows.

Jolting herself out of her shock, Penny struggled down the embankment, her dogs racing at her heels, as the bus tipped on its side and plunged into the water.

* * *

It was roughly a twelve-minute drive via the Yesler Way from the FBI offices to Lake Washington Boulevard. A call came through from Marcia, updating us that the transit company was having difficulty with its communications with the bus. They'd been experiencing communication system problems on and off over the past two days. But neither Will nor I could have anticipated what awaited us. As we rounded the bend that ran alongside the water, we were confronted with the sight of the bus in the lake, with cars and cyclists coming to a stop and people running down the embankment to the water's edge.

We leaped from the car, Will calling 911 while I made a hurried call to Marcia. The bus was on its side, its front half submerged, the rear part of the vehicle above the surface level. Children's traumatized faces pressed against the windows and as we approached, I saw that there was water filling up inside. Were there smashed windows or was the submerged front door open? The rain was beating harder now. I knelt, unlacing and removing my shoes and stripping out of my FBI blazer, and I waded into the water and dived, ignoring the pain from my bruised muscles. Underneath the water, I could see that the bus door was open, but it was wedged against the bottom of the lake. It was impossible to get into the bus that way. And the bus was filling up fast. And then I saw the face of one of the children, submerged in the water, her body still, her eyes closed. Eerily reminiscent of the image in the mural. Was the girl unconscious? She must have been knocked out. Why weren't the others pulling her to the bus's rear which wasn't yet filled?

They don't know she's stuck there. They're simply consumed by panic.

I squinted through the water, becoming aware, behind the girl, of the driver slumped against the steering wheel, the side of his head smashed in. Instinctively I knew that he was dead. I broke the surface and raced back to the shore, calling to Will. "We've got to get those kids out. There's an unconscious girl, under the water–"

Will whirled toward the other onlookers. "Everyone who's got a car here, get us your tire jacks." Even as he said it, he was sprinting back across the grassy strip to our vehicle, retrieving the jack from the trunk.

He raced past me and began smashing the jack against one of the bus's rear windows, fumbling on several occasions as he pushed himself through the pain of his injured arm. He raised his good arm again and again, striking the metal against the glass. It cracked, and he punched out the shattered remnants of the glass, blood covering his knuckles, then he moved to the next window, once again pounding the glass.

My heart was racing and there was a hammering like a drum in my temples, but I knew I had to steel myself and calmly, methodically, swiftly act to free those children.

I will not let any one of them drown in that bus.
Not one child.

The first onlooker returned, breathing heavily, armed with their car's jack and I took it from him and thrashed my way back through the water. I located the window closest to the front of the bus that was still just above the waterline, raised my arm, and swung the piece of metal with every last ounce of energy. Once. Twice. *That girl is drowning.* Three times. On the fourth bang, the glass shattered.

With the second window, alongside the first, now broken, Will had the space he needed to reach in and start pulling the children through.

I didn't have time to create more window space. I figured – hoped – there was enough width to the window for me to wriggle my way through. There was a moment when I was sure I'd miscalculated. I was halfway through and stuck.

The girl will drown.

I wanted to scream in frustration but I wriggled and scraped and my hips hurt like hell, and I managed to squeeze all the way through. The moment I was fully on the other side, I lowered myself into the submerged part of the vehicle. I grabbed hold of the girl and pulled her above the waterline. I scrambled over the seats to where I could position her against one of the backrests, which was on its side, and began performing CPR, alternating chest compressions with mouth-to-mouth.

Please breathe. Please breathe.

I was aware that the water level was rising rapidly, and that at the higher end, the children were clambering through the smashed windows with Will's assistance. I heard sirens in the distance.

Please breathe.

I kept on with the CPR, overcome with desperation, seized now by a sickening fear that I'd lost her. The girl was as still as death, her tiny face ashen.

I couldn't stop, not yet, but I was suddenly conscious that the rising water had almost reached us, swirling now around the edges of the seat, and then the bus lurched forward, shifting deeper into the water.

I heard Will's voice, shouting, "Ilona, you need to get out of there."

Another round of mouth-to-mouth breaths and then I resumed the chest compressions, but I could see no sign of a response and I knew I was out of time.

The bus lurched again.

And then came the miracle I would never forget, the split second that changes everything and serves as a constant reminder that no matter what, you never, ever give up, not until you've exhausted every last possible option. The girl coughed up water and then she gasped for breath.

"It's okay, honey, you're okay." I brushed my fingers over her forehead. "What's your name, honey?"

The girl's voice was weak. "Kira."

"Okay, Kira, I need to get you out of this bus. Okay?"

The girl nodded feebly, her eyes wide with fright.

I put my arms around her shoulders and drew her close, and I climbed over the side-turned seats, leading her to the upturned rear of the bus. There were just a few of the children still scrambling through the window into the arms of Will and several other men and women.

Will reached in, taking hold of Kira and I followed, emerging into a steady stream of rain.

"We've got all the children," Will said. "The driver?"

"He's dead."

The mural image of the submerged child had been real, I'd seen her under the water. I'd saved her. But we hadn't stopped the crash. There'd been one fatality. How could the Artist be the cause of this? And if the Artist was psychic, if this case proved Zach's theories of the supernatural, and the Artist was seeing future disasters, then no matter how much we figured out in advance, we couldn't change the inevitable.

Which seemed to be exactly what this artist wanted.

Chapter Twenty-Four

There was a look of surprise on Will's face as he surveyed the kids. I watched as he went forward, approaching one of the girls. "Amanda?"

The girl, sitting with her knees pulled up, stared back at him, her face impassive.

He ruffled her sandy hair. "I'm Will. I worked with your dad. Do you remember me?"

She gave an almost imperceptible nod. She was shivering. In shock. They all were.

"Are you okay?"

She nodded, following up with a tentative, "Yes."

Will tapped numbers into his phone. "Let's get your mom and dad over here, yeah?"

I went forward. "Hey, Amanda. I'm Ilona. You look very cold. Need a hug?"

The girl nodded again and I reached out and embraced her. "Let's warm you up."

There was a bustle of activity all around us, as emergency workers comforted the children and locals rushed forward with blankets. The rain had petered back to be no more than a drizzle, as though in sympathy. Rescue teams waded into the water to assess the situation with the partially submerged bus. News vans pulled up by the side of the road.

Will spoke into his cell.

As he ended the call, I said, "Her dad's on the way?"

"Yes."

"And you worked with him?"

"Don Frankel. Same team as me when I was with the CCRSB. There were a couple of occasions when I met young Amanda. Way back when."

I hugged the girl close. "Coincidence," I commented.

Will didn't reply. He was staring off. The expression on his face was one I knew well. A look that said something wasn't right about this.

"What is it?" I asked him.

He shrugged it off. "Nothing."

"Nothing doesn't have a facial expression like that."

"Just seemed a little odd that the daughter of a colleague was on the bus."

"FBI family members have been known to catch buses. Especially school buses," I said drily. "It's just a coincidence."

"I don't believe in coincidences when I'm working a case." His eyes fixed on mine. "And neither, if you're honest about it, do you." He was clutching the arm that had been badly bruised the previous day, and he winced in pain.

"Your arm?"

"It's fine," he said dismissively.

I was worried about him but I decided not to push it. Not at that moment, anyway. "So, what do you think this so-called coincidence means?"

"I've no idea," he said. "And that's what worries me."

My eyes wandered over the frantic activity surrounding us, and I noticed a blue sedan with white trims and branding on its side in the form of an insignia – a crown – and the words, 'Sovereign Insurance'. Two men alighted from the vehicle. The one that strode in front of the other was a tall, black man, with broad, handsome features. Both were dressed in suits, immediately putting them out of place with the onlookers and fire and rescue crews.

"That same insurance company," I said to Will.

He nodded but said nothing and we approached the two men, who were now scanning the scene. Will and I flashed our FBI creds and I introduced us to the man whom we'd first seen.

"Myles Craddock," he responded, offering his hand, and gesturing to his offsider whose name I didn't catch.

"You're the insurers of the bus?" I said.

"Yes," said Craddock. "We're here to assess the damage."

"Fast response," Will noted.

"We don't waste any time with an incident like this." Craddock had a confident, authoritative tone. "And as it happens, we were already on the road, returning from a meeting." His eyes flitted over the mostly submerged bus and the children, huddled together, being attended to by the medics. "I understand all the children are safe but the driver died."

I swept back a strand of wet hair that had fallen across my cheek. "It was touch and go there for a while," I told him.

He loosened his tie, taking a deep breath. "An absolute tragedy, thank God it wasn't even worse."

"You've had several clients involved in extreme accidents this past week or so," I ventured. "The overpass crash, the train derailment, and the factory gas explosion."

Craddock had an intense manner about him and his eyes fixed on mine. "We get thousands of claims a week, most of them fairly routine cases, nothing like this, nor like those other three you mentioned." He glanced at his colleague, then returned his gaze to me. "I've been with the company ten years and I've never seen a series of incidents like this, so close together."

I knew that Sovereign would have multiple claims to pay out so there could be no possible benefit to the company. Was it a mere coincidence they were the insurer for the victims of these tragedies? Will was right when he pointed out that being one of the state's largest insurers, it wasn't strange that they had clients in each of the accidents.

"You're looking at potentially a great deal of claims," Will observed.

Craddock flinched, shifting his attention to Will. "Yes, especially to the train operator. And possibly to all the people injured on that train. But the company has a structure in place to deal with multiple payouts in tragedies like this."

"What's that?" I asked.

"Are you familiar with catastrophe reinsurance?"

"No," I admitted.

"It's when an insurance company takes out insurance of its own to reduce its financial exposure in the event of catastrophic events. That means natural disasters, such as floods and hurricanes, as well as man-made calamities like terrorist attacks, and accidents like the railroad crossing tragedy."

"How does that work?" I asked.

Craddock spread his hands. "Take Sovereign, for example. We have a contract with a reinsurance company. Not cheap. The premiums are massive, but without the cover, a mass number of claims from a major catastrophe, like an earthquake, could potentially cripple our operations. The reinsurance firm spreads that risk among several other insurers, selling bonds, and investing the proceeds in interest-yielding accounts."

I thought about this for a moment. "If there's a higher number of disastrous events in a given period," I speculated, "as well as mass claims from something like the train crash, then…" I took a breath, considering how best to pose my question. "Then that would provide a selling point for the reinsurer to sign up new contracts from more clients."

Craddock shrugged. "I suppose so." He gave a brief, half-grin, "You have a suspicious mind, but I guess that's to be expected of a federal agent."

"You said yourself these reinsurers charge sky-high premiums. So, there are big dollars to be made."

Craddock squinted with skepticism. "Surely, you're not thinking these accidents have been engineered by the reinsurer? This bus crash and the suicide of the girl who drove onto the rail crossing aren't something that could be manipulated. Nor could the truck that went over the overpass, or the factory gas explosion. Is this because of those media reports about a psychic graffitist? That's nonsense, isn't it?"

"There's no suggestion that the accidents have been deliberately caused by a third party," Will said, always the voice of moderation whenever I let fly with conjecture, "but we're examining these incidents due to those murals, and we have to consider every possible line of inquiry. One of the murals did feature your company's logo, which is only the most tenuous connection, I know, but does invite closer inspection."

"Of course." Craddock gestured toward his colleague. "We have to get to our examination of the scene, but if it helps your inquiries, I know the CEO of our reinsurer – David Handler of Haven Insurance Services – and I'm sure he could shed more light on their side of the business if that helps."

"Thanks," I said, "that could prove useful."

Will cast a conspiratorial eye over me as we headed back to our car. "Interesting angle about the reinsurance company."

"Your diplomatic way of saying it was way over the top."

"Maybe a tad."

"When I saw the Sovereign car pull up, it struck me as very coincidental," I said, "and you don't believe in coincidences."

"You think there's a pattern?"

"Yes, but I'm just not seeing what it could be. In those murals, the edges of every one of the images interact, with all of them swirling around the screaming man. Similarly, I'm certain there's something about every one of these disasters that links them. And connects them to the Artist. But what?"

We were back in the car, Will driving, and I closed my eyes momentarily, imagining the murals, but it was the rendition of the screaming man that filled my mind, a gruesome portrait backlit by a blood-red sunset. In my imagination, a wail erupted from the twisted mouth of the man, a primal scream that sent ice-cold shivers shooting through every nerve end.

I glanced at Will. "If I'm right, the answer to who the Artist is and how these horrors are painted in advance lies in each of those paintings."

Will's cell, propped in a holder under the dashboard, rang. Nadine's name appeared on the display for incoming callers. Will answered the call with a touch of the screen.

"Hi, Nadine. I'm in the car, with Ilona, I've got you on loudspeaker."

There was no mistaking the unease in Nadine's voice. "Will, there's been someone sitting in a car across the street from the motel, for over an hour, watching my room."

Chapter Twenty-Five

"Are you sure they're watching the motel?" Will asked.

"Yes," Nadine said. "They keep looking this way, and I've got a feeling this car followed me earlier. It pulled over there not long after I came in and… I can't be certain, from this distance…"

"What is it?"

"It looks like it could be Leo Vasquez."

"Stay inside," Will instructed. "We're only ten minutes away."

The ten minutes seemed longer, with Will hovering just over the speed limit, forcibly restraining himself from speeding, his hands clenching the steering wheel.

I attempted to ease his anxiety. "She's not in any danger from Vasquez, Will," I said.

"We don't know that. One minute he's trying to sue the FBI through the Supreme Court, and then he launches a civil case against Brett. What the hell's he doing outside that motel? How would he even know Nadine is Brett's sister, or where she's staying?"

We pulled over behind the vehicle, which was a Toyota Landcruiser, and approaching its front, we saw immediately that it was, in fact, Leo Vasquez. Will tapped firmly on the driver's window and Vasquez, startled to see us standing there, lowered the window. Looking into the car, I noticed some hi-tech equipment and a laptop on the passenger seat.

"Mr. Vasquez, you need to get out of the vehicle where I can see you," Will ordered.

"Why? There's no law against sitting in a parked car."

"Out of the vehicle, now."

Reluctantly, Vasquez stepped slowly out of the Landcruiser, making no attempt to mask the sneer on his face. "Once again, federal agents harassing an innocent, grieving member of the public."

Will's eyes scanned Vasquez's body for signs of a weapon. "Why are you watching the motel room where Brett Rochester's sister is staying?"

"I was thinking maybe of having a word with her, if and when she came out of the room."

"If that was the case you could have gone over and knocked on the door."

"I didn't want to disturb her."

"That's not the reason," Will countered. "Why do you want to speak with her?"

Vasquez shrugged. "Just thought… maybe she could persuade her brother to do the right thing, fess up that he acted irresponsibly, putting the public at risk, killing Olivia."

"What's the reason for the computer equipment in the car?" I asked him.

He shot me a hard look. "I'm in accountancy and I get a lot of urgent calls when I'm out of the office, so I sometimes pull over to attend to a request remotely. Also not a crime."

"How did you know Nadine is Brett Rochester's sister?" Will asked him.

Vasquez glared back at both Will and me. "I don't have to answer your questions."

"Did you keep a watch on the FBI building for when Agent Rochester arrived and left?"

Vasquez clenched his teeth, anger simmering. He didn't respond.

"Did you follow Agent Rochester, see him meet up with his sister, and then follow her, see where she lived, figure out she was Rochester's sister from social media posts?"

"I'm not a stalker."

"You've stalked Brett Rochester and now his sister. Just as you did when I was with Brett on that parking station roof."

"I just want justice for Olivia."

"It was an accident," said Will. "A dreadful, tragic accident. You don't think the agents involved haven't been haunted by it ever since?"

"You expect me to have *sympathy* for them?" The words came as a spit of contempt.

"No. But you need to stop this intimidation against FBI officers, Leo. You're on the verge of breaking some serious laws."

"Like any criminal, Agent Rochester needs to be held accountable for his actions. And you know what, Agent McCord? I'm done talking with you."

I was conscious that another car had pulled up and parked a couple of houses back and in my peripheral vision I saw its occupant step from the car and approach us.

Will turned, as I did, and as a quiet aside to me, he said, "It's Gabriel Vaughn."

"Who's he?"

"Leo's friend. He was there the night Leo confronted me and Brett at the parking station."

I recalled Will's description of Vaughn from that encounter. Vaughn had a lean physique and a tangle of dark hair. Will had also described him as intense, but the man who reached us now, walked with a relaxed gait and an open expression.

He nodded in the direction of Will and me, and then said to Vasquez. "Leo, what's going on?"

Vasquez grunted. "Nothing. What are you doing here?"

"Your family called me, looking for you. They're worried. They wanted me to check you were okay and tell you to go home."

Vasquez's face reddened. "I don't need everyone checking up on me and I'm headed home now, anyway. I'll speak to you tomorrow, eh?"

He waved at his friend but shot angry glances at me and Will as he turned and got into his car. Will and I stepped clear as Vasquez pulled out from the curb.

Vaughn sighed and came closer, his gaze focused on Will. "Agent McCord, let me just mention that night at the parking station. I tried to dissuade Leo from confronting Agent Rochester but he wasn't listening. Yeah, he has a temper and I went with him that night to make certain he didn't do anything stupid."

Will gave the slightest of nods. "Okay," he said. "How did you know to find him here outside this motel?"

"Leo and his wife, Miranda, have GPS locators for each other, and for their kids, on their phones. Like I said, his wife is worried about him, and she gave me the location, asked me to see what he was doing."

"He's on the verge of committing a serious offence," Will said.

"I was wondering if you could help with regard to his complaint."

"Mr. Vaughn—"

Vaughn raised his palm. "Hear me out. And please, call me Gabriel. What I want to say is that despite all Leo might have said and done, he's an honest man. He wouldn't falsify a claim like the one he's made against Agent Rochester out of some twisted sense of revenge. He just wants justice, his perception of it, anyway, for his sister. I believe he's genuine when he says Rochester has been coming around to his house, and that he threatened him while waving his gun."

"Gabriel, the FBI's Office of the Inspector General is investigating Leo's claims."

Vaughn spread his hands. "I know that. But I saw how on edge Rochester was that night at the parking station. There must be other instances of erratic behavior that would support Leo's claims, and as you've been in high-stress situations with him, perhaps you've seen or heard something in the past, something—"

Will raised his hand. "Let me stop you there, Gabriel. No, I haven't. I've no reason to believe, not for a moment, that Agent Rochester would act in a criminal manner."

Vaughn's shoulders slumped and he cast a brief, pained expression at both Will and me. "People under immense stress can act out of character," he said, his voice low.

"We appreciate your belief in your friend," I said, "but we really have to leave this matter to the OIG."

Vaughn took a deep breath. "It seems so." His body language was no longer as relaxed as when he'd approached us. He gave a conciliatory gesture. "Thanks for hearing me out, anyway." There was the briefest of pauses and then he left without another word.

I thought back on what Will had told me, about the incident with Brett losing control. "I don't know Brett anywhere near as well as you do. The incident you described before doesn't mean Brett's harassing Vasquez. But you're certain, in your own mind, that Brett would never go off-book and threaten a citizen?"

"Certain," Will said, but for the first time since I'd known him, his eyes lacked the conviction of his words.

Nadine, casually dressed in a T-shirt and jeans, came across the road toward us. "I didn't think it was a good idea for me to confront him."

"You did the right thing, staying out of his way, and calling me," Will said. He filled her in on the exchange that had just taken place.

Concern was etched all over Nadine's face. "You don't think he'll go tearing off to Brett's place now, do you?"

"Unlikely now that we've intervened," I assured her, "I'm sure he'll just head home. But we'll let Brett know to keep an eye out and we'll report this to the police. Vasquez's all stirred up inside but I don't think he would have walked over to the motel and knocked on your door. Eventually, he would have just driven off."

Will's eyes were on mine. He didn't say anything straightaway but I could tell from his expression that he wasn't convinced of that.

* * *

Arriving home at his apartment, Will removed his jacket, poured himself a scotch and dry, and lowered himself onto his sofa. He hadn't been able to stop thinking about the troubles that were swarming around Brett and were now entangling Nadine. Even though he'd gone to Nadine's motel when she'd phoned him, and even though he'd spoken to the OIG in support of Brett, Will didn't feel he was doing enough. Not nearly enough.

He'd known the Rochester family for a long time. They'd always been there for him and he would always reciprocate.

Will first got to know Brett during one of the most intense, exhilarating, and unforgettable times in his life. His mind was cast back to one particular day, unseasonably hot at over 95 degrees, a day with a relentless sun blazing from a cloudless sky.

Will prided himself on his physical fitness but after a grueling hour, he was exhausted, with every muscle, nerve, and tendon groaning, his mouth as dry as desert sand, thirsting for water, even just a drop. Sweat beaded his forehead and flattened his short, dark brown hair against his scalp.

He and his partner had traversed the gravel road for what seemed an eternity, climbing the steep hill and then down the other side, before reaching the rambling farmhouse where a woman and a child were the hostages of a man who'd lost all sense of control, a man seething with anger, a man armed with a sawn-off shotgun.

"One of us should take up the rear," Brett said, breathing heavily.

"Cover me," Will said, and brandishing his firearm and keeping low, he moved stealthily in a wide arc, to avoid the eyes of the madman who was moving in and out of the front door, watching.

The back of the house was unguarded. Will relayed what he was seeing to Brett via their comms. "I'm going in. Keep him distracted."

"Roger," came Brett's reply.

Brett stepped out from behind a fence and called to the man on the porch, identifying himself as FBI, and instructing him to put down his shotgun and raise his hands. Anticipating the man would fire a warning shot, Brett was quick to move back behind the fence pressing his body flat against the earth, but the gunman didn't fire just one shot. A hail of bullets peppered the ground.

Hearing this, and with Brett's commentary on his actions coming over the comms, Will sprinted to the back door, quietly opening it and peering inside. He moved in, scanning the area, and saw the woman and the child in the living room but something about their expressions alerted him that something else was going on. It was at that moment that another figure, a woman, appeared from one of the bedroom doorways, a pistol raised. She fired at Will.

"You're dead, and your partner is about to be blown away by not one, but two armed perps," the Quantico training instructor said, clipboard in hand, stepping from another room.

The simple but essential lesson learned was that the brief given to the trainees had been missing one vital piece of information – there was more than one hostage taker in the farmhouse. Neither Brett nor Will had considered, or planned for, that eventuality. No matter the intel, unforeseen factors always needed to be considered.

Will and Brett had been going around and around the same gravel road, and up and down the same hill, before being instructed to move on the farmhouse. Not the façade of a dwelling but a real house, of which there were dozens, along with shops, streets, and paid actors, all comprising the town of Hogan's Alley on the Quantico grounds, a town created by the FBI with its own zip code, for these exercises. This one was designed to test the trainees' responses when they were exhausted and confronted in the field with life-or-death situations.

Will had met Brett on the first day of their course at Quantico but it was during that particular exercise, several weeks later, that they'd really bonded. Brett had looked distraught, not that he would have likely been killed had the situation been real, but that he would have lost his colleague.

"Always expect the unexpected," Will had said. It had become something of a catchphrase between them.

Tonight, Will was unnerved by the feeling that those four words had never been so insightful as they seemed right now.

Chapter Twenty-Six

I had told Will I was going to phone Lars Andersson's granddaughter, Danielle, at midnight, which was 8 a.m. in London. I'd intended to have a restful evening in my apartment up until then, but my mind wouldn't switch off.

Astrid Karlsen told us that Edvard Munch's paintings had constant themes of depression, anxiety, and a preoccupation with death. Zach had looked into the facts of Munch's life. The great Norwegian artist, afflicted with health problems as a child, had grown up in an abusive household.

"You don't mirror a famous artist's style this closely unless you both admire and feel a spiritual connection to them," Zach had surmised.

But Munch hadn't predicted disastrous events with his art. He hadn't debased public and private property. The graffiti artist may have identified with Munch's observation of the dark side of nature, but it seemed to me that was where any similarity ended. There was something far more disturbing in the graffitist's embrace of the horrors that can lurk in everyday life. A joy. A game. Was it bitterness? Hatred?

Was the Artist experiencing those disparate images in visions? I exhaled heavily with frustration.

There has to be more to it than that.

I sipped a glass of white wine and tried to turn my mind to other things. But the events of the past few days kept crowding it. The horror of seeing those kids in that submerged bus. The sickening moment when the train collided with Sally Corcoran's car. The metal debris that felled Will. I reminded myself to check with him, in the morning, on his arm. It was clear he was in pain but ever-stoic Will wasn't going to admit to it or let anything prevent him from staying on the investigation.

I dozed without realizing it because all of a sudden the alarm I'd preset as a precaution sounded. It was midnight. I tapped Danielle's number into my phone and she answered almost immediately.

I introduced myself and explained that her grandfather had given me her number and that I had a few questions about a fellow art student that could be helpful to us. "Okay. Of course." I could hear the surprise in her voice. I knew she'd been in England for a few years and I could detect traces of a British accent creeping in.

"Danielle, your grandfather told me that you attended art classes he was running when you were quite young?"

"That's right."

"And you told him about a girl who said she had a friend who could draw events before they happened?"

"I haven't thought about that for years, but yes, I do recall that. And I remember it led me to have a big discussion with my grandad about psychic stuff."

"Do you remember the girl who told you about those future sketches?"

"Ah, let me think. We were friends for a while but it was a long time ago now." There was a brief silence on the line.

I waited.

"Estevan. That's it. She was Puerto Rican. Rosa Estevan. A bubbly girl and she really loved to draw."

"Your grandfather said she didn't attend many of his classes."

"Her parents were separated. I'm pretty sure, from what I remember, that she and her mother moved away and, of course, at that age, we didn't keep in touch."

"You've no idea where she is now?"

"No, not at all. Can I ask what this is all about?"

"We believe Rosa's friend, the one who supposedly drew the future, might be able to help us with an investigation we're running."

"Really? I wondered at the time if Rosa made it all up, seeking attention."

"Do you recall if Rosa told you this friend's name or where they lived?"

"No, sorry. You believe there actually was a friend who did drawings like that?"

"If there was, and we're hoping Rosa can clarify that, then it may be connected to the case we're working on. Either way, thank you for speaking with me. You've been a great help."

I ended the call and sank back into the comfort of my sofa. It might be a long shot, and it might be a false trail, but if we could locate Rosa Estevan, then we might be able to track down the neighbor who could sketch events before they happened.

I wondered if the graffitist was out there again tonight, painting another mural. Another prophecy of disaster. If they were, they'd avoid being anywhere near the locale where I'd spotted and chased them the night before. They could be anywhere. It was a large city, with no shortage of the lower storied buildings that suited the Artist's needs. Even so, I was covered in bruises on my back, arms, and legs, and exhausted, I knew better than to go out climbing and roaming the rooftops on a fool's mission.

I stripped down and crawled into bed, certain I'd be asleep within minutes. And yet all I seemed able to do was toss and turn. A searing sensation of dread tormented me, more of an ache than the bruises. I rose, pulled my lace gown around my shoulders, and padded out onto my balcony. The night was calm, with no breeze, and the cold night air felt refreshing. I looked out on the cityscape but all I saw was the back of Sally Corcoran's head, in her car, facing the oncoming train, and the thundering, looming image of the train bearing down on us. And the terrified faces of those children pushed against the windows of the submerged bus. I dropped to my knees, shaking all over, tears in my eyes as I tried to imagine the sheer horror felt by Sally, of the lasting horror that would be imprinted on the minds of those school kids. What was happening? This wasn't like me, to be as deeply, personally affected as this by the traumas I witnessed in our investigations. I'd had plenty of experience of trauma before. I'd been in near-death situations on previous assignments. I'd learned to create an emotional and mental barrier to distance myself from those memories, those fears. But this was different. I'd been staring at people who were themselves staring horrific deaths in the face, and in the case of Sally I'd been powerless to help her. What if that had been me?

I sobbed as I tried to close my mind to the memory of that physical impact of the train hitting. Both Marcia and Will had warned me that the full shock of what I'd witnessed would come home to roost. I'd been certain that the mental partitioning that I'd mastered in the past was enough to shield me from the emotional whiplash.

I could not have been more wrong.

Chapter Twenty-Seven

The Artist

On the morning that she and her parents were moving to live in another house in another part of Washington, the girl was in the backyard when her neighbor called out to her from the fence. She was able to peer through a hole in one of the wooden palings and her neighbor grinned and told her to keep the sketches she'd been given of the falling boy and the burning house. "It will help you to remember me."

"I'll remember you," the young girl said.

"No, you probably won't. But keep those drawings in a special place, maybe a drawer or a case, and whenever you open them up, you'll remember."

"I don't want to remember the boy falling into the river. Or the yucky fire."

"Why not?" the older child asked.

The girl didn't like the odd way her neighbor was staring at her. "Because they're scary. Why did you draw them?"

"Because I like drawing what is going to happen."

"No one knows what's going to happen tomorrow," the girl protested.

"Don't they?" her neighbor teased.

"No." But the young girl wasn't certain. She wasn't certain at all.

Twenty-two years later

Sometimes I think back to the boy who fell into the river and drowned. And the fire in the house across the street from where I lived. So long ago. I'd sketched both of those events in the days before they occurred and gave those sketches to Rosa. She'd been so spooked and I'd lain in bed the night after those drawings had become reality and I'd laughed my head off. There were a lot of people, I'd realized way back then, who liked watching horror movies because they enjoyed being frightened. They considered it entertainment.

I did too, but more than that, I enjoyed being the one creating something that scared others. The look of fear in their eyes. Whether they were young or old, male or female, I didn't care. It was the sheer dread that engulfed them that was like a tonic to me. And even more so, that sense of power over everything around me. There was nothing I couldn't do. If you know what is going to happen then the fate of so many people, perhaps of the whole wide world, is in your hands. Or in my case, in my crayons, paints, and spray cans.

I wasn't just drawing future disasters. I was painting them into existence.

I wondered where that young girl was now. She'd be a young woman. Was she still in the state of Washington? Was she watching the breaking news reports that showed my graffiti murals? Did her mouth drop open at the speculation that the image fragments in those murals depicted disasters that were just days, or less, away? Did she cast her memory back to the sketches I'd given her?

Even if she did, she'd been too young to remember my name or anything about me. But I hoped she remembered the falling boy and the roaring flames of the burning house. I hoped it made her heart thump with fear.

Chapter Twenty-Eight

Day Four

Despite gaining only a few hours of sleep, I woke early, set on gathering as much intel as possible and tracking down the Artist.

I knew from experience that the best time to catch a CEO was early morning before they became embroiled in one meeting after another. They were always in their offices early, before the mile-a-minute entrepreneurial day erupted. I phoned Will to say I'd miss the team's early morning briefing, as I wanted to drop into Haven Reinsurance's offices on my way to the Bureau. When interviewing witnesses or suspects, it was almost always done with two agents in attendance but for compiling general information from people, it wasn't essential. A quick visit, by me, to see David Handler was all that was needed.

Haven Insurance Services was housed in one of the newer and taller commercial buildings on Virginia Street in the city. I'd expected the fastest-growing reinsurance agency in the state to occupy maybe two or three levels. Instead, I was surprised that their allocated space was less than half the floor space on level seven.

From the elevator I took a left turn, through automatic sliding doors into a spacious and ornate reception area.

Adorning the walls on either side of the reception desk were several paintings, all by well-known classic artists. My eye was drawn immediately to one of the paintings near the furthest corner. The style was unmistakable and I'd seen a reproduction of it in Astrid Karlsen's art book. I moved toward it for a closer look. *Anxiety* by Edvard Munch. A group of people, their faces wretched with despair, the dark hues of color swirling behind and around them adding to the depressive tone.

"A print, of course," the receptionist, watching me, said. She was a striking-looking, dark-skinned woman with long, lustrous tresses, impeccably dressed. "The original is hanging in the Munch Museum in Oslo."

I glanced about at the other paintings. "Someone has a penchant for the modern masters," I commented.

"Our CEO, Mr. Handler. An avid collector. I think he'd love to, one day, be able to purchase the originals." She smiled. "All of them."

I walked across to the desk and showed my credentials. "I'd like to have a brief word with Mr. Handler."

The young woman tapped at her keyboard, her eyes on the screen. "Do you have an appointment?"

"No. But this really won't take long."

She phoned through to her CEO's office and told her boss there was an FBI agent asking to see him. A moment later, a man in a perfectly tailored suit appeared from the corridor that ran from the far corner.

I introduced myself.

He made a gesture. "Please, come on through, Agent Farris."

Like the foyer with its ornate appearance and paintings and prints by masters, Handler's office was all muted colors and elegant fixtures, with another classic painting on the wall opposite his desk.

"I'm told that Haven is the fastest-growing reinsurance agent in the field," I said as I took a seat opposite him.

Handler was fortyish, with a magnetic smile, piercing eyes and a tangle of thick, dark hair swept back off his forehead and smoothed down. A wave of youthful vigor emanated from him even as he sat behind his broad desk. Every inch the consummate salesman.

"I won't rest until we're the biggest," he said.

"I'm not sure you'll stop even then."

His smile broadened. "Not a chance."

Casting an eye back toward the small area outside his office, I said, "But your business doesn't take up a lot of space. I guess I expected to see a large, sprawling, multi-level suite of offices and meeting rooms."

"I run a small, tight, passionate team of super sales professionals. Everything else is contracted out. Admin, accountancy, contracts, legal, IT. That's the model. It means I don't have to worry about a great deal of hiring and firing in those areas, or the sick days and the vacations, the wages, the payroll tax. No distractions, just a one-hundred percent focus on selling. Building what will soon be the nation's biggest reinsurance agency."

"Myles Craddock from Sovereign filled me in a bit on reinsurance and how it works."

"Yes, he phoned, said I might get a visit from the FBI, wanting to draw on my expertise. Anything I can do to help the great law enforcement agency of our country, I'm up for. Perhaps, in kind, you can even point me in the direction of those concerned with the Bureau's insurance needs."

I gave a non-committal grin. "Now that's one thing I don't know anything about." Moving on quickly from that, I said, "I see you are a connoisseur of fine art."

He chuckled. "Ah, you flatter me. A connoisseur? Just an enthusiastic collector of great works."

"You may have seen media reports about some elaborate graffiti that features the screaming man from one of Edvard Munch's most famous paintings."

Handler clasped his hands together, a quizzical look on his face. "No, I haven't. Graffiti? Really?"

"The graffiti paintings predicted several disastrous accidents that have occurred over the past week and a half. One of those was the overpass crash. Another was the train derailment."

"Good God. But... how?"

"My colleagues and I are investigating how the graffitist has been able to do this. We're looking for an artist who has displayed great skill in mimicking Munch's work. I didn't know that you were someone with their finger on the pulse of the art market, but given that appears to be the case, have you encountered anyone who fits that bill?"

Handler scratched his chin as he gave the question serious thought. I watched his eyes closely for signs he knew more about all of this than he might let on. His response surprised me.

"To use a modern expression, there was something of a primal scream inherent in Munch's work. A sorrow. A darkness. An ethereal quality. And going back a few years there was a local artist who was making a bit of a mark in that regard. An interesting man with an interesting story — a tragic military background — but he retreated from the commercial art scene. I'm not sure why but I believe he wanted to pursue spiritual matters. For whatever reason, what you've just told me, brought that man to mind."

"Are you referring to Garrett Gainsford?"

"That's him. You know Gainsford?"

"I've spoken with him."

"Have you seen any of the art he painted in a similar style?"

"No."

"He didn't speak of it?"

"He did, but he didn't show us anything and he didn't compare his work with Munch's. He pointed out that the authority on Munch here in Seattle was Astrid Karlsen."

"Yes, well if anyone can mimic the work of great artists it's Astrid. Remarkable talent. A great teacher. I think Astrid would have liked to have her own work acclaimed like the works of those masters but you have to be highly original to achieve that."

I nodded my understanding. "What I specifically wanted to ask you about, is whether there is any financial benefit to insurers when faced with multiple accidents, or disasters, that require big payouts."

He winced. "There's no benefit to the industry in payouts."

"What about as a selling point for insurance firms to extend their reinsurance arrangements?"

"Ouch," he joked. "Now that's a Machiavellian way of looking at things. Goes with your territory, I suppose." He leaned forward with a surreptitious grin. "Surely you couldn't be suggesting that a reinsurer, like ourselves here at Haven, would stage a terrorist act for the potential marketing opportunities."

"You'd be surprised at some of the things the FBI has unearthed during its one-hundred-plus years. But no, that would be a stretch. However, in your opinion, is there another reinsurer, or any other kind of contractor out there, who could benefit greatly from a series of calamities occurring in a short time frame?"

"Not in my view. The industry is tightly regulated and is regularly under review. Washington State's Office of the Insurance Commissioner makes certain of that. As for other contractors related to our field, well, there are private investigation firms sometimes used by insurers, and there are researchers who create predictive modeling, to suggest premium rises based on the number of claims in a given period. But really, Agent Farris, nothing that would suggest criminal behavior that could benefit any of them."

"Does Haven employ the services of private investigators or predictive modelers?"

"As a reinsurer, we do not need private investigations. However, we have used a research firm for modeling, among other types of analysis. As I said, when it comes to our in-house operation, we're purely sales-focused."

I had the feeling I was going around in circles. And ever since I'd seen that print of a Munch painting in the foyer, I'd been acutely aware that if Handler or his firm had any involvement with the accidents or the murals, then the last thing they'd want is to be displaying a painting that would stick out as an obvious link.

I rose, extending my hand. "Thanks for your time, Mr. Handler. You have definitely given me some food for thought."

"Call me David, and speaking of food, perhaps I could buy you lunch later on. And you can feel free to keep picking my brain while we eat."

I smiled graciously. "Thank you, but I'm afraid I'll have to pass on that, I have a busy day ahead."

"Of course. Perhaps another time."

I smiled again, but said nothing further, as I headed out.

I could hardly believe the man had tried to hit on me while I was there in a professional law enforcement capacity. But then a smooth, charismatic character like Handler wouldn't allow social filters to get in his way. Some women might be either flattered or annoyed but I shrugged it off. I had bigger things on my mind. I wasn't getting a sense that the insurance angle held the answer to how the Artist could predict these disasters, or whether the accidents were being initiated in any way. A false trail? But there was something about Handler's operation – economical, singularly focused on their core skill, and using external providers for backup services – that stuck in my mind.

Chapter Twenty-Nine

Will was with Marcia and Zoe at the main console when I entered our ops center. "We've got addresses for Rosa Estevan. Home and business," he said. "She's still in Seattle, not that far from here."

I shrugged off the good fortune that she'd been easy to locate. You had to catch a break sometime. "Let's go see her," I said. "I'm feeling optimistic."

"Let's hope she's got as good a memory as Lars's granddaughter had," Will said.

"Have you checked in with Detective Radner–"

"Yes. No reports as yet this morning of any more murals turning up."

We headed down to the parking basement and Will asked me if I'd gleaned anything from my meeting with David Handler. As he drove, I filled him in on Handler's collection of reproductions, on display in the Haven foyer, and the print of an Edvard Munch painting that was featured there.

"You think this guy, Handler, or someone in his company, has something to do with all this?" Will asked.

"No."

"Okay. But the Munch painting there is another apparent coincidence so what are you thinking?" He waited for a response, eyes on the road ahead, before adding, "Not like you to hold back."

"Not holding back. Thinking it through."

Will nodded his understanding. There was nothing awkward about the silence that fell between us as we left the city perimeter, heading toward the neighborhood of Rainier Beach along the I-5 S. Will understood, as did I, the need to sometimes momentarily shut out everything around us, to mentally follow a potential trail. Letting it lead us to someplace that might otherwise remain a shadow in our subconscious. It was a skill we'd both been aware we had when we'd worked together at the CCRSB.

"It's a standard investigation process," I said presently, "to look for connections between the incidents – the people, their employers, the school, the transit company. I think the Artist seems to understand enough of this to know we'd identify the same insurance company being connected to one or more of the people in the accidents, and then to the reinsurance agency, and the Munch painting in the foyer there."

"You think we're talking about a law enforcement professional?"

"Maybe. Or perhaps someone who's studied investigative procedures. Garrett Gainsford suggested we were dealing with someone who held a grudge against law enforcers. With the fragmented images giving us just partial clues, we're being taunted, and maybe we're being intentionally led down one rabbit hole after another."

Will picked up on my line of thought. "So, the Artist intended for Haven Reinsurance to be a red herring."

"We'll look further into Handler – we have to – but I suspect we won't find anything. And while we're chasing that down–"

"There will be more murals. More disasters."

"Most likely."

Will glanced at me momentarily before focusing back on the road. "I'm sensing that, like me, you're still not sold on these murals being drawn from visions."

"Something else has to be going on," I said. "Something in the connections."

Will touched on something else that Gainsford had said to us. "Part of a cat-and-mouse game."

I craned my neck, easing the tension in my shoulders. "Something in plain sight, Will. When we get back to the office, we need to take another look, a fresh look, at every one of those accidents."

Minutes later, Will pulled over outside a nondescript white stucco single-story building, on the upper part of a sloping road. Stepping from the car, I could glimpse just a strip of the waters of Puget Sound.

Rosa Estevan ran a dance school and, as her classes were mostly run after school hours, for children, her mornings were spent in her office, handling the business's paperwork.

"My least favorite part of this whole thing," she said as she led us across the dance hall to the not-so-spacious, cluttered room behind it.

If she was surprised to have a couple of special agents wanting to ask her about a childhood friend, she didn't show it. I got the immediate impression she was a young woman who took most things in her stride. She was a tiny bundle of energy, with large blue eyes, dark brown skin, and a head of loose curls.

"Rosa, you told some of your fellow students at Lars Andersson's classes that you had a friend who could draw future events," I said.

"Oh, yes, I remember. Freaked me out. No one believed me, of course."

"Do you remember who it was?"

"Yes. My neighbor. He lived next door to me before my mother and I moved away, closer to the city."

"*He.* So, it was a boy."

"Yes. And he went to the same school as me but he was a little older."

"Do you recall his name?"

I watched her closely as she mulled this over. She shook her head. "No. It's kind of on the tip of my tongue, and then it isn't if you know what I mean?"

"I do."

"I didn't know him real well, we didn't hang out very much or anything. But we sometimes used to sit and draw. We were both into drawing, I guess that's why we were friends. At least, I thought we were friends. But I was very young, around eight or nine."

"What did you mean by 'I thought we were friends'?"

"He knew, the first time he showed me a drawing that came true, that it scared me. But then he did it again, showing me another drawing of an awful thing, and then, when that thing happened, he seemed to enjoy having frightened me. So, he wasn't much of a friend. He was kind of spooky."

Will and I exchanged a glance at this.

"What drawings of his did you see that you believed were predictions of the future?" Will asked her.

Rosa told us about a boy she and her neighbor had seen fall from a bridge into a river. The boy had drowned. And about the house across the street from hers that had burned down, killing one of the occupants. Both had been sketched by her friend before they happened.

"Another time," she said, "he drew a picture of a car and a cat's claw and a street sign. And two days later, a cat belonging to one of the other neighbors was almost hit by a car, around the corner, a bunch of kids saw it happen and didn't stop talking about it."

"And that was the street with that particular sign?" Will asked.

"Yes."

"Are you sure the drawings you saw were sketched by this boy?" I asked.

"Yes, of course…" But her voice faltered and there was another pause, this time lasting a little longer.

"You watched him draw those pictures?"

I waited. To me, her hesitation was like a silent alarm going off.

"I couldn't say I ever did. He always showed me his drawings after they were done."

"So, you never saw him sketching one of those directly?"

"Not that I can remember. Probably not."

"That doesn't mean he didn't sketch them," I said, "but it's important we cover all the bases."

"I understand."

"Do you, by any chance, still have any of those sketches?"

"Good Lord, no." Rosa chuckled. "I threw them out long ago."

"Was there anyone else, a brother or one of his friends maybe, who could have drawn them?" Will asked.

"He didn't have a brother," Rosa said, "just a sister. Older than him."

"Was she into art?"

Rosa's voice brightened. "Oh yes. I remember she was an art student somewhere or other. But I never saw any of her drawings."

"How well did you know her?" I asked.

"I didn't really know her at all. Would have seen her around occasionally, maybe said 'hi,' but like I said, I was eight, she was quite a bit older, and I never had any more than that to do with her."

"And you don't recall her name either?"

"No. Sorry."

"And you indicated before," I said, "that you and your mother moved away from the area not long after all this."

"That's right. I was kind of glad not to be living next door to that boy any longer."

"Where was this that you were living, before your move?"

"Near Tacoma. Buckley, in Pierce County."

I brought up the photos of the murals on my phone and showed them to her. "I appreciate, Rosa, that it would be hard to recall too much about those drawings all these years later. The style wouldn't be the same, as the artist would've been much younger, but was there any similarity with these?"

She took a moment, appraising each of the photos. "Not sure, style-wise. Don't remember. But the positioning of the different images reminds me of the sketch with the cat and the car. The others hadn't been like that. But these photos have reminded me of something else."

"What's that?"

"The boy's cat sketch. The images of the car, the street sign, and the cat were circling a set of eyes."

"Like someone watching?"

She nodded.

I felt a chill. *Someone watching.*

"You must have wondered how the boy was able to do this. Whether or not he was psychic?"

"To be honest, once I moved away, I stopped thinking about it, and it was a long time ago."

"Okay, thanks for taking the time to speak with us, Rosa. It's been a great help."

"Has it?"

"Every detail gathered in an investigation helps."

Outside, Will and I sat for a moment in his car. I was thinking back over the details we'd been able to draw out of Rosa Estevan. "A boy and a girl, living next door to Rosa, all those years ago. Drawings of accidents that became reality within days."

Will was silent and I could tell from his expression that, like me, he was sifting through the information we'd gleaned from Rosa.

"One of those sketches, like the Artist's murals," I mused, "had fragmented images of the scene that almost became roadkill."

"And, with the watching eyes," Will added, "that sketch could have been an early version of what would later become the screaming man."

I closed my eyes and imagined one of the scenes that Rosa had described. Rosa and her neighbor sitting on the shore by a river, watching as a boy fell from the bridge into the water.

Rosa's neighbor: a boy who delighted in the disasters he drew before they occurred, and who enjoyed scaring the little girl next door. Did that boy draw those pictures? Were they psychic visions? Did that boy become the graffitist who now delighted in playing his cat-and-mouse game with the FBI?

* * *

Many thought that an artificial intelligence system, specially created for a new FBI unit, would take a large team and an enormous budget but Zoe Marshall had proved otherwise.

Zoe, alone, could write reams and reams of complex code. Those intricate lines of coding created a set of algorithms that could analyze huge amounts of data in milliseconds and also drew on that process for self-learning. As a result, Themis was in a constant state of improvement without massive funding. It memorized the details of every single unsolved case and compared them with every newly reported crime.

It also meant Themis was a highly targeted search engine.

One of the main functions of Zoe's and Marcia's interactions with Themis was to issue prompts. These were instructions to gather specific information that one of the agents wanted – such as configuring the license plate numbers that led us ultimately to the submerged bus. Its self-learning algorithm would also issue self-prompts when it thought it beneficial.

But Zoe would never let her creation do all the thinking for her. That was never the intention. She envisaged Themis as another agent off which she could bounce ideas, observations, and theories.

Right now, she had Themis slowly scrolling each of the mural photos across her monitor. She took her time, examining once again each of the images in those murals. There was always something new to notice, she thought. Maybe it was the intensity of a particular color in the background, or something about the angle of one of the images.

She found her attention being drawn to the area just beneath the top left corner of the overpass truck mural and of the factory explosion mural that was alongside it. Her eyes followed the outer rim across the top of the two murals. Something familiar. She looked then at the train mural and the school bus crash mural, her gaze focusing on the same area and then tracing the outline of all of them.

She looked over to Marcia. "Can I borrow you for a moment?"

Marcia pushed herself up from her chair, noticing the puzzled expression on Zoe's face. "Of course you can."

Zach had looked up from his PC screen when Zoe had spoken to Marcia.

"You too, Prof," she added.

"So, what's going on?" Marcia said as she rounded the horseshoe-shaped console but Zoe's focus had already diverted back to her AI.

She activated the mic and, unconsciously doing something she didn't realize she'd been doing more and more of late, she spoke to the machine as though speaking to a co-worker. "Themis, there's something I need you to do…"

Chapter Thirty

The second we strode into the ops room Will told Zoe the Pierce County address that Rosa Estevan had lived at when she was eight years old. "Find the name of the neighbor who owned the house next door, on the northern side, and we need to know the names of that owner's children. Program Themis to search through birth records and local school data—"

"On it," said Zoe.

"As well," I said to her, "run a check on records in the same county of a boy drowning in the river after falling from a bridge." I was about to elaborate, telling the group about one of the sketches Rosa had seen as a young girl but the curious expression in Marcia's eyes, boring into me, alerted me that something else was going on.

It took Zoe mere seconds to code the instructions into the system. "Won't take long, but while Themis is crunching data, there's something else."

I could tell from the looks on the faces of Marcia and Zach, who were sitting at scattered angles around Zoe, that whatever the 'something' was, it had unsettled them.

"Sitting here staring at these murals, one after the other," Zoe said, "I began to notice a certain uniformity to the overall design. Our eyes are naturally drawn to each of the fragmented images but I started to see a shape to the murals as a whole." She clicked on the mouse and a line appeared around the outer edges of the five murals. "So, I had Themis put on her graphics hat and draw a line around the contours of each of the paintings. And then I had Themis hide the paintings." The system highlighted the areas of the drawings. And then the images vanished, leaving only the outline around the edges. A silhouette. An outer frame I knew well, a shield crested by an eagle. The tiny hairs on the back of my neck rose. A shiver passed through me. "The shape of an FBI badge," I said.

Zoe's eyebrow lifted. "It's not something anyone's likely to have picked up from looking at one or two of these murals just once, but when you're continually viewing them, analyzing, and then with a third and fourth mural, you start to see it."

I drew in a breath. "The Artist is sending us a message."

"Yes. Letting us know these murals are specifically for us. For the Bureau."

"Why?" Marcia voiced the thought for all of us.

Zoe swiveled a full 180, facing us, her back to her console. "I think it's the Artist's way of issuing a challenge, knowing there would be either police or agents studying the murals, expecting that at some stage the Bureau would be called on."

"His challenge, all along," said Will, "for us to figure out the disaster being prophesized and stop it. But why, specifically, the FBI?"

"Maybe we should think of it like the brain game," Zach suggested, switching to his criminologist mode. "That's the reason for just a vague set of images. The first part of the game is for us to work out what the disaster is while the clock ticks down to the event. The second part is for us to try and prevent it. But at the same time, he's teasing us, intimating we can't succeed because it's all preordained. He isn't just challenging us, he's throwing down a gauntlet, proving he's better than we are, driving home that he's the one with the smarts and we're powerless against the inevitable." He was talking at his usual breakneck pace. "But I believe it's showing us something more than that."

I jumped in before Will could. "Spit it out, Prof."

"He's making a point that one lone figure is a greater force than all the agents of the FBI put together. I think this is a person who has a deep-seated grudge against the Bureau and they intend to go on proving their superiority. To this artist, they're making a mockery of us as we race to try and figure them out."

"A grudge. The same suggestion Garrett Gainsford made," Will said, his eyes fixed on Zach, "but if that's the case—"

Zach held up his palm. "I know, I know. If that's the case, then it also suggests these images may not be the result of psychic visions. To keep doing this, envisioning disasters a day or two ahead, it would appear the Artist has to be manipulating them, as impossible as that seems. Like the Devil's work."

"Doesn't help your quest to prove psychic phenomena." Zoe's tone held a conciliatory note.

Zach gave a wry smile "And here I was, thinking you didn't care."

"I don't." Her eyes twinkled.

Zach ignored the jibe and shrugged in frustration. "Proof will come. One day. Perhaps not this time around. Even the genuine seers of this world aren't able to conjure up visions from the future when and where they wish. Never been any evidence of it working that way."

"Never been any evidence of it working any kind of way," Will said.

Zach pursed his lips, as though about to launch into a response but then seemed to think better of it.

Biting down on his lower lip, Will looked at the badge-shaped outline on the large screen. "If the Artist holds this much of a grudge against the Bureau, then this could be a lot more than a cat-and-mouse battle of wits." His gaze settled on me. "It throws a whole different light on Agent Frankel's daughter being on the bus that went into the lake."

"You think agents are being targeted?" Marcia's expression was grim.

"But how is the Artist doing it?" I said, more to myself than to the others. "Zoe, let's get all the images back up on the screens."

Everyone's attention was riveted on the photos.

I looked again at each of the accidents. Sovereign's name could be linked to some but not all of the accidents. Yet every one of those disastrous events involved a vehicle of some kind. Was *that* the common denominator I was looking for?

If so, what did those vehicles – or the drivers – have in common? It wasn't the insurance company. The same was true of Haven, the reinsurer. Like Sovereign, it could be connected to some, not others. It wasn't the employers of the drivers. The drivers all worked for different companies. Sally Corcoran worked for a hospital. The overpass truck driver and the driver that hit the factory were in completely different lines of work, one a truckie, the other an office worker.

I was still sensing a pattern, though. Like the images in the murals. Each fragment was a clue to the whole. Like the screaming man, observing each of those images, seeing the greater picture.

Was there an even greater picture behind each of these murals, hiding in plain sight?

"Themis has accessed the police records on the boy who drowned in that river," Zoe announced. She tapped a key and asked the AI, "What have you got for us, Themis?"

Themis's Greek-accented female voice, firm and authoritative, said, "Blair Tyrrel, nineteen years old, fished from the bridge every afternoon after work. He and his buddies were known to cast lengthy fly lines into the river from the twenty-five-foot-high footbridge in the natural reserve. After the accident, police confirmed that the railing of the bridge, in the area where the young men always leaned, had been severely vandalized."

"That's the first definitive piece of information," I said, looking at the others, my gaze stalling for a moment on Zach, "that the murals aren't the work of a psychic, but someone who's created the conditions for the accidents, and that the boy who sketched that drawing could have grown up to become our graffitist."

Zoe scrolled to another screen on her monitor. "Real estate records. Rosa Estevan's neighbors were named Scanlon. But there are no records associated with that name, or school records, of a brother or sister with that name."

"Perhaps the boy and girl were relatives living with them," Marcia suggested.

"Or adoptees," said Zach.

"See if you can track down the Scanlons," Will said to Zoe.

I took a deep breath, exhaled, and pulled up a chair at the far end of the console that was the centerpiece of the Themis setup. I needed to take a little time and pore over each of those images. My thoughts kept returning to the badge-shaped outline of the murals.

Someone with knowledge of law enforcement procedures. And yet someone who hated law enforcers.

Garrett Gainsford had first suggested, in his peculiar rambling way, that the Artist held a grudge. Gainsford himself was both ex-soldier and ex-police officer, he was both a person involved with the local psychic community and an artist – Handler had mentioned his ethereal style – and it seemed he'd had a tense relationship with his SPD superior, Detective Radner. He fitted the profile. Had his suggestion that the Artist held a grudge been part of a cat-and-mouse game, something he laughed about privately?

I began sifting back mentally through every aspect of the accidents we'd attended. Agent Don Frankel's daughter had been on the submerged school bus. Will told me he and Frankel had worked together on a CCRSB unit that included Brett Rochester. I'd since learned from Will that Frankel had been with them that night when Brett tragically shot Olivia Vasquez. Don Frankel had testified in Brett's defense at the internal hearings, as had Will. There was no doubt whatsoever at the size of the grudge Leo Vasquez held against Brett Rochester. But he wasn't an artist. Was he? Did he harbor the same level of enmity against the other agents connected to that incident? Will and I both knew that he'd become increasingly erratic.

Could either Gainsford or Vasquez have something to do with all of this?

I knew it was a common assumption that killers with twisted minds were unemployed loners, living with parents or relatives, and socially inept. A wildly inaccurate stereotype. More often than not, these killers had good jobs, good incomes, and were comfortable in most social situations. Their dark side was well hidden under layers of normality. But they craved an excitement of a kind that wasn't socially acceptable. And sometimes they developed a grudge against a person or a particular group or an institution. They became filled with resentment, perceiving themselves as victims, driven by an ego that wanted to prove their superiority. That appeared to be what was going on here. A meshing of secret, twisted desires merged with an all-consuming hatred of authority.

Will pulled up a chair alongside me but said nothing, his focus also on the murals.

I shared my thoughts. Will acknowledged what I told him, mulling it over.

"I think it's worth having a chat with Detective Radner about Gainsford, gather some more background," he said. "We'll check out childhood backgrounds, and see if there's any connection with Gainsford or Vasquez to the area where Rosa Estevan lived. And then we'll pay Gainsford another visit."

Chapter Thirty-One

Detective Paul Radner waved Will and me to his visitor chairs as we entered his office. I'd called ahead and Radner, as always, was glad to help. I'd once been called in to assist Radner when his officers were attempting to stop a teenage boy from jumping to his death off a city building. After that, Radner called on me to assist with his search for reckless urban climbers, an obsession of his since the death of his daughter. Despite the secret life I kept hidden, I was no fan of hot-headed, daredevil climbers, who took risks while putting others in danger.

"So, you want to talk to me about Garrett Gainsford?" Radner said.

"Yes," said Will. "We understand he was with the SPD, reporting to you?"

"Several years ago now." Radner didn't give the impression this brought up pleasant memories. "Gainsford would've made a great cop but he didn't have the right attitude. For starters, he wanted to question every order he was given, every approach the department took on its investigations, and he wasted time arguing." The detective spread his hands in a gesture of frustration. "I might've sympathized. Look, the guy had a rough trot in the army. His unit members were wiped out by a land mine. They'd been given the wrong route, his commanding officers had screwed up. I gather the brass covered their asses and were hardly reprimanded. Gainsford railed against the system, he became increasingly difficult and was eventually discharged. He joined the SPD but he was still in headbutting-the-authorities mode."

Will bristled. "Dangerous."

Will and I both believed in the importance of protocol and working as a team. Lives depended on it. Will was more a stickler for it than anyone I knew, whereas I'll admit to sometimes flaring up against the restraints those same protocols put on us.

"Don't we both know it," Radner replied to Will's comment. "To be honest, he was a pain in the ass and a future with the SPD just wasn't on the cards. But I hoped – and I still do, for his sake – that he can find a way to beat those demons. I've no idea what he's up to these days, but if the UCU is asking about him, I've no doubt I'm about to find out."

I explained to Radner how Gainsford was involved with both the art and psychic communities, and how his background, and known grudge against authorities, fitted the profile we were building of the Artist.

Radner exhaled a long, slow breath. "That, I was not expecting to hear."

"We're simply gathering more information on him at the moment," Will said, "and on another guy with a very serious grudge against the FBI. We're also casting a wider net for others who match the behavioral characteristics."

"Who's this other guy holding a serious grudge?" asked the detective.

Will told him about Leo Vasquez and the tragic events that led to Olivia Vasquez's death.

"I know the case, of course," Radner said. "And that guy, Vasquez, we had him here in a holding cell several nights back."

"What?" Will leaned forward.

"He got into a fight in a bar with a bunch of paramedics who were having an after-shift drink. Vasquez was drunk and loud and accused them of failing to save his sister. They didn't know what the hell he was talking about. My officers were called and they brought him in. Vasquez's friend sold us a sob story about the grief

Vasquez was going through, and pleaded with the sergeant not to press charges."

"And they let him off?" I asked.

"With a warning that next time we wouldn't be such pushovers."

"Was the friend Gabriel Vaughn?" Will asked.

Radner checked the details on his computer. "Yeah. Vaughn."

"He's trying to keep his friend out of trouble," I told Radner.

"And it's becoming more and more obvious he's got his hands full," said Will.

"Which night was Vasquez in the cell?" I asked.

Radner pulled up the details on his PC and told us the date.

I looked at Will. "Not one of the nights the murals were done," I said.

* * *

"What approach do you suggest we take with Gainsford?" I asked Will as we pulled up in front of Gainsford's cottage at Bitter Lake.

"I say we tell him we'd like to pick his brains a little more about the local artists he knows. We give him a description of the profile we're building, as it stands at the moment."

"And we make it obvious, without saying it, that he's a perfect fit for that profile."

"Yes. We see what kind of response he has to the profile. He's a quirky, outspoken character. I don't think he'll be able to *not* speak his mind. Whether it reveals anything about him to make him a bona fide suspect, we'll just have to wait and see."

"I like it."

He grinned. "I thought you would."

And just like that, it was as though, in that instant, we were the couple we'd been over two years ago. But just as quickly the moment passed.

Will rang the doorbell and when there was no response he knocked loudly, and then knocked again. We listened but there were no sounds of life coming from within.

The door in the cottage alongside opened and a middle-aged woman came out, her hair pulled tight in a ponytail, her make-up heavier than it needed to be.

She glanced over at us. "You looking for the strange one?" she said.

"Garrett Gainsford," said Will. "You know him?"

"Don't know his name, he keeps to himself. I just know him to say hello to if and when we pass on the street. Psychic guy, apparently, and has a few people come by several times a week for appointments, readings, whatever you call them. Not my cup of tea. He strikes me as a little odd but he's no trouble, pretty quiet, and I can tell you I've had some weirdo neighbors in my time. But you won't find him here for a while, I'd say."

"Why's that?" I asked.

"I saw him load some stuff in his car earlier. Does that every now and then and he goes off, usually away for a few days, sometimes longer."

"Thanks for letting us know," Will said.

I recalled Astrid Karlsen mentioning that Gainsford sometimes satisfied his wanderlust by going away somewhere for days or weeks at a time, off the grid. I exchanged a glance with Will and I could tell he was remembering that same detail.

Our previous visit to Gainsford had alerted him to the fact the FBI was looking for the graffiti artist responsible for the murals. Had Gainsford gone off on one of his supposed spiritual wanderings, getting away from it all, or was there another agenda at play here?

Chapter Thirty-Two

On our return to the UCU, Will and I were briefed by Marcia on what she'd learned about the childhoods of Leo Vasquez and Garrett Gainsford.

Both men had been raised in the Seattle area but neither had lived in the same suburb as Rosa Estevan nor had they gone to the same school. Marcia hadn't uncovered any connection between either man or their families with Rosa's neighbors of the time, the Scanlons.

Vasquez's father had been with the military, stationed at the Joint Lewis-McChord Base near Tacoma. The family lived on the base and Leo's father was often away on missions.

Gainsford had lived at that time just a couple of suburbs away from Rosa.

It seemed like a dead end. Regardless, I asked Marcia to make a few more inquiries, at the local schools, and the military base. I wasn't certain what we were looking for, but any possible association, at any time, with either the Scanlons or with the Estevan family was the main driver, along with any reason those families might have had a bad experience with the FBI.

Zach was still seated at one of the monitors, conversing with Zoe. Whenever we called on his expertise, Zach would work around his university commitments while consulting with us. Sometimes, and this was one of those occasions, he would arrange for one of the other lecturers to take his classes so that he was free to put in a full day with the UCU.

Will and I pulled up chairs alongside them. "Given that we're looking for someone likely to have a grudge against the FBI, Zoe," Will said, "let's get Themis to compile a list of people arrested by the Bureau, who've been released from prison in, say, the past year, and who currently reside in Seattle. And then, run a deep dig into those people, their jobs, any courses they've attended, their online presence. We're looking for any connection to art or psychic interests, or both."

"I think there's more to it than an ex-prisoner with a grudge," Zach said. "We also now know the Artist wants to engage us in a battle of wits. And the badge-shaped murals aren't just to mock us, this artist wants to prove they're better than us, this is a contest. And as Ilona said before, this person has an in-depth understanding of investigative procedures."

Will's voice was grave. "Prof, you're not suggesting the Artist is an agent?"

Zach shook his head. "Not necessarily. Otherwise, they would almost certainly be using their position to create chaos from within the Bureau. I'm certain this person is operating outside both the agency and the SPD but has made a study of how trained agents think, how an investigation is conducted."

"What about someone who wanted to be an agent but didn't make the grade?" I suggested.

"There are thousands of FBI employment applications rejected every year," Will pointed out.

"We could start," said Zoe, "by focusing our attention on applicants who were accepted into Quantico but, for whatever reason, didn't complete the training."

"The extent of this grudge means they were most likely forced out," Will said.

"Prioritize it," I said to Zoe. I turned to Will. "We know that after he was demobbed from the military, Gainsford joined the SPD. What we don't know is what other applications he may have made. Did he apply to the FBI?"

"Easy enough to search FBI applications for Gainsford's name," Zoe said, and seconds later she advised that Gainsford's name didn't show.

"I think we need to find out just where Garrett Gainsford is," I said to Will.

"What's your gut telling you?" he asked.

"When we spoke with Gainsford, he referred to the Bureau as the F-B-oh so glorious-I – sure, it was in a jokey fashion but, regardless, the guy had an edge that seemed… off. And we've since learned about his whole anti-authority attitude. My gut's telling me something else is going on with him."

"Agreed. We need to know more. I suggest we pay Astrid Karlsen another visit and see if we can find out a little more about what he gets up to."

* * *

"You want to ask more about Garrett Gainsford," Astrid said as she opened the door, beckoning us inside. "You're starting to worry me."

"Why's that?" I asked, as Will and I entered the studio space.

"I'm getting the distinct impression you suspect Garrett of something criminal."

"We're not at that point yet," Will said, "but we've developed some serious concerns."

Astrid gestured to the seating that was positioned along the walls, and she sat with us. I reiterated what we'd learned about Gainsford, and my antenna going up when he'd seemingly taken off on one of his strange disappearances not long after speaking with us.

She held herself still, her body stiffening and creases forming around her eyes as I voiced our concerns.

In a low voice, she said, "It's the paranoia… I should've suspected something like this might trigger it."

"What paranoia?" I asked.

She crossed her legs, leaning forward, raising an eyebrow as she stared at us. "Garrett had this crazy notion, which he raises now and then, that his ex-military bosses were keeping tabs on him, that they wanted to make him pay for the aspersions he'd cast on them. He even thought it stretched to the SPD, following on from his tenure as an officer there. I don't know how many times I pointed out that it was his imagination getting away from him, that the army and the police didn't care about any of that, it was all in the distant past. I thought – I hoped – that he'd started to move on from all that, immersing himself in his meditations and his art."

"You think our visit triggered his paranoia?" Will asked.

"You're the FBI. What I fear now is that he started overthinking your visit. Maybe he started thinking that your questions about the art and psychic communities were a cover for checking on him on behalf of the army. Or perhaps his PTSD got him imagining that you suspect him of being this mysterious artist. And he's freaked out and gone off into hiding. He's done this before but if he's really freaking out this time then he could be a danger to himself."

"Or to others?" I wondered.

Her expression was mixed and she didn't answer.

Will kept his voice gentle. "Have you any idea where he goes when he's on these sabbaticals?"

"He usually heads north, likes to hike and camp in the woods. And he'll often spend a few nights at a cabin that I have in the Mt. Baker-Snoqualmie National Forest. Something my parents left to me, but I very rarely get up there. It's secluded, off the beaten path, just what Garrett craves when he's in one of these dark moods. He'll hole up there until he feels less troubled. I let him use the cabin whenever he needs to, and he knows where the key is kept."

This came as a surprise and I raised an eyebrow, focusing my gaze. "That's more than just a little generous,"

I said. "I'm aware you've known Garrett for a while but I have to ask, is there more to your relationship?"

"We've been a sort of couple, on and off. Neither of us has proven good at maintaining relationships, and his PTSD doesn't help. But we've always been friends."

I looked at Will. "I think it's in all our best interests if we find Garrett and have another chat with him."

"Can you give us directions to this cabin?" Will asked Astrid.

Astrid bit her lip. "It isn't certain he'd be there."

"I think it's worth a try," I said.

"He isn't the graffitist you're looking for," Astrid said. "Garrett's not the type to go sneaking around at night, spray-painting walls."

"But you can't know that for certain," I said.

Astrid twisted a lock of hair. "What worries me is that if he is there, and if his mind has gone as dark as I know it sometimes can, then how will he react if he sees FBI agents approaching?"

"Does he carry a weapon?" Will asked.

She lowered her head, staring hard at the floor. "He keeps a rifle at the cabin." Looking up again, she shifted her body and I could sense the unease coursing through her. "Let me go with you, it'll be quicker if I show you the way, and if he is there, then far less confronting for him when he sees I'm with you."

Chapter Thirty-Three

I wasn't certain whether I was pushing the wrong barrow with this, but there was something about Garrett Gainsford's background and attitude that was ringing alarm bells, even more so now that Astrid had opened up about the extent of the paranoia he suffered.

It was just under an hour northeast along the I-5 N and the WA-522 E to Gold Bar. Heavy clouds had spread across the sky, allowing only scattered sunlight over this area of the Mt. Baker-Snoqualmie National Forest. Leaving the main road, we drove along a narrow, winding road with thick swathes of forest on either side. Spooked by our concerns, Astrid thought it best if we left the car further back on this road, just out of sight of her cabin. By approaching on foot, Astrid could call out to Garrett once outside the cabin, and then calm him of any anxiety about me and Will being with her.

Stepping from the car, I caught glimpses of the river through the trees, the sound of the rushing water louder than I'd expected. The air was fresh, the haze of the mountains just visible in the distance. As the cabin came into view, we sighted two SUVs parked alongside it.

"Is one of those Garrett's?" I asked Astrid.

"Not certain." There was no mistaking the confusion in her tone. "But there shouldn't be anyone else here."

"I'm sorry, Astrid, but my spidey sense is tingling, so I can't let you go up to the door on your own. You stay back here, with Will, and I'll go first and check things out."

Astrid looked uncertain but didn't protest.

"No sudden moves," Will cautioned me.

I shot him a steely eye. "I have done this before."

I walked forward in a casual manner but before I'd gone far, the front door was flung open and a figure stood in the doorway, cloaked in shadow, brandishing a rifle.

"Don't come any closer." It was a deep growl of a voice, but it wasn't Garrett's.

"I'm here to see Garrett," I called out to the man.

"He's not here." The figure stepped forward, the faint light revealing a beard and a head of shaggy hair. He raised the rifle. "Now I suggest you leave."

My pulse quickened. What the hell was going on here? I held up my badge and identified myself as FBI. "Sir, you need to put the weapon aside, it's an offense to threaten a federal agent."

I heard the sudden rustle of leaves and the crack of twigs nearby, signaling movement in the forest. From the grove of trees on my right, a man appeared, also armed with a rifle. I could tell immediately from his physique, his bearing, and the way he held his weapon, that he was military-trained.

The man at the doorway aimed his firearm at me. "Last time I'm going to say this. *Leave. Now.*" His finger rested on the rifle's trigger.

I heard Will shout, "Ilona. Hit the ground," as a shot rang out and the man at the door stumbled back, the rifle falling from his grasp. I threw myself at the ground, expecting, as did Will, that there would be shots fired by the man at the tree line. There wasn't. Instead, he turned and fled into the woods.

I darted forward to the man who was now sprawled on the small porch at the front door. Will had a crack aim and his shot had served its intended purpose, grazing the man's shoulder, and disarming him without causing a major injury. I cuffed him to the porch railing, activated my comms, called for backup, and saw Will, signaling to me as he sprinted into the forest on the trail of the other man. I was going to follow but something gave me pause. We didn't know for certain that Garrett wasn't inside the cabin, using these two men, whoever they were, as shields. I glanced back along the road. Astrid was standing frozen, her eyes wide.

I slipped my 9mm Glock from its holster as I moved cautiously into the cabin. The interior was larger than I'd anticipated, rustic and sparse of furniture, with a fireplace in the far corner, and a large table taking up the space along the adjoining wall. There was a stream of papers and folders spread out across the surface of the table. A short hallway ran from the other side of the space, with doors to a bedroom and a bathroom. I checked both of those. Empty, but the open bedroom window and dirt and scuff marks on the windowsill indicated that someone had climbed out of it. Garrett?

I peered out on a tangle of forest growth, once again glimpsing the river through the trees. In the soil beneath the window, I saw boot prints. I went back through the cabin to the front door and crept around the side to the back, my eyes scanning the surroundings, my ears pricked for the slightest sound of movement. I trekked in the direction the tracks seemed to lead. As I entered the woodland, I called out, "Garrett? It's Special Agent Farris. I'm simply here to ask for your help. I have some more questions about the spiritual and arts scenes." There was no response. I kept moving as stealthily as I could and then, after a few minutes, there was the sudden, brief sound of feet shuffling and branches creaking, not far ahead of me and further back from the river.

"Garrett," I called out again. "Speak to me."

Nothing. I was certain he was following the direction of the river while staying deep undercover in the forest, and I decided to surprise him by running forward, closer to the riverside. I then cut back into the deeper woodland, hoping to be ahead or just behind him. As I did, a shot broke the calm, its bullet grazing the trunk of a tree just a foot away from me. Birds screeched, wings flapping furiously as they flew from the treetops.

"I won't let them take me." It was Garrett, his voice edged with fear. Who was he talking about? The two men who'd been at the cabin?

"Who are you talking about?" I called back.

"The military. And I know they've sent you."

"Garrett, you need to calm down and listen very closely to me. I have not been sent by the military, I'm here to help. Put down your rifle and come out into the open and we can talk about this. If you resist and you keep firing at a federal agent, you will only make things worse for yourself. Your friend, Astrid, is here and she can verify everything I'm saying."

"You've brainwashed her."

"Garrett, no–"

Another shot rang out, the bullet embedding itself in the tree that I was perched behind. There was a burst of noise, branches snapping as Garrett ran. I followed the sound, rushing through the foliage, leaves scraping my face and my hands, and then I saw him, hurling himself in desperation through the undergrowth. I holstered my pistol and sprinted at top speed, closing on him, then I launched myself forward, grabbing him just below the knees and tackling him to the ground. He thrust out his leg, his boot landing a crushing blow to my cheek. I reeled back but just as quickly rolled, reaching out and pushing him face-first into the dirt, straddling his back and pulling his hands behind his back.

"Stay down," I shrieked into his ear.

I didn't have another set of handcuffs on me so I held him firmly. Thankfully, he didn't seem as fit as he would have been during his military days. I waited until his breathing slowed and the tension in his body slackened. I managed to position myself so that I could kick his fallen rifle further away from us.

"Okay, let's see if we can make it back to the cabin without any grief," I said.

I pulled him to his feet, pulled out my revolver, and kept it trained on him as we marched back through the woods. Minutes later, I saw Will running toward us. His face broke into relief when he saw me.

"All under control here," I assured him. "What about the man who ran?"

"I got him," Will said, "and our backup's here."

* * *

Detective Radner and several SPD officers had arrived and they'd taken Garrett and the other two men away, while Will and I searched the contents of the cabin. Astrid sat near the large table, staring silently into space, stunned by what we'd found in the large storage cabinet in the hallway. It was stocked with a small arsenal, comprising several pistols and rifles.

Will and I pieced together a scenario, gleaned from the arsenal and the papers and folders on the table.

Two of the folders had photo IDs of the other two men we'd encountered at the cabin. Both ex-army, both dishonorably discharged, both had been counseled for PTSD. It appeared Garrett had teamed up with them and they'd met at the cabin regularly. It wasn't hard to speculate that the three men had a shared paranoia that the military was out to get them.

The other folders were of three senior army executives. They'd been responsible for mission data that proved disastrous for units the three men had been with.

There were reams of printouts, containing surveillance photos of the homes of those army chiefs, and information on their daily routines. Two of those men were now retired, and one of them still held a command position.

"Garrett and his new friends were planning to attack those executives, presumably believing the army men were intending to harm them."

Astrid's voice was strained, her face grim. "Garrett would never have gone through with such a thing."

"Maybe not," I said, "but there is enough evidence here to show intent."

"What will happen to him?"

"That's for the courts to decide," Will said, "but his PTSD will be taken into consideration."

"You still think he could be the one spray-painting those murals?"

"It's clear from all this that his focus was on these military chiefs. He believed they were a threat to him. The graffiti murals don't seem to fit in with that, but we'll have a chance to question him further when we're back in town."

Chapter Thirty-Four

I filled Marcia and the others in on what had transpired, over the phone, as Will drove us back to Seattle. We dropped Astrid off at her studio, and my heart felt for her as, ashen-faced, she turned at her front doorway and waved.

We spent thirty minutes questioning Garrett Gainsford in an interview room at the SPD. His face wore a haunted expression, a shadow of the man we'd spoken with just days earlier, and his spiral into this depressive state was unsettling to observe. He remained convinced that the army had been following both him and the other two men and that they'd had no choice but to plan an attack on their tormenters. But there didn't appear to be any link between any of that and the graffiti murals or the prophesized disasters.

The moment we walked back into the UCU, Zoe flashed us a grin as she tapped away at her keyboard. "Some interesting news on the search for common denominators. Themis has highlighted an external services provider that she's matched to at least one of the firms in *each* of the disasters."

"What have we got?" Will asked.

"The hospital that Sally Corcoran worked for, and the company who employed the driver who smashed into the factory, have something in common with the companies that operate the school bus, and the gravel truck that crashed onto the Interstate – Sovereign Insurance isn't the only external service provider some of them have in common. Each of those companies uses the same firm for its IT requirements. Advance IT. And so does the college where Astrid Karlsen runs her art classes."

I shifted in my chair, locking eyes with Zoe. "Okay. What's the extent of the IT services?"

"Troubleshooting system failures and glitches. Computer hardware repairs. But also repairs to the staff's personal laptops and cell phones, given they're also used for work matters."

"How does that tie in with the Artist and his paintings?"

"I need to access Advance's service records to find out. Look for any links to the people involved in the accidents. We'll need a warrant."

"We could just ask the manager to cooperate."

Zoe shot me a pained expression. "Giving them a chance to delete files. I don't like getting all conspiracy theorist on you, but we don't know who's involved – or if anyone is – but this is a much more all-encompassing link. Either way I think it's best if we turn up unannounced, with a warrant, before anyone can react."

"Then we get that warrant," I said.

"Leave that to me," said Will.

If there was one thing that Will excelled at more than any SSA I'd ever worked with, it was tracking down the right judge at the right time and persuading them of the need for an urgent search warrant. He headed back to his office to make the necessary calls.

I was back on my feet, standing a little further back from the monitors now, and I moved slowly from one screen and one set of images to the next.

The lake. The school. The factory. The explosion. The rail-crossing suicide. My eyes raced over the images. The license plates. The front of the truck crashing through the overpass barrier. The driver's license. The boy joyriding in his uncle's pickup truck.

"They all involve a vehicle of some kind," I said, revisiting an earlier thought. "And always one particular item to lead us to someone involved in the disaster. Like a driver's license or a license plate or a street sign. Never more than just a few words or numbers. Just enough to point us in a particular direction. Often associated with a vehicle."

Did this mean we should be looking for a mechanic? A car dealership? A transport company employee?

"We can also take a close look at the make of every one of the vehicles involved in the accidents." Zoe tapped away furiously.

The individual models and product details appeared in columns on the big screen. Sally Corcoran's car was a sedan, as was the vehicle that smashed into the factory gas container. It was a truck that went through the overpass barrier and plummeted onto the freeway. It was a school bus that crashed into the lake and a pickup truck that the kid had been driving on the Mt. Vernon property. Nothing we didn't already know. All different makes and models and manufacturers. Just as there was no connection between the drivers, all from different walks of life.

Will walked back in. I noticed he was moving stiffly, wincing. Still in pain. "We've got the warrant," he said.

* * *

Advance IT was located on the outer rim of the central business district. As I'd expected from a progressive tech firm, the offices were all glass walls and doors, plush carpets, and from the reception foyer, it was easy enough to see through to part of a larger area where workers sat at rows and rows of monitors.

The CEO, Ryan Shelton, came out to greet us once he'd been alerted by the receptionist that the FBI had come calling. I introduced myself and Zoe and presented the warrant. He was a young man, sandy-haired, with bright blue eyes, and a designer jacket that seemed color-coded to match the light, designer stubble on his face. But he was not happy about the warrant.

"What on earth could the FBI possibly want with my company?" he said.

I explained that his firm was not in our sights, but that information on the firm's clients could be useful to us on a case. Reluctantly, he led us through another door and down a corridor to a windowless, white-walled room that held the firm's servers, as well as a command PC unit.

"You can access everything on our database from here," he said with mild irritation. "And any questions, my office is just along the hall."

"It will be a lot easier for us," Zoe said, "and much less of a disruption to you, if I set up temporary remote access and then I can sift through your files, from our office, for the data specific to our investigation."

Shelton seemed relieved by this and said he was more than happy to assist, but his hesitation and the film of sweat on his brow made me wonder whether he had anything to hide.

Later, as we headed back to the UCU, I said to Zoe, "Did Will seem to you to be struggling with his pain this afternoon?"

Zoe gave a slow nod. "Yeah. Deep bruising like that is painful, but as the doctors said, there's always a chance of infection developing. He probably should be having a couple of days of body rest at home, not putting in full-on days at the UCU, especially not after he's had to physically restrain a runner. Not sure how you convince a workaholic of that, though."

"I might go around to his place tonight and tell him just that," I said. "Let him know that the rest of us can deal with this."

Zoe grinned. "Good luck with that."

It was getting late and the others had left when Zoe and I walked back into the ops room. Zoe fired up her monitor.

"Maybe you should tackle this fresh in the morning," I said.

"I won't be pulling any all-nighters. But if I go home now with my brain doing cartwheels I won't relax anyway."

I'd only had a couple of heart-to-heart conversations with Zoe but from those I knew that, as a teenager, she'd run for a while with a street gang whose leader kept getting the group into more and more dangerous situations. Flying high as a college student on a scholarship, she'd left the gang. She was devastated, just a few months later, to learn that one of the guys was killed during a gang robbery and the others were in jail.

Creating an AI with a special designation for policing became a passion project for her, a personal dedication to the kid who'd lost his life.

* * *

Back in my apartment, I showered and pulled on a T-shirt and jeans. I wandered onto the balcony and glanced momentarily at the sliver of the Seattle wheel that I could see from my place. It wasn't like me to be sentimental but something about the intensity of the last few days had brought forth a sense of the fragility of everything.

The lingering shadow of melancholy I sometimes suffered when I thought back on the loss of both my parents, was making its presence felt. I was touched again by the awful dread, as I had been two nights before, of what it would have been like if Will's injury had been far worse, and of what the future would look like if he was no longer around. I'd been determined, since joining the UCU and working closely once more with Will, that I did not want to rekindle the relationship we'd once had. I did not want to feel that sense of loss that engulfed me when we'd ended our romance over two years ago. We'd drifted apart because we'd been more committed to the cases we were working on than we were to each other. He'd once told me that I needed to learn to switch off from the job. I was older and more experienced now – hell, we both were – and I was starting to wonder if I should relax those defenses. If anything was to transpire with Will again, maybe I should at least be open to it.

I decided to follow through on what I'd said to Zoe, and visit Will, persuade him to take a break, and look after his health. Despite my fall from that rooftop, my bruises were nowhere near as bad as his, thanks to the awning that had broken my fall.

At the same time, as I pulled my car out of my building's parking station, I couldn't prevent my mind from envisaging what the morning might bring. The thought that sooner or later we were bound to face another mural, another set of images, another race against the clock to unravel their meaning, was like an all-encompassing weight, pressing down on me.

Chapter Thirty-Five

Every now and then, the constant ache from the bruising would flare up worse, no doubt the result of Will continuing to exert himself. He'd taken painkillers before leaving the office and the pain had subsided by the time he reached his apartment. After fixing a light meal he sat down at his laptop and scrolled through enlarged visuals of the images in each of the murals. He mulled over Ilona's comment that a vehicle was a common denominator in each of the disasters. He pulled up the vehicle product details that Themis had compiled. He wondered about the latest information highlighted by Zoe, that Advance IT was a service provider to many of the people and companies connected to each accident. His eye was drawn to the outer edges of the mural shaped like an FBI badge, and to the letters inscribed in each mural, mirroring the first letters of Edvard Munch's words.

Can only have been painted by a madman.

He wasn't expecting a visitor but his doorbell rang and he was pleasantly surprised to find Nadine standing there when he opened the front door. He smiled, and said, "Hi," but noticed straightaway that her return smile was half-hearted and there was deep anxiety in her eyes.

She joined him on his sofa. "I had a call from Brett's wife, Carol, a little while ago," she said. "She sounded distraught, Will. Not just because he's been so on edge about Vasquez, but because he's been phoning our brother, Luke, every night and not getting an answer, and his flatmate said Luke hasn't been there much lately, he's been out more and more with the guy who organizes those street races. Carol said Brett's been out late, driving around, trying to spot any street race activity, looking for him." Nadine drew in a breath and took a moment to compose herself. "Have *you* heard from him?"

"No." Will pondered what she'd told him. "Carol is worried Brett's going to get himself in more strife?"

"She's terrified that's what's going to happen."

"Have you or Carol tried calling Brett?"

"He isn't answering but apparently that's been the case the last few nights, and then he's been getting home at some ridiculous hour, like 3 a.m., and then up at six and heading into the Bureau."

"So, he's exhausted." Will eased the tension in his neck by rolling it from one side to the other. "Let me try. If he doesn't want to talk to either of you while he's out cruising, maybe he'll pick up if he sees it's me on the line."

"That's what I was hoping," Nadine said.

Will made the call and he'd guessed right. Brett answered.

"Brett, everyone's worried about you and that includes me."

Will had the call on loudspeaker so Nadine could hear but she remained silent, not wanting Brett to know she'd gone there to enlist Will's help. Again.

"You don't need to worry about me," Brett said tersely.

"I know you're worried about your brother but cruising the streets half the night and burning the candle at both ends isn't going to help you – or him. Nor will it put you in the best frame of mind to deal with the internal investigation. I've got an alternative suggestion."

"What's that?"

"I'm going to speak to Detective Radner at the SPD and a few of the agents at the Bureau and see if I can get a combined team together. A group to track down info on these races and the organizers, and move to shut it all down."

"It's hardly in the Bureau's remit," said Brett.

"But it's in all our best interests to put a stop to them. They're dangerous and the illicit race scene seems to be growing."

"The guys who are running them are adrenaline junkies and jerks and they're putting a whole hell of a lot of people in danger. Including Luke."

"Agreed. So, I'll start canvassing for agents and officers to shut it down," Will said, "but Brett, you need to go home and be with your wife and children. They need you. Will you do that?"

Brett hesitated. "Yeah."

"Now?"

"Yeah."

"We'll talk again tomorrow, okay?"

"Okay."

Will ended the call and stared at Nadine. "Two birds with one stone. We'll put together some real action on stopping these races, and give Brett – and you and Carol – some peace of mind about keeping Luke out of serious trouble."

Nadine took both of his hands in hers, her eyes fixed on his. "What did we Rochesters do to get such an incredible family friend as you?"

Will grinned, letting his tension ease further. "Pure dumb luck, I guess."

The doorbell rang again.

"Never rains but it pours," Will said, as he went to the door.

This time it was Ilona who waited on the other side.

Will ushered her in and Ilona looked momentarily surprised when she saw Nadine on the sofa. Will explained what had been going on with Brett, and his idea for helping out with the growing street racing problem.

"I'm also here on a mission," Ilona admitted, "but one that puts a bit of a spanner in the works where your street race team is concerned."

Will shrugged. "Let's hear it."

Ilona made her case for Will to take a couple of days off and get plenty of body rest while his bruising healed.

"I'll second that," Nadine said, "and there's no reason you can't still recruit eyes and ears to suss out the street races with me doing the organizing. We can make the necessary phone calls from right here on your couch. After all, Luke is my brother too, not just Brett's."

"I'm not a work-from-the-couch kind of guy." Will was defiant. "And I'll be in the office tomorrow, but" – he held up the palm of his hand to block any objection from Ilona – "I will stay in my office, or close to it, and I'll make my calls from there, and leave any field work to you and Zoe."

Ilona conceded his point. "Okay, I suppose. At least you'll have Marcia in there to make certain you're pacing yourself."

Will gestured to the door. "Now go and get some rest yourself. I'm not the only one nursing serious bruises."

"I won't be far behind you," Nadine said to Ilona.

* * *

I was parked further down the street and once back behind the wheel, I sat for a few minutes, feeling a pinch in my stomach at the amount of time Nadine was now spending with Will as they shared their concern for Nadine's brothers. There wasn't much doubt she wanted to rekindle her relationship with him.

A few minutes later, Nadine came out the front door of the apartment block, Will walking with her down the short flight of steps to the sidewalk. They spoke for a moment and then Nadine leaned in and pecked Will on the cheek, a tender moment, and she lingered a little longer than was necessary. And then she kissed him on the lips. Will didn't seem to respond, nor did he angle away. The kiss was brief and then, with a wave, Nadine headed off in the opposite direction along the sidewalk to her car.

Maybe my initial thoughts when I joined the UCU had been right. Keep my relationship with Will strictly professional.

When I first began working alongside him again for the first time in over two years, there'd been an awkward moment or two when Will reminisced about our past – the last thing I'd wanted to do – and apologized for the lousy way he'd handled things during our breakup. Lousy as in uncommunicative. His feelings of remorse had come as a surprise to me as Will wasn't exactly the type to be overly emotional, either on or off the job. He hadn't put it into so many words but there was a strong sense that he wanted to give things between us another try at some point.

I'd given a clear indication that wasn't on my agenda but I hadn't expected the spark which still seemed to be there between us.

I'd started to wonder if, a little older and a little wiser, this might be a time and a new phase of life for me, for the both of us, to loosen up and see how things developed. As though to encourage me, my memories took on a life of their own, bringing forth a recollection of an early moment in my burgeoning relationship with Will during our CCRSB days. After work, we'd grabbed takeout coffees from a bar near Pier 57 and Will made a spontaneous suggestion we take a late-night ride on the Seattle Great Wheel. I'd always been pleasantly surprised by this other, little-seen, fun side to him.

The night was still, the cool air refreshing. We marveled at the lights that glittered across downtown Seattle and the luminescence from the Wheel's LED lights glittering across the waters of Puget Sound. We were huddled close together when Will leaned in a little closer and kissed me, and I returned the kiss. It had always been one of my most cherished memories of those early times.

And now, just as I was opening up to that spark again, Nadine Rochester was back on the scene.

Chapter Thirty-Six

Day Five

Will was already in the office when I arrived, and I was relieved to see him looking bright and moving more easily. "I trust you're taking it easy, as promised."

He had been exiting his office, into the corridor, as I arrived. Ignoring my greeting, he motioned urgently for me to follow him. "Zoe's got something," he said.

In the ops room, Zoe's fingers were flying across the keyboard, her head jutting forward, eyes glued to her screen. Marcia and Zach were standing expectantly behind her.

Zoe turned to face Will and me as we came alongside her, and she spoke at a pace to rival Zach. "Sally Corcoran, the drivers of the truck and the school bus, and the man who smashed into the factory, had all had their phones repaired or been supplied new ones by Advance IT over the past two years. A couple of them recently. The others over a year ago."

"Meaning?" asked Will.

"I need to look at those phones."

"Zoe, the car that crashed into the factory was burnt out, and nothing in it survived," I pointed out, "and Sally Corcoran's was destroyed when the train hit. The school bus—"

"Everything was underwater." Her eyes brightened. "What about the truck driver? He died and the crash caused an almighty pile-up."

"But the phone might still be intact," I admitted. Another thought sprang to mind. "There's also the phone that belonged to the boy who died on the Mount Vernon property. I'll get Marcia to contact the boy's uncle and see if he still has it."

The truck driver's phone was still intact. I phoned Detective Radner who confirmed its condition and that it was still in police evidence at his station.

Before I could say I was on my way, he said, "I was about to phone you, Ilona. I've just got off the phone from one of the street cops—"

"Another mural?"

"Yeah." He told me the address. "If you want to meet me there, I'll sign the phone out of evidence and bring it with me."

"You go," Will said to me, "and take Zoe with you."

* * *

It was another alleyway, not far from where the previous mural had been found. After taking a night off, no doubt to confuse matters, the graffitist was at it again, continuing his journey from one side of the city to the other, just as Aiden Sharpe was doing for his graffiti discovery podcast.

We had brought the UCU's camera and Zoe took the shots, uploading them straight away to the mainframe back at the office.

As expected, the outer rim of the mural mimicked the contours of an FBI badge. The images were of a spinning tire, its skid marks creating a circle, a mass of faces surrounded by flames, one of those an obscured face of someone wearing a Dodgers cap, and once again partial numbers from a license plate. And the screaming man, tying it all together.

Radner handed me the plastic evidence bag that contained the overpass truck driver's phone. "You got any idea what you expect to find with that?" he asked me.

"There are connections in each of the accidents pointing to Advance IT," I said. "Phones belonging to victims that were either bought or repaired at Advance. What, if anything, that means, we don't know, and of course, it's just one potential lead at the moment."

"I had a call a little earlier from Agent McCord," Radner said, with a grin, "or, as I'm starting to think of him, the man who never sleeps–"

"He likes to tackle things early," I interjected.

"He outlined his idea about a group of us consulting on these street races. I'm certainly on board, the SPD can use all the help it can get tracking down those guys." He took a breath and gestured to the mural on the wall in front of us. "I look at those images up there, and you know what I'm seeing?"

My eyes roamed over the images and I immediately saw where the detective was coming from. "A drag race."

"It's as though the Artist knew what was in Agent McCord's mind and painted this to mock him."

I felt a shiver as I considered the implication.

My phone rang and I saw Brooke Goodman's name on the incoming caller display. I answered.

"Breaking news," Brooke said. "Aiden and I are standing in front of a brand-new mural."

I glanced about but I didn't see either of them. "I'm already there," I said, "but I don't see either of you."

There was a note of confusion in her response. "Ilona, Aiden and I are the only ones here."

"Where?"

She told me the address, and as she did, I shot a glance at Radner, gesturing to the painting on the wall. "This isn't the only new mural this morning."

* * *

The second mural had an image of a strip of water, interlaced with a broken bridge railing, and a lifeless, outstretched hand. Lying beside the hand was a portion of what appeared to be an FBI badge, mostly obscured but revealing just the last three letters of the name on the badge.

ORD.

The same last three letters were in McCord.

I didn't know if Zoe or Detective Radner had picked up on it but it was clear to me that it hadn't, as yet, occurred to either Brooke or Sharpe. I didn't intend to share the thought at that moment. But there was enough of the eagle in the shape of the badge for them to see it was an FBI insignia.

"I've asked our podcast followers to message with any new murals they sight," Sharpe said by way of explanation, "and this came in at the crack of dawn from some jogger."

"Aiden called me and we high-tailed it over here to shoot some video," Brooke added. "But now you're telling me it isn't the only one?"

I told her about the images in the other graffiti painting.

"Given we know these murals are predicting real events," Brooke said, "showing a potentially fatal accident involving a federal agent is more than just a little ominous. This has to be deliberate." It was typical of Brooke to deliver a question as a statement to draw a reply she could pounce on.

I remained silent. The last thing we needed was commentary from me getting quoted on Sharpe's *One Voice* podcast, creating broader panic.

Regardless, Brooke and Sharpe would be following up on their previous podcasts, reporting on what they'd found, and deliberating on what it meant and whether another disaster was imminent.

And I knew that somewhere out there, the Artist would be watching and enjoying every minute. And planning the next move.

Chapter Thirty-Seven

Detective Radner returned with Zoe and me to the UCU, to join us in discussing, with Will, the possible street race inference in one of the murals. I knew Will had already examined the mural photos that Zoe had uploaded but the anxiety on his face alerted me there was something more.

"What is it, Will?" I asked as Radner, Zoe, and I pulled up chairs in his office.

"The Dodgers cap."

"It means something?"

"It sparked a memory that Luke Rochester is a dyed-in-the-wool Dodgers fan."

My breath caught in my throat. I thought of Agent Don Frankel's daughter in the submerged bus. Frankel had been on the same team as Brett Rochester and Will. If it was Luke Rochester and Will who were subjects in the last two murals, could it be that the Artist was targeting family members or agents associated with Brett?

Will held up his hand, signaling for quiet as he made a call. He had it on loudspeaker and when the call was answered straight away, he said, "Nadine."

"Will, what is it?"

"I remember that Luke was a committed baseball fan and that he had a Dodgers cap."

"Still has it. Wears that damn thing everywhere. Why? What's this about?"

Will exchanged a glance with me. I could tell that he saw no reason to hold back leveling with Nadine. "We've sighted new murals this morning. One of them has a Dodgers cap."

"Okay. So?"

"It also has a spinning tire, skid marks, and watching faces."

"Like a street race?" As realization dawned, she said, "Oh my dear God. No."

"We can only speculate, at this point, what it means but I'm not taking any chances where Luke is concerned. What can you tell me about this friend of Luke's who organizes the races?"

"Nothing. But Luke's roommate might know something."

"What's his number?"

"Will, the roommate has spoken with me before. So, it might be best if I'm the one making the call."

"Okay, ring him now, anything you can find out could help us in tracking down Luke." He ended the call and glanced at Radner, Zoe, and me in desperation.

Radner was incredulous. "How could this artist know that Rochester's younger brother wears a Dodgers cap?"

None of us had an answer.

"Will," I said, "you had to have noticed that the badge depicted in the *other* mural had the last three letters of your name."

He nodded. "But I'm not the only Seattle agent whose name ends in those letters."

"Who are the others?"

"I've already got Marcia checking that out."

Zoe rose, holding up the evidence bag with the truck driver's phone. "And I've got some diagnostics to run on this," she said, heading out to her console.

Marcia passed her in the corridor just beyond Will's office door. There was an exchange between them, I couldn't hear what was being said, but what I did pick up was that it related to the phone. Zoe made a triumphant sound and raced off, then Marcia entered the office.

"Okay," she said, "we have three other agents in the building here with names ending in 'ord'. Ford, Bradford, and Guildford. The first, Mike Ford, is on vacation in California, and while disbelieving of the prophetic nature of what I told him, he's agreed to stay clear of any cliffs or bridges. The second, Jock Bradford, is currently in the hospital for surgery on an old leg injury. Regardless, I've instructed him, and the hospital staff there, to alert us immediately if that status changes."

"And the third?" I asked.

"Tate Guildford. Rookie. Mostly on desk assignment."

"Get in touch with Guildford's superior," Will said to her. "Make certain he isn't assigned to anything outside the building until we say otherwise. And call him, give him the same order not to go anywhere near cliffs or bridges when he's off duty. And to be doubly certain, I'll ask for some agents to keep watch on him."

"I can cover that, with a couple of my officers," Radner offered.

I couldn't hide my frustration. "But none of those are the likely targets, Will. *You* are."

"We don't know that for certain," Will said, "but regardless, I won't be going anywhere near cliffs or bridges either."

His phone rang. "Nadine," he said to us as he activated the speaker again. "What did you find out?"

"Luke's roommate didn't know much but he did know that Luke's friend's name is Luis. He didn't remember the surname but thought it sounded Spanish. And he said this guy was a player in some South End gang and he'd been cautioned by police on a few occasions."

"Cautioned over what?" Will asked.

"The roommate didn't know any more than that."

"Okay, we'll check it out."

"Will, we've got to find Luke, make sure he's safe," she said.

"We will."

As Will ended the call, Radner said, "I'll get my guys to check our records for anyone they've questioned named Luis." He moved into the corridor as he made the call.

I turned to Marcia. "It sounded, just before, like you had some information for Zoe."

"I managed to contact Ty Jansen's uncle at Mount Vernon; he still had the boy's phone and he offered to bring it in. He just dropped it off and I've given it to Zoe to run her diagnostic on it, as well."

"Had the uncle or the boy used Advance IT?" I asked.

"The uncle hadn't but he remembered his nephew had bought the phone from a place in the city. He was able to locate a receipt among the boy's belongings and it was from Advance."

Radner walked back in, his phone still in hand. It hadn't taken long for his officers to give him an answer. "Luis Mendez. Believed to be a member of a street gang. He's been questioned a few times over petty crimes but never arrested. The gang's in the SPD's sights, suspected of being involved in bigger things."

"Has he been connected to these illegal street races?" Will asked.

"The gang's suspected of being involved, yeah."

"You get an address for Mendez?"

Radner nodded. "Maple Valley."

"Let's go."

"Will, you need to take it easy. *I'll* go," I said.

"You stay close to Zoe, checking out Advance IT," he said. "I'll be a passenger, with the detective here driving and I'll organize to pick up Nadine on the way. I'll be fine. We just want to locate Luke so we can keep him away from any of these damn races."

"I'm your partner here, not Nadine." The moment the words left my lips I regretted them.

Will paused, a look of confusion on his face. "Luke is Nadine's brother," he reminded me.

I flashed a look at Radner. "Will's bruising needs to heal."

Radner's expression seemed a little perplexed by my reaction, and he glanced at Will, before looking back at me. "I won't be letting any of us get in harm's way, Ilona."

"Then let me know when you've got Luke safe and sound," I said to both of them, avoiding Will's glare.

I breathed a sigh of relief after they'd left. I needed some space after making that gaffe. Letting my defenses down. Not my style.

"You sounded a mite tetchy then," Marcia said.

"Just concerned about Will."

"Because of his injury? Or Nadine?"

"The former."

Marcia was never one to back away from being forthright. "I'd say it's both."

"Maybe I care about some things more than I should."

"Maybe you and Will need to have a heart-to-heart when this is all over," Marcia countered.

"I think it's Will and Nadine who'll be having the heart-to-heart." I took a deep breath, feeling more fragile in that instant than I was used to. "The truth is, I know it's Will's name being intimated in that mural. That terrifies me and I'm damn frustrated that he isn't taking it more seriously."

Marcia came forward and placed a reassuring hand on my shoulder. "He's worried. He's just masking it. If there's one thing you two are both masters of, it's hiding your true feelings." She took my hand and led me from his office. "Let's just make certain that we stop this graffiti psycho before anything further happens."

I wanted to believe her. I'd never taken on a case that I wasn't one hundred percent determined to solve. But I couldn't shake the feeling that we hadn't been able to avert any of the previous disasters. We still had no idea how the Artist could be engineering accidents caused by such random events, or whether, in fact, they really were psychic premonitions. But if that was the case, and if the future was preordained, then Will McCord was in far more danger than any of us wanted to believe possible.

PART THREE

Chapter Thirty-Eight

Maple Valley was a thirty-minutes' drive southeast of Seattle. Mendez's address was a rundown farmhouse on a spacious block with a large shed and several vehicles scattered around the property. The cars were a variety of models but what they shared in common were the multiple scrapes and dents and the caked-on dirt.

"Looks like Mendez lives here with a few others," Radner remarked as he, Will, and Nadine stepped out of his car.

Will strode forward, rapping loudly on the front door but his instincts had already told him there was no one at home. He turned to a crestfallen Nadine. "No luck."

Nadine took in the rustic surroundings, and the haphazard array of vehicles. "With the mural depicting Luke, and what we know about Mendez, not to mention these cars, I'd say we have probable cause to break in."

"I agree," said Will.

"Whoa," called out Radner, coming up behind them, "you're not crashing that door with that bruised arm." He swept past the two of them. "Stand clear."

Will and Nadine stood back as Radner took a run and swung his leg, kicking the front door and then ramming it with his shoulder. The door, old and rickety, gave way with little protest.

Once inside, the three of them split up, searching through the main living area and the three bedrooms for anything that might reveal a clue to where and when the next street race was planned.

Will was rummaging through the drawers of a bedside nightstand when he heard Nadine call out.

"There's a brochure in here on one of the chairs," she said. "There's been a regional motor show running the past three days in Tacoma."

Will walked into the bedroom. "I guess that explains where these guys are if they're not in day jobs. And I expect they'll be heading back here this afternoon."

Radner approached from the living room. "It still doesn't tell us if and when the next drag race is happening."

Will peered out the front window at the cars scattered there. "I'm no motoring guru but I can tell the Ford out there's been hotted up and looks like it's done a few of these races." He turned to Nadine and Radner. "I brought a few RFID trackers with me for good luck." He grinned. "I'll affix one to the Ford and the others to another two that look most likely. If and when they head off to a race, we'll know. In the meantime, I say we take a break, grab a late lunch, and head back out here later; hopefully we find these guys have come back and Luke's with them."

Nadine didn't look to Will like she was satisfied but she shrugged, not having a better option, and the three of them walked back out to Radner's vehicle. As they did, they heard a motor gunning, and then a Mustang with blacked-out license plates thundered from around the rear of the shed, spraying a thick cloud of dust over them as it flashed by, careering off the property's frontage and out onto the road.

"Quick, get in," Radner ordered Will and Nadine, and seconds later, pedal to the metal, he gave chase.

As they turned onto the road, Will sighted the Mustang in the distance, but it appeared to be stationary. He saw a flash of movement beside the vehicle, a figure, and then a hail of bullets from a long-range rifle shattered the windshield. Radner lost control as he slammed on his brakes, his car spinning off the road and coming to an abrupt stop just inches from one of the thick-trunked spring maples.

From the back seat, Will said, "Are either of you hurt?"

Radner had gashed his forehead, and blood trickled down his cheek. Nadine was in shock but miraculously unharmed. They both turned to face Will.

"I'm okay," Nadine said. She twisted toward Radner. "You're hurt."

"A scratch," Radner said, dismissively. He cast his eyes over Will.

"I'm fine," Will said.

"I guess this is your idea of taking it easy," Radner quipped.

Will shrugged and stepped from the car and cast his vision over the road. The Mustang was gone.

"Who the hell was that?" rasped Nadine.

"Whoever it was," Will said, "I'm worried they're onto the fact I've tagged the cars back there."

He shook off the jolt that had reverberated through him with the impact of the bullets on the windshield. That, and the gnawing sense of horror Nadine could have easily been killed, as could have Radner. He glanced back at her. She was visibly shaken, and gazing out on the landscape, wrapped in her thoughts.

"Let's find out," he said, "if there's a Mustang, and any guns, registered to Luis Mendez, or anyone else at that address."

Chapter Thirty-Nine

On his return to the UCU, Will briefed Marcia and me on what had transpired. Radner had returned to the SPD where he was searching for information on any known contacts of Luis Mendez. Will told us that Nadine, although still shaken from the ordeal, had gone to see Brett at his home, to fill him in on the latest.

It wasn't long before Will received a call from Radner, and he shared the update with us. As expected, there wasn't a Mustang or any weapons registered to Luis Mendez. The farmhouse was a rental and a check on real estate records showed the tenant as Mendez, with no one else listed as living there. Nor were there any other vehicles coming up on the system as being housed at that address.

Gang members, I guessed. Couch surfers, moving from one gang member's residence to another. But for what reason had Mendez fled from the scene, firing on Will, Nadine, and Radner in the process? If, in fact, it had been Mendez. All it had done was draw attention to the farmhouse. Now, an official search-and-seize warrant had been issued and CCRSB agents were on their way to the property. This would be a far more exhaustive search than what Will and the others had undertaken when on the spot. It would extend to the shed and all the vehicles scattered about the grounds.

On a hunch, I had Marcia prompt Themis to compare the partial license plate numbers in the mural to registered Mustangs. There were dozens with those partial numbers but one in particular stood out. A black Mustang that had been stolen just a few weeks earlier.

Will was waiting at the office for the results and whilst we all hoped Luke would turn up there later, it was beginning to look doubtful.

Marcia and I headed out to the ops room. We saw that Zach had come in at some point and was uncommonly quiet, not even sharing banter with Zoe. He was absorbed in the data on one of the PCs at the far end of the console, keying commands and perusing documents.

"What are you up to over there, Prof?" I said.

He leaned back in his chair, pivoting to face me, and then launched into one of his rapid spiels. "There's a question I keep coming back to. Why Edvard Munch's painting? Why the figure from *The Scream*? Right from the start we've been looking for a psychic or an artist who can emulate Munch's style who is worth investigating, but even with Astrid and Lars helping we've so far come up empty-handed."

"Take a breath," I said.

He conceded this with a shrug but his speech barely slowed. "Munch's work fits into the pan-European movement of early expressionism in the late nineteenth and early twentieth centuries, and it's one of the main precursors of that movement. I wanted to run a search of people who follow that movement, and I've been compiling a list of galleries, auction houses, and special interest groups that identify with it."

He swiveled his PC screen so Marcia and I could see the spreadsheet he'd created.

"I've spoken with a number of establishments that specialize in early expressionism," Zach continued, "and they all mentioned a small hobby collective called EAAS, the Expressionist Art Appreciation Society. A group that collects and shares information on the expressionist art world, and advises when paintings and prints are up for sale."

I nodded. "Worth following up on. Do you have the names of the people in this EAAS?"

"They don't have a website, in fact, very little online presence at all. Astrid isn't a member, it's too disorganized and hobbyist for her, but she did have a phone contact for the group's secretary in her files which she's passed on to me. No answer yet, but I left a voicemail message and I'll keep calling because I'm thinking this might be just the kind of thing that would appeal to the Artist."

"Why's that?"

"Because it's a little-known entity. It suits this graffitist, who I don't believe has been open or public about their paintings. Perhaps the reason we couldn't find anyone with this artist's talent, from Astrid's and Lars's classes, is that this person is largely self-taught, and prefers anonymity. And that fits the profile of many graffitists out there. Hiding in plain sight while taking potshots, through their paintings, at authority. This is someone who – we suspect from a young age – enjoyed creating works that depict suffering. Someone who gravitated to the depressive tone in Munch's work. A fan, a disciple, whatever you want to call it. I've come to think of them as the Devil's Artist and they know to keep that dark side of their psyche hidden. But I think as well as that, something traumatic in their childhood fed into this, and more recently, there could have been something equally as harrowing triggering these murals and this obsession with federal agents."

I thought of Garrett Gainsford's military trauma and his tumultuous time with the SPD. I reflected on Leo Vasquez's grief over his sister Olivia's death and his vendetta against Brett Rochester.

From her position in the center of the horseshoe-shaped Themis console, Zoe had seemed oblivious to us as she ran her diagnostics through the two phones. All of a sudden, she half-rose from her chair, pumping her fist in the air. "I don't believe it," she shouted.

"What is it?" I asked.

"I had a suspicion; it was why I needed these phones–"

"Zoe!"

She swung around to face Marcia, Zach, and me. "Get Will in here."

"I'm here," Will said, walking in, having heard Zoe's exclamation.

"Advance IT has installed a hidden mic on these phones," Zoe said excitedly. "Put simply it means that as long as these phones are turned on, someone from Advance can remotely access them and listen in. And I'm guessing someone at Advance has done that to all the phones they've repaired or supplied new. Hundreds. Probably thousands."

Will didn't hide his surprise. "Someone's been listening in to hundreds of people's phone calls?"

"Not just phone calls. There doesn't even need to be a phone call underway. The listener can hear everything in the immediate surroundings of the phone – conversations, ambient sounds like doors opening or closing, kettles boiling, everything."

I'd heard of these kinds of mics and, of course, high-level tech of this kind is used by government agencies for covert ops. But what was this about? And then it struck me. "Whoever's been listening in, knows who these people are, knows their routines, and—"

"What they're *about* to do." Zoe ticked off points on her fingers. "The Devil's Artist knew Sally Corcoran's routine, driving to her hospital shift at the same time every day that week, and that her route crossed the railroad crossing. And corresponding train schedules can be accessed by anyone." A second point. "The Artist knew the same school bus picked up basketball kids every Wednesday and that the road ran alongside that lake." A third. "They knew the factory-crash driver's route on that particular day, and via his phone's GPS could track his movements in real-time. For that one, it's no stretch the Artist was following, and could see the moment the car was about to pass the factory." Another point. "There were several buses on the Interstate that the Artist could have been watching in the lead-up to the gravel truck's crash over the overpass."

"I get the drift," I said, "but that still doesn't explain how they knew the accidents were going to happen."

"Nor how they could have made them happen," said Will.

The fragmented images from the murals filled my mind: the interwoven edges of each of the pictures surrounding the screaming man, whose hands covered the sides of his head, his eyes wide in anguish.

Someone watching. And listening.

"People with psychic abilities can see, feel, or hear things about people, and about future events," Zach said, "but there are also theories about people with a different kind of extra-sensory perception. Psychokinesis, which is the ability to move objects, or pyrokinesis, a psychic ability to cause fires."

"Sorry, Prof," I said, "but if a hidden mic enabled our graffitist to know people's conversations and movements, then what other trick could there be for engineering these events? Zoe, we need to look into all of the Advance staff."

Zoe could be incredibly intense but I'd rarely seen her this impassioned. The realization that all these deaths had somehow been engineered was tearing away at her on the inside, as it was me.

"One step ahead," she said. "I downloaded the staff data, figured we'd need to run it against the people in the accidents and the insurance company and the art student lists." Her fingers tapped over her keyboard. "Got Themis scanning for matches."

No corresponding names or connections were highlighted. Not even the state manager of the IT firm.

"Advance IT has offices in several cities," I noted, "but how many employees here in Seattle? Fifty? Sixty?"

Zoe tapped again on her keyboard. "Sixty-eight."

"Run a search through the staff names for Gainsford, Mendez, and Vasquez."

Zoe tapped furiously. "Leo Vasquez," she said.

Marcia shifted the glasses on her nose, peering over Zoe's shoulder at the screen. "I thought Leo Vasquez was in accountancy?"

"Bringing up his job description." Zoe tapped away again. "Yep, he's an accountant. Finance division. Runs the payroll, among other things."

"Let's go have another talk with Vasquez and with the Advance manager," Will said to me.

As we turned to leave, Nadine strode in, looking frustrated. "That brother of mine has to be one of the most stubborn men on the planet."

"What's he done?" Will asked.

"I filled him in on what happened at Luis Mendez's address. He insisted he was going out there to be on hand after the CCRSB's raid."

I watched as Will mulled this over. "There's probably no harm in that," he said. "None of the gang members are there. Brett can watch as the agents carry out their search. It will give him a sense of involvement in clamping down on whatever's going on there."

"I suppose so." Nadine didn't sound convinced.

"Ilona and I need to pay a visit to Leo Vasquez's workplace," Will told her. "As soon as I'm done with that, I'll head back out to Maple Valley, and keep a watch on Brett."

"I'll go with you," she said.

"Okay. If you want to wait here, I'll call you when I'm on the way back, and we can head off then."

Before Will and I had made another move, Zoe called out to us. "Guys, there's breaking news coming in on the internal comms."

Chapter Forty

The communique informed all agents of an unfolding critical incident. On their approach to the Mendez rented farmhouse, CCRSB agents had sighted gang members hurriedly removing crates suspected to be of cocaine from the rear shed into two SUVs. The gang members had opened fire as the agents took up positions surrounding the property. And then it sounded like all hell had broken loose.

The FBI Special Weapons and Tactics (SWAT) team had been deployed to the scene.

"God, no," said Nadine. "Brett."

Will flashed me a look. "I'm heading out there, just to make certain Brett hasn't got himself in the line of fire."

I looked at Nadine. "We're *both* going with you," I said to Will.

As Will, Nadine, and I left, I heard Zoe quip, "The boss's idea of keeping rested."

She wasn't wrong. I knew how determined Will was to look out for Brett, and how a critical incident like the one at the farm could suddenly escalate into a tragedy. I knew Will was ignoring the pain he was in. We simply needed to make certain Brett was nowhere near harm's way, and if he was, to get him away from it and let the SWAT team do their job.

From the car, I phoned Detective Radner and, as Will and I had been diverted from going to see Vasquez, I asked Radner if he could help out. He agreed to take an officer with him and go to see Vasquez and question him as to where he'd been at the times of all the accidents.

I was acutely aware of an unearthly quiet as we pulled up on the road a little further back from the property's deep frontage. The SWAT vehicles were stationed just ahead, adjacent to the property's access road, where a command point had been set up. We could see the positions that some of the agents had taken around the perimeter.

Alighting from our vehicle, the silence was broken by the lead agent's order over a loudspeaker to the gang members.

"Wait here while I check things out," I said. I sprinted across to the command post, which was no more than an area in the middle of a circle of vehicles, with shields mounted. I conferred with the agent-in-charge and then ran back across to our car. "Brett hasn't been here," I told Will and Nadine.

"I think Mendez is one of the gang leaders and so he won't have come back here himself," Will said. "He'll have sent others to try and load up the gear and get away before the Feds raid, which they've failed to do. What we know about Mendez is that he's a street racer, a drug dealer, and a gang member, so I expect he was using an alias, anyway. Brett will have figured all that."

Nadine wrung her hands. "So, where the hell is Brett?"

Will exhaled in frustration. "Doing the very thing we said not to do. He'll have gone looking for Mendez, by himself, hoping to find Luke in the process."

"He doesn't know where to look, or even who he's looking for," Nadine said.

"He'll go to the apartment Luke shares with that other guy," Will said. "He'll look for clues as to where Luke and Mendez might be, or where Mendez is planning to hold the next race."

"So, we go there?"

"Yes."

"Hold tight for a moment," I said. "When I was over there a moment ago, the SWAT guy told me they're about to storm the property."

Seconds later we watched as the SWAT team launched several gas canisters onto the ground around the rear of the farmhouse. Under the camouflage of the billowing smoke, garbed in oxygen masks and brandishing shields against gunfire, they rushed the shed. I expected a hail of gunfire from the gang but there was none. Just raised voices and shouts and soon after the gang members, hands cuffed behind them, were led out by the agents.

But the gang's leader was still out there somewhere and Brett Rochester was out-of-control, hunting him down.

The sun was low on the horizon and I looked out at a dark bluish and reddish sky, twilight settling. Will gunned the motor and turned the car around, heading back along the country road the way we'd come.

* * *

Luke's roommate may or may not have been a stoner but he had the look, with heavy eyelids, long, unkempt hair, and a laid-back drawl. Even so, his expression was one of paranoia when he opened the door to us, with Will's badge thrust in his face. "Not again," he complained.

"What do you mean by that?" Will demanded.

The roommate's name was Roland and he told us he'd only had a visit from an FBI agent a short while before. "The dude pushed his way in, threatened to arrest me if I stood in his way, and went rummaging like crazy through Luke's room."

"Did he identify himself as Agent Rochester?"

"Yeah, the same surname as Luke. What's this all about, anyway? Don't you guys need a warrant?"

"Agent Rochester is Luke's brother and he simply wants to find him, he believes Luke could be putting himself in danger. You'd want to help us with that, wouldn't you, Roland?"

The young man lost the attitude and nodded. "Well, yeah. I've told Luke myself that street racer friend of his, Luis, is a crazy-ass dude."

"Do you know if Agent Rochester found anything of interest in Luke's room?" I asked.

"If he did, he didn't tell me."

"Roland, would you mind if we took a look in there for ourselves?" Will asked in a tone designed to get Roland onside.

Roland shrugged. "Okay, I guess."

We didn't have to search far. Brett had done the work for us. In clear view among a sheaf of papers were real estate pages and maps of industrial sites and large recreation parks around the greater Seattle region. The kinds of places we knew these street races were usually held.

"Nothing we didn't already know," Nadine said. "The problem is there are hundreds of these. Why did Luke have them?"

Will gestured to a small desktop printer in the corner of the room. "Mendez has been using him as a lackey, I'd say, to run errands, do internet searches, and print stuff off."

"Even if it's at one of these locations, the next race could be tonight or next week," I pointed out. "We just don't know. And after today's events, Mendez might be laying low for a while."

"I'll take these home with me," Will said, "and take a look through them. The larger ones are the ones Mendez will be prioritizing. You need internal roads with plenty of runoff to stage one of these with the flair this guy will want. And somewhere accessible enough to attract his followers. Mendez is a show-off, he likes a crowd. And we'll get a BOLO out for Mendez and a Mustang with blacked-out license plates."

As we walked back to his car, Will said to me, "Leave this with me and Nadine. You should get back to the office, check on the dig into Advance, and get some rest."

"You're telling me to get rest?"

"I'll make sure he doesn't do an all-nighter," Nadine assured me, "and I'll make sure he eats."

Will ignored our concerns. "When we've established the larger potential venues, I'll call the private security patrols they use, and request they arrange more drive-bys."

I stared at Will for a moment. The glare in his eyes told me it wasn't worth trying to argue with him, and I knew Nadine was as concerned about him resting those injuries as I was.

"I'll call you if we turn up anything further on Advance," I said.

* * *

Brett had driven to half a dozen of the larger industrial sites around the city and he'd seen nothing. No strange activity whatsoever. His heart sank with the realization that this kind of random search was a long shot. If he'd hoped to get lucky, then it seemed luck was not on his side. And despite regularly calling Luke's phone he'd received no response.

Until now.

His heart leaped when he saw a text message appear on the display. He pulled over to the side of the road and read the text.

> *Brett, I've gone with a friend to a street race. I'm there now but something weird is going on. I want to leave but I can't start my car. Can you come and get me?*

Luke had been nothing but antagonistic toward Brett for months. For Luke to have made a cry for help like this then, there had to be something very strange and threatening going on. The text message ended with the address of an industrial site that was on the northern side of the city.

Brett pulled out, turned the car, and sped toward the Whitman Industrial Center in Pinehurst.

Chapter Forty-One

Will's phone buzzed. Looking at the display, he saw it was the number for Luke's roommate. He hadn't been expecting a call from him. "Roland, what is it?"

The roommate sounded out of breath. Panicked. "Luke was back in here, but only for a few minutes."

It wasn't the response Will anticipated. "Did he say what he's doing?"

"He was hyped up to the max, I think he was high. He said his friend Luis was on the run from the cops, that Luis had a whole drug arsenal in a shed at his rental property, and he was there when people broke into the house. He figured they were cops or agents, and he took off. Fired shots apparently, though I haven't seen anything come up on the news about that. But now I see there's been a raid on the place. I told Luke to stay in, it would be safer than running around with this mad dog Luis character, that his brother had been here looking for him, but Luke went off again, saying he and Luis needed to blow off some steam, and that there was a race on. He'd only come back to get his car and grab his car keys."

"His car?"

"Yeah, he keeps it parked in the alley behind our apartment block. He usually leaves it here when he's off running around with Luis, but he said he's going to enter it in the race tonight. I'm freaking worried about him, man."

"When was this?"

"About a half hour ago."

"And you waited until now to call me?"

Roland was breathing heavily. "I don't want to get him into trouble, man. I've been pacing back and forth, trying to decide what to do, who to call. Am I in trouble?"

Will ignored his question. "What does Luke drive?"

"A silver Camry."

"Roland, where did you get your phone from?"

"What? My phone?" The sudden change of topic had thrown him. "A place in the city. I can't remember the name off the top of my head. Luke's is from the same place."

"Was it Advance IT?"

"Yeah. That's it."

The Artist had been listening in and monitoring Luke's and Roland's conversations.

A race on.

The Artist had known in advance about the plan for tonight's race.

"Did he say where this race was being held?"

"No. He knows I'm not into that whole scene."

"Thanks for letting me know, Roland. I'll see what I can do." Will's mind raced through the possibilities. His eyes flitted again over the street maps and real estate pages. He checked his watch: 10 p.m. He and Nadine had been so focused on trawling through the various sites that they hadn't eaten earlier. Food had been the last thing on his mind but Nadine had gone out to get them some late takeout from the 24/7 bar and diner a few streets away.

His focus kept coming back to the industrial estates in and around Seattle that had lengthy, wide internal roads for the passage of trucks. These inner roads were often hidden from view from the main roads by the buildings that lined the outer edges of the sites.

There was a sub-culture out there; people liked to turn up and party at illegal races, they'd be given a heads-up about the event up to twenty-four hours prior either via social media or – more likely in Mendez's case to keep it under the radar – via private messaging a few, relying then on their word of mouth.

Luke was out there with loose-cannon Mendez, and Brett was already out cruising the streets, on the lookout for signs of people gathering for a race. The images from the mural flashed through Will's mind. The spinning tires, the skid marks, the faces consumed by fire. He thought again of Agent Frankel's daughter in the submerged bus. Now it was Brett's brother in the crosshairs.

Will had to find that industrial estate but there wasn't time to wait for Nadine. He knew where the sites shown on the map were. He raced out to his car. As he drove, he activated his phone's loudspeaker, called Nadine, and told her what he was doing.

"Will, you should've waited–" Nadine began to protest.

Will cut across her. "No time, and instead of being with me, there's something else I need you to do."

"What?"

"Family members of agents could be among those being targeted. Like Luke. Like Don Frankel's daughter. I'm worried Brett's wife and kids might also be in danger."

"Surely not."

"Let's not take any chances. Go around there, stay with Carol and the kids, make sure they're safe."

* * *

Brett's brow knitted as he approached the Whitman Industrial Center. There was Luke's Camry, stationed on the street, near the entryway. But there was no sign of any activity anywhere. The industrial park's grounds were silent and empty, just the night lights illuminating patches of darkness.

Brett stepped from his car and ran forward to the Camry, keeping watch on the immediate surroundings. The street was quiet. Reaching the car, he flung the driver's side door open and peered in. No sign of his brother.

What the hell? Where is Luke?

He was suddenly aware of a reflection in the passenger side window, a figure looming behind him. Luke? He began to turn but before he could complete the movement he felt a sting to the back of his neck. The effect was immediate. His vision blurred and he felt a heaviness descend on his limbs. He flailed, trying to reach out and hold onto the car door but his hand closed around empty air, and he slid to the ground. His mouth was dry. He tried to fight against the drowsiness, but it was too strong. He was vaguely conscious of the figure manhandling him into the back seat of the Camry.

Before he lost consciousness altogether, he caught a glimpse of the face of his attacker. A face he knew but he could not fathom why he was seeing it here. Now.

And then everything faded to black.

Chapter Forty-Two

Will started with the industrial sites on the south side of the city and began driving past one after another, circling west, heading north, taking a punt that Mendez would avoid the areas closest to Puget Sound. Mendez would want to allow as many roads as possible heading in all directions if he needed to make a fast escape. Will had passed a half dozen potential spots but had seen no action when a text from Brett's number appeared on his phone with the accompanying ping.

Luke's been in touch, needs help. I'm headed there now.

An address for the Rockburn Commercial Estate, north of the city, followed.

Will breathed a sigh of relief. He had a location, and Brett had been sensible enough to contact him. His goal right now was to ensure the safety of Brett and Luke. He pulled over briefly and called the SPD night dispatcher, telling him the address of the street race. The SPD could deal with Mendez and the racers.

He checked the clock display on the dashboard as he drove. 10.20 p.m. The industrial estate was just five minutes away. He pressed down on the accelerator and sped toward the scene.

* * *

He could hear the roar of motor engines as he turned into the entryway to the Rockburn Commercial Estate. Cars blocked the internal street ahead, beyond which a seething mass of people seemed to sway in the semi-darkness. Will turned his car around and retreated to a spot where he could safely pull over. He couldn't see Brett's car anywhere. There wasn't time to phone Ilona or anyone on the team, he couldn't waste a second in locating Brett and Luke. He fired off a brief text to Ilona that he'd been contacted by Brett and would update her once he'd got the Rochesters to a safe place. He stepped from the car, there wasn't any option but to advance on foot, with the spectators' vehicles blocking the action. But this was safer. He was just another anonymous face in the crowd.

The industrial park's internal road was like an enormous rave party in the open, with flashing, ricocheting lights, briefly illuminating random faces, casting staccato silhouettes across constantly moving shapes. There must have been a hundred people, mostly youths. The cacophony of voices was deafening, almost drowning out the roar of engines and the screech of tires that came from the center of the gathering. There, in a wide diameter, lined by the cheering onlookers, were two souped-up streetcars drifting at high speed in a circle. They veered dangerously close to one another before gyrating away, then repeating the cycle, the hoods and sides of the cars sometimes colliding, the grate of metal on metal another thrill for the crowd.

One of those vehicles was Luke Rochester's silver Camry. The other one was the Mustang.

Will pressed ahead, wondering what he could do now to stop this from continuing. He was surprised when the Camry suddenly braked, skidding and sliding as it ground to a halt.

Will ran toward the Camry. The surrounding crowd was momentarily confused, looking on in awe as the other car, the Mustang, zig-zagged away. Will pushed through the crowd and squinted as he approached Luke's car. The heavily tinted windows meant he couldn't see inside the vehicle. He couldn't see anyone behind the wheel. Or anyone in the Camry at all.

Reaching it, he flung the driver's side door open.

No one was behind the wheel.

Sprawled on the back seat, unmoving, was Brett.

"Brett!" Will shouted. "What the hell are you doing? You need to get out of here. Now."

No response. Brett lay immobile but the expression in his eyes spoke volumes. Fear. Panic.

"Brett?"

Brett's mouth moved slowly, his speech unintelligible. A word that sounded like it began with an *R*. Remorse? Remain?

Will reached back, his hand gracing Brett's shoulder. "Brett, what's going on? Can you move?"

Only Brett's eyes moved. Desperately wanting to convey… something.

Will glanced back at the crowd. They were spreading out, most of them gravitating to the Mustang which now coasted to a stop. The driver stepped out, raising his arms and clenching his fists in a triumphant gesture, a cigarette in his mouth, a wild mane of hair trailing his shoulders, and the crowd roared its approval.

He turned toward the Camry, palms upraised, his fingers beckoning the other car to challenge him further. And then he was back behind the wheel, shooting forward, turning the wheel into another high-speed spin and drift, creating another widening circle.

Then, the unexpected. Catching the surrounding crowd off guard, the Mustang accelerated, breaking out of the circle, narrowly missing onlookers, and thundering away along the inner road. Reaching the far end, the Mustang spiraled in a 180-degree turn and charged back, its speed ramping up to what must have been over 100 mph. It then swerved toward the gas station that stood alongside the nearest warehouse, revolving as it did so that it was the car's rear that smashed into one of the gas pumps, shattering it.

Will gasped in disbelief, stunned by the enormity of what was nothing less than a suicidal act. The driver at the wheel with a lit cigarette. The Mustang's petrol tank underneath, toward the vehicle's rear. The sheer force of the impact rupturing fuel lines. The shattered gas pump. A perfect storm.

There was what seemed a long, eerie, silence – in fact, it was only a few seconds of time distorted – and then the Mustang burst into flames, followed by an ear-splitting explosion. Plumes of fire and shards of shrapnel billowed out from the Mustang and the demolished gas pump, knocking down large numbers of onlookers.

Will, only partway into the Camry, was flung back, the searing heat like a dragon's breath against his flesh. He hit the ground and lay stunned, looking up at a night sky lit by the flames with thick plumes of smoke billowing across it.

He pushed himself to his feet. The entire warehouse was quickly engulfed in fire, and another, smaller explosion came from within. The main front wall crumbled. Bloodcurdling screams filled his ears and he saw several human shapes writhing, their clothing alight, the fire fanning out around them in ferocious waves.

He slid into the driver's seat, pulled the door closed, and pressed the ignition starter.

"I'm getting you out of here," he said to Brett.

He gunned the engine, backed up, and turned toward the exit. The crowd had already dispersed and was running from the encroaching inferno.

Will sped out of the industrial estate, spying his car by the side of the adjoining road where he'd left it. He would have to abandon it. He needed to get Brett to a hospital. And where was Luke? There had to have been a driver but Will hadn't seen anyone getting out of the car. But then it wasn't likely he would have, given he'd been confronted by the darkness, the flashing lights, and the thick crowd surrounding the dueling street racers.

From the back seat, Brett tried to speak. Slurring the R-word from before. Remain? Why the hell would he be urging me to stay, Will wondered.

It was then that he heard the click as the doors automatically locked and the Camry accelerated. Too fast. Will pressed down on the brake pedal. Even as he did, the speed increased further, careering through the street, swerving erratically even though Will's hand on the steering wheel was steady.

Will applied the brakes again and wrestled with the steering wheel to no avail.

Brett's slurred speech attempted the gargled word again. It was then that Will realized with mounting horror what it was Brett was trying to say.

Chapter Forty-Three

On my way back to the UCU, I'd received a call from Radner. He'd been to see Leo Vasquez, got the man's alibis for the nights the murals had been painted, and he'd get them checked as soon as he could. There weren't many like Radner, prepared to sacrifice his personal time to pitch in and help the FBI on one of our cases.

It was no surprise to me, either, that Zoe and Marcia were still in the office, working late, or that Zach was hanging around. Whenever the UCU was in the midst of an investigation, the whole team put their personal lives aside and was committed to finding a solution. For that reason, I'd bought a few boxes of takeout pizza back with me.

"You're a genius," Zach said, waving me over to his spot. He wasted no time biting into a slice as he gestured to his screen with his other hand. "I got a call back from the secretary of that obscure art-appreciation society, the EAAS, and I had her send over her list of members. There are more than I anticipated. A few thousand, at least." He indicated a column on the spreadsheet that detailed where there'd been an interaction, such as a phone call or email, from any of the members. It appeared at a glance that most had been inactive for a long time. He leaned in, taking note of some of the names. "I've been scrolling through some of the pages and I'm recognizing the names of a few CEOs."

Marcia looked over at us. "Not so unusual when you think about it. Those guys are often purveyors of expensive art."

"One of them," Zach said, "is that Haven Reinsurance guy. David Handler."

"What exactly does being a member of this art appreciation society entail?" I asked.

"Not much. They don't appear to have get-togethers or anything like that. The secretary is an enthusiast and she sends out a newsletter once a month with news on paintings that have gone on sale. She reproduces feature articles of interest on expressionist art both classic and contemporary."

"Let's feed this list into Themis," I said to Zoe, "and see if it locks onto any names connected to the other data we've compiled."

I handed one of the pizza boxes around to Marcia and Zoe and they tucked in eagerly. All of a sudden, we all realized how hungry we were. But we were all equally aware that it was now late evening and the clock was ticking. Where were Brett and Luke Rochester? Was there going to be a street race somewhere tonight? I pulled up a chair and ate, my eyes locked, first, on the mural that seemed to be depicting a race and a fire, and then on the other mural, the one with the last three letters of Will's surname, and the broken bridge railing, and the dying, outstretched hand. And, of course, the screaming man.

Someone watching.

Leo Vasquez or someone at Advance IT?

"Any ideas on where that bridge might be?" I asked Zoe.

"I've got Themis compiling images of bridges all over the state and drawing comparisons with the drawing." She took a bite of pizza and when she'd finished chewing, she added, "But the wispy, ethereal style of the painting makes it vague for identification."

We knew it was likely that all the accidents had victims with phones with hidden mics. There were no phones featured in the murals. But there was the one common denominator that I'd zeroed in on before. The motor vehicles. "Have you found anything that links the vehicles?"

"I've run through the makes and models of the vehicles involved. All models are from the past five years and what I realized is that they've all got onboard electronic systems with internet connectivity for entertainment and navigation." Zoe held up the truck driver's cell. "This is linked to the truck so that the phone operates as a remote for the vehicle. So, it can automatically open and close the doors. That's routine. But I've been running a deeper check on the extent of its connections to the onboard systems. Got a diagnostic back on that now."

I waited as Zoe scanned the report.

"The phone doesn't just have the hidden mic," she said. "It's been transfigured to hack into all the onboard electronics. And that means it would be the same for the phones of Sally Corcoran and the other drivers, and the Mount Vernon lad."

"So, with remote access to those phones," I said, "the Artist could also connect to the vehicles' systems?"

"Yes." She paused, turning over the implications in her mind. "An IT engineering guru with the know-how could then hack most of those onboard electronics remotely via the phone. DARPA, the Defense Advanced Research Projects Agency, has been developing apps along these lines for years. And I suspect the Artist has built their own – set up in their home, totally separate to the Advance infrastructure. A command point linked to a laptop and not unlike a high-end video game. Using a car's GPS to display the road ahead on the screen. Tapping keys to lock or unlock the doors. Kill the brakes. Disengage the automatic speed lock so that a car's acceleration increases. And most importantly, take control of the steering."

I thought of the surprise Sally Corcoran would have felt when her car braked for no reason and stopped at the rail crossing. Her shock when the doors locked and then the car accelerated onto the track as the train bore down on it. The school bus driver's horror when despite his attempts to keep the bus on the road, it seemed to have a mind of its own, accelerating and steering the bus off the road and into the lake. The Mount Vernon boy's confusion when his uncle's pickup truck sped toward the ridge. The Artist, waiting there, must've coaxed him from the vehicle and smashed his head with a stone before pushing him over the edge.

Not just someone watching but someone listening, planning, following, and then painting the tragic result in advance of setting it all in motion. Not a prophet but a sick mind, an instrument of the devil, as Zach said.

I had no doubt now that the images in the latest mural were of a street race. How many of the souped-up engines there could be controlled by the Artist? The possibilities were horrifying.

"Any luck with the list of members for that art-lovers society?" I asked Zoe.

She checked the result. "No matches with any of the other data."

So, neither Garrett Gainsford nor Leo Vasquez were on the EAAS list. That didn't rule them out, but it didn't incriminate them further either. I sank back into the chair and mentally retraced my earlier visit to Advance IT. It occupied an office space smaller than what I expected, as had Haven Reinsurance. And, like Haven, it didn't have the number of workers that I'd anticipated, given its broad client list and the services it provided. David Handler had told me Haven Reinsurance outsourced its non-core activities. Did Advance IT do something similar? It didn't outsource all of its non-core needs, as it employed Leo Vasquez there as an accountant. But like many of these high-tech firms, it would have a roster of freelancers, called on as needed to cover the services it offered.

I sat back up. "Zoe, we haven't turned up anything with the Advance full-time employees, but what about freelance providers? Add them to the mix."

Mere seconds later, Zoe said, "Good call. They have hundreds of freelancers in several different fields, including IT practitioners."

"Run those against everything else."

I watched the data scroll at super speed across the screen, expecting nothing. We were coming up against one dead end after another. And then, Zoe squinted at the screen, and turned slowly toward me, a curious look in her eye. A yellow box had formed around one of the names.

"A match?" I asked.

"One name," she said. I rocketed out of my chair and joined her, with Marcia and Zach walking over from their spots.

A name that appeared as an Advance IT freelancer as well as in the EAAS membership data. Not the name I was expecting. "What else can we find out?" I asked.

"Themis is already accessing every database we need to put together a profile," Zoe said.

Even as she spoke, my phone buzzed. Nadine calling.

I answered. "Nadine, what is it?"

She told me she'd returned to Will's apartment with takeout, to find him gone, and about the phone call she then received from him. My heartbeat drummed in my ears. Will was acting out of character, driven by his need to protect both Brett and Luke. The badge-shaped outline of the murals filled my mind. What if there was a connection between the images in those last two murals? We hadn't considered that.

"I'll phone Will," I told Nadine, "and I'll arrange to go and join him."

Zoe and Themis hadn't been idle while I was talking to Nadine, and I could tell from how she whipped her head toward me that Zoe had found something else on the name we'd been viewing on the EAAS list.

"Not just an expressionist art fan," Zoe said, "but would you believe, a former applicant to join the FBI."

"What?" I moved closer to her monitor. "When?"

"Three years ago. The application was unsuccessful."

A grudge against the FBI, but not just because they'd failed to be selected for training at Quantico. There was also another reason. "I need to make one urgent call before I go and track down Will," I said to the others.

Chapter Forty-Four

The call I made was to Leo Vasquez. I checked my watch as I listened to the ring. It was after 10.20 p.m. I was betting Leo wasn't an early-to-bed kind of guy and I was right. He answered after just a few rings, his voice bright. I had the call on speaker so Zoe, Marcia, and Zach could listen in.

"Leo," I said, "did you know your friend, Gabriel applied to join the FBI?"

If Leo was surprised to be receiving a late-night call from me, he didn't initially show it. "I remember that. Didn't make the grade."

"How did he react?"

"At first, he was really pissed off but he soon calmed down. That's Gabriel. Always the calm one."

"What happened after he was turned down by the FBI?"

"What the hell is this all about? And now, at this time of night? I already spoke to that Radner guy from the SPD this afternoon."

"It's important, Leo. I know you have your issues with the Bureau but I'm asking you to put those aside for a moment and trust me on this. What did Gabriel do next?"

"His background was in IT, always had been, so he decided to stick with that for a while, took on freelance IT work. And then, well…" I heard him expel a breath. "Olivia died."

"What was the relationship between your sister and Gabriel Vaughn?"

"What is it to you?"

"Leo, you need to cooperate with me. Lives depend on it."

"Lives?"

"What was their relationship, Leo?"

"They had been seeing each other."

"Did you ever mention that?"

His voice rose in anger. "Why would I? What has any of that got to do with her being gunned down by federal agents?"

"They were in a serious relationship?"

"Yes. I always sensed that he blamed himself for what happened, which is nonsense, of course."

"Why would Gabriel blame himself?"

"Because of the stupid game."

"What game?"

"When she was a little girl, Olivia's favorite game was hide and seek. She created a silly, adult version of it that she played with Gabriel. When they were out and about, she would sometimes run off ahead of him, and hide just out of sight."

"And was that what she was doing that evening, when she ran ahead and went into the alley?"

"Yes." He paused and I could sense his frustration. "I always thought it was childish but it was something she loved doing."

I allowed a moment to pass before I resumed questioning. "Leo, is Gabriel into art?"

"He's always dabbled. So did Olivia."

"When did you and he first become friends?"

"I'm not going to answer any more of these questions—"

"Leo, this is a serious investigation and I need your full cooperation. Do you understand me?"

His response was hesitant. "We were around fourteen, maybe fifteen. He came to live in the same suburb."

"And where did he live before that?"

"His dad was stationed on the army base in Tacoma, same as my dad. But I remember he said he and his mother often stayed with friends or relatives."

"The Scanlons, in Buckley?"

"Yeah."

"Because they didn't like life on the base?"

"Something like that. And his father was a difficult, verbally abusive man."

I let the silence gather over the line while my mind joined the dots. Growing up in a home with an abusive parent, something he would later learn he had in common with Edvard Munch.

I placed the palm of my hand over the phone's mouthpiece and said quietly to Zoe, "The school Rosa Estevan attended when she lived next door to the Scanlons. Check the student records, I expect we'll find Vaughn's name on them, and then get Themis to find class photos online from a yearbook, anything of the kind, that might feature Gabriel Vaughn at around that age."

"I'll run a search."

"If you find anything, send it to Rosa's phone, and ask her if she can identify him as the boy she knew."

I suspected there was a whole other side to Gabriel Vaughn. A kid who enjoyed inflicting harm on others and who painted pictures depicting his darkest desires. Maybe that side had then been dormant for many years but when Olivia was shot, something snapped. His other, darker half awakened if, in fact, it had ever been asleep.

The adult Gabriel, grief-stricken by his girlfriend's manslaughter and his sense of guilt, had become the doomsayer again. His hatred spiraled.

"Themis has photos," Zoe said, "of the other, older classes at that school from that time. Gabriel is in them. Contacting Rosa now."

I moved my palm away from the phone mouthpiece and heard Leo's voice becoming more and more agitated.

"What's this all about, Agent Farris?" he asked again.

"Did Gabriel ever tell you where he lived before his father was stationed at Tacoma?"

"He lived for a while in Norway. His father was on a training mission to a US army base there."

"Do you know where Gabriel is right now?"

"No. Why would I?"

"Thanks for your help, Leo, but I'll have to call you back," I said. I ended the call abruptly and turned to Zoe. "Does the surname Vaughn show up on any of the old student lists we have from Astrid or Lars?"

Zoe's fingers danced across her keyboard, and then we waited as Themis crunched through the data. It took mere seconds.

"Sandra Vaughn," Zoe said. "Studied for a while with Lars Andersson, many years ago."

"Gabriel's older sister," I said. Rosa had told us that the boy who lived next door to her had an older sister who was also into art. "She studied painting. And I'd say she passed on a lot of that teaching to her younger brother." Even if she'd noticed her little brother's fascination for death in his sketches, she probably just thought she had a weird kid brother.

In Norway, the family most likely visited the art galleries in Oslo, where an impressionable kid made a connection with Munch's work.

Leo Vasquez wanted to bring the FBI to heel with litigation and public humiliation. Gabriel Vaughn, quite the opposite, kept to the shadows, wreaking havoc with his graffiti and his masquerade of psychic premonitions, again taking up his childhood trick of sketching accidents and then making them happen. Targeting Brett and Frankel along the way.

And Will McCord.

Zoe's phone pinged and glancing at the text message, she said, "Confirmation. It's Rosa. She's identified Gabriel Vaughn's class photo as the boy who drew those sketches. And I've been running a search on Sandra Vaughn. She's married with two kids, and she's been living down in Florida for the past five years, near their widowed mother."

I reflected for a moment on the shock that Sandra Vaughn and her mother would feel on learning that Gabriel was a mass murderer.

My gaze took in Zoe, Marcia, and Zach. "I think Gabriel Vaughn hatched his plan long ago and Advance's clients were perfect. A diverse range of people and companies, including Brooke's employer, *The Seattle Times*, and the college where Astrid Karlsen taught. Hundreds of cell phones were sent to him for repair or replacement."

"All implanted with the hidden mic and the GPS," Zoe added. "When any one of those people also used their phone as a remote for their vehicle, Vaughn could hack into the onboard systems."

I drew in a deep breath. "When he listened in on Brooke's conversation with Aiden Sharpe about the graffiti project, he uncovered the perfect way to communicate his intentions for his twisted game with us."

"The truck driver was on heart medication but the assumption his heart attack caused that accident must have been wrong," Zoe said. "It was the shock of the accident that then most likely induced the heart attack."

My phone rang. I didn't recognize the number but I could immediately identify the laid-back drawl of the voice. "Roland, what is it?"

"Luke's back here with me. I couldn't get a hold of Agent McCord but I thought you guys should know, so—"

"Roland, is his brother, Brett, with him?"

"No. Luke was mugged and his car's been stolen."

"Put him on," I said.

A moment later, another voice, not the laid-back drawl of Roland, but sharper, and anxious. "Hello?"

"Luke, I'm Special Agent Farris. I believe you texted your brother, Brett, a while ago, and gave him the location of a street race. You were in distress. Is that right?"

"I don't know what you're talking about. I was pricked with a needle when I went down to my car, put me out for… I don't know how long…"

"Have you got your phone?"

"No, it was in my car. The jerk that drugged me has got my car *and* my phone."

"Luke, this is important, your brother's and Agent McCord's lives are on the line. You need to tell me, *right now*, where that race is taking place."

Chapter Forty-Five

I tried phoning Will as I raced down to my car. No answer. Neither Brett nor Will could now be contacted. Will told me he'd received a text from Brett. It had to have been sent by the Artist, another lure.

What was Gabriel Vaughn planning? A massive disaster at the street race. But where did the bridge and the water from the other mural fit in?

I was at the Rockburn Commercial Estate within ten minutes.

The area was cordoned off. Fire trucks and emergency workers were everywhere, the night sky lit by the flames. I pulled to a stop just short of the perimeter. People were wandering about on the road, some in shock and being comforted by others, some simply standing and staring at the spectacle.

I saw Will's car by the side of the road. Empty. I got out of my car and scanned the crowd. No sign of him. I tried his phone and his comms again. Nothing. What had happened to him?

I scanned every car in the vicinity. No silver Camry.

I moved toward the burning area. A fireman at the cordon raised his hand to halt me. I could see the smoking remains of the Mustang. I produced my badge.

"I don't expect the driver of the Mustang got free?" I said.

"No, ma'am. They're about to remove the body, as soon as they can stabilize the surroundings."

Luis Mendez and Luke Rochester were the perfect fodder for Gabriel Vaughn's plans. What had his next move been with Will and Brett?

I ran to one of the emergency workers who was directing the others. I flashed my badge, told him I was looking for another agent, and asked whether he'd seen a blue-striped silver Camry. He hadn't.

My eyes wandered over the ring of onlookers, kept back now behind a police cordon, watching the firefighters battle the blaze. I ran into the crowd, frantic, holding my badge high, shouting, asking if anyone had seen the Camry. Several voices said, "Yeah." I zeroed in on one of them, a young woman with pink-dyed hair, tatts, and great big star-shaped earrings. "You saw the Camry?"

"Most of us did. Weird. It stopped dead during the spin-off and some dude ran up and opened the driver's door. Then the Mustang burst into flames and next thing I know the Camry's taken off, almost mowed down people as it raced past."

"Could you see who was in it?"

She shook her head, glaring at me like I was some sort of crazy lady, her eyes then drawn back to the fiery spectacle.

I pushed through the crowd and back onto the main street, to my car.

Vaughn must have got hold of Brett's phone. Vaughn knew Will would drop whatever he was doing to go and help Brett.

Some dude ran up and opened the driver's door.

I could only assume that Vaughn had fled the scene but that Will, for some reason, got into the Camry. Now Will, and maybe Brett, must be trapped in a vehicle remotely controlled by Vaughn.

I got into my car, my hands gripping the steering wheel in anxiety. I cast my mind over the details in the second of the last two montages discovered. An indistinct car crashing and flipping over the barrier of a bridge, the steel girders beneath showing the upper curve of an arch. And the corner of an FBI card with the letters ORD.

Where was the Camry headed? Where was that bridge?

I video-called Zoe and quickly told her what had happened. I watched as she brought up a photo of the montage on her PC screen, positioning it beside a group of photos that she enlarged, one by one, as a direct comparison to the bridge shape in the graffiti image.

"Themis's search has come up with a few similar structures, over water, within striking distance of Seattle. But I think *this* one checks all the boxes. 180 feet high over the water, around eighty or so minutes north."

"The Deception Pass Bridge," I said.

It spanned the gap between Fidalgo and Whidbey Islands, north of Oak Harbor, but to law enforcers, it was also known for something else. A spot that attracted troubled people looking to end their lives, with several incidents most years, so much so that community care groups had left stones along the railing, painted with messages of hope and salvation.

But the crash of a Camry into the icy waters below wasn't going to be another suicide, nor was it a forewarning from a psychic's vision. This would be a meticulously planned, premeditated murder.

"Zoe, I suspect Gabriel Vaughn is on the road, controlling the Camry while following it in his own car. But how the hell is he driving one vehicle while remotely driving another?"

"By switching in and out of a self-driving autopilot. I'll know more when I can see whatever command point he's set up at his apartment."

"Take backup and get over there. You need to find a way to hack in and wrest control of the Camry from him before it reaches Deception Pass."

"On it. Will you be meeting us here?"

"No. I'm heading to that bridge."

"He's got a head start on you, Ilona."

"Yes, but he'll be keeping both vehicles within the speed limit. He doesn't want to attract a police pursuit because of speeding, not until he's within reach of the bridge. Then he'll stoke it up, big time."

"I don't think you can get there in time, but even if you could, what can you do?"

"I'll call you when I get there." I ended the call and gunned the motor.

I phoned Detective Radner. He came on the line, his voice low, in late-night mode.

"Where can I get a chopper this time of night?"

He became alert. "The hospital's medevac, on their rooftop helipad, might be available. Quicker than the chopper from King County that the SPD usually uses. What's going on, Ilona?"

"I need to get to Oak Harbor," I said.

Chapter Forty-Six

The Artist

Rosa held the phone in front of her eyes, looking at the school photo of the boy she had now been told was named Gabriel Vaughn. It rekindled a distant, vague memory that she'd known her neighbor as Gabe. The agents hadn't sent through a photo of what he looked like now and she was glad about that. She really didn't want, or need, to know. She opened up her laptop and navigated to the *One Voice* podcast about the murals, painted as graffiti on city walls, that supposedly prophesized horrific events. She shuddered as she viewed the images.

And now, she couldn't prevent the images of those long-ago sketches from her childhood from leaping into her mind. A memory sprang forth of another sketch, one she'd forgotten about. On the morning she and her mother left that home in Pierce County, the strange boy had given her a sketch of a brick shattering a windshield, and of a skidding car. Later she learned of a brick thrown from an overpass in the same area, that had caused a fatal accident.

A shiver ran through her and she hoped that her memories of that odd child and his sketches would fade again into a locked room in her mind.

Elsewhere

I wonder if Rosa, a young woman now, has seen the murals and heard the news, and the podcast that has been so useful in showing what I am capable of. Does it remind her of the sketches she was given? Does it cause anguish?

I remember when I was very young, playing in the front yard of a friend's house, when I heard the sudden screech of car wheels. I looked across the street to where a small dog had run in front of a car, the driver swerving and narrowly missing the animal as it darted off into someone's yard. My friend, a boy the same age as me, ran onto the sidewalk, concerned for the dog. But I'd simply sat there, on the grass, with an odd thought. What would it have been like if the car had hit the dog?

Later, at home, I'd picked up my sketch pad and my crayons and I drew the street and the swerving car – my illustrations very crude in those days – and I drew the dog being struck. And not just that. I drew the anguish on my friend's face. This tragic alternative outcome sparked my curiosity. What if by drawing such a scene I caused it to then become a reality?

It was just a few months later when my father, my mother, and my sister moved to Norway and I will never forget our visit to the Edvard Munch Museum, or the first time I saw the anguished face of the screaming man, as he looked out on all the everyday horrors of our world. I was too young to fully grasp the subtle complexities of Munch's art but I began to imitate aspects of his style. When I was older there was a part of me that, looking back, understood the perceptions of that macabre figure, surrounded by chaos.

Drawn to news photos of freak accidents, both current and historic, I began painting them, always imagining the face of my friend in that yard, and the young girl, my neighbor, freaked out by my drawings.

But nothing prepared me for that fateful day when the one random event that I could never paint exploded right in front of my eyes, in a Seattle alleyway. And from that moment, I knew that I couldn't be satisfied with painting havoc after it had occurred. Just as I could no longer look the other way and ignore the very forces responsible for this, that had rejected me, believing they were so superior.

Not any longer.

Chapter Forty-Seven

The Camry was driving just under the speed limit on the I-5 N, attracting no undue attention, its doors locked, and its steering perfect. No matter what Will did, attempting to brake or pull the car over to the side of the freeway, he could elicit no response. He had recognized that the word Brett was trying to say wasn't remorse or remain. It was *remote*. Will realized that the Artist was somehow controlling the car. Were they also following and watching? Will squinted at the rearview mirror. There were a few headlights behind him.

I'd wager one of them is the Artist.

He tried calling Ilona on his phone. The previous attempts had failed to connect and he got the same result again. There shouldn't have been a problem with a signal in this area but the bars still weren't showing.

Something else is going on. The signal's been blocked.

If the Artist could remotely control the Camry, then was he also able to impact the signals of any devices in the vehicle? Will knew there was tech like that available and the Artist had proven themself a cyber whizz.

Even though he had no control of the Camry, Will didn't want to take his eyes off the road. He racked his brain for any way he might be able to take control of the car. He briefly turned to glance at Brett, lying immobile in the back seat.

"Brett, I know it's hard for you to speak, but did you see who did this?"

There was a spark of recognition in Brett's eyes but his slurred speech distorted the jumble of words that followed.

"I haven't been able to take any control over the car," Will said. "The Artist has hacked the Camry and it seems he's blocked the signal of any phones in the car."

"Luke?" Brett managed to say.

"Sorry, I don't know where Luke is but it's obvious the Artist stole his car, so I'm going to assume your brother is safe, somewhere."

Will looked desperately at the freeway ahead. Where was the Artist driving the vehicle?

It was when the Camry veered onto State Route 20 that Will knew where they were headed. His mind recalled the images in the mural. The outstretched hand. The broken bridge barrier. The water.

Chapter Forty-Eight

The twin-engine H135 Airbus had a top speed of 156 mph, which meant it could deliver me to the Oak Harbor area at around the same time the Camry would be on the approach to the bridge. I was seated beside the pilot in the cockpit, looking out on the eerily tranquil moonlit waters of Puget Sound when a video call from Zoe came through on my phone.

"We're at Vaughn's apartment," she said, "and all the evidence you'd ever need is right here."

She positioned the screen so that I could see the walls, which were covered in the Artist's sketches and paintings, and photos of his spray-painted graffiti. The sketches were black and white crayon. The paintings were in oils or pastels. Paintings of well-known historical disasters. The twin towers. The San Francisco earthquake of 1905. Wildfires. Hurricanes. The sketches, not as elaborate, rough, most likely from his teen years, were of a house fire, and a stark view, from across a river, of a boy falling from a bridge.

The sketches that Rosa Estevan had described.

I clenched my jaw. These were the visions, not of a psychic but of a psychopath.

"He has a control point set up here on his PC," Zoe said. "He can access any of the phones and hack the connected vehicle's controls. And he's configured his system so he can also operate it remotely, from his own phone or his laptop, which is what he's doing right now. I can see the actions he's taking on the accelerating, braking, and steering of the Camry, unfolding on the screen. Probably has a laptop set up on a dashboard tray extension, within easy reach."

"Can you override his actions?" I asked.

"I'm looking into that now. There should be a way but he's got firewalls set up to safeguard against anyone trying to hack *him*."

"We don't have much time."

"Just as well I work well under pressure," Zoe said but there was nothing lighthearted in her tone.

I didn't respond, I needed to let Zoe do her thing without any further pressure from me. I figured the Camry was no more than ten minutes away from Deception Pass Bridge and that Gabriel, following, was close enough to observe the Camry and ready to send it hurtling at high speed over the side of that bridge when the moment was right.

"Where are you now?" Zoe asked.

"Heading toward Whidbey Island," I said.

Marcia came into view on the video line. "I've been using Themis to run simulations of smashing a Camry at high speed into the barriers at that bridge. It's most probable the car would flip and go over the side. And if it doesn't work the first time, Vaughn can simply turn the car around and try again, and again, until it does, and there's unlikely to be any other cars, if any, on the road at this time of night."

"We have to make sure it doesn't come to that." The scenes in the mural wouldn't stop leaping into my mind, not just as painted pictures but as twisted three-dimensional images. This time, though, it wasn't the bridge and the water that became eerily real. It was the screaming man. His eyes wide. His hands pressed to the sides of his face.

Would that be my face instead, watching Will in the Camry crash over the side of the bridge?

* * *

The H135 landed on the wide asphalt strip of the Oak Harbor PD's driveway and parking area. I stepped from the chopper and Sheriff Ray Contiff, a burly, brusque man, escorted me to one of the white Ford Interceptor patrol cars. I was only half listening to his protests at what I'd outlined. There isn't a word in a thesaurus that could have described how immovable in my intent I was at that moment. I felt like a blinding streak of lightning with a missile-like focus on one thing and one thing only. Preventing this disaster. I could not – *would not* – let Will McCord die. *No.*

I insisted on trying to intercept the remotely controlled Camry by myself. I didn't want anyone else's life in danger, and the simple fact was, I didn't know what I was going to do out there. I *did* know that I didn't want to feel restricted in any way by having someone sitting beside me in the vehicle. The sheriff and a deputy would be of far greater use driving one of the other patrol cars, following me, and acting as backup.

My best option was to somehow forestall the Artist's attempts until Zoe could wrest control of the Camry away from him. *If* she could. But I couldn't entertain the notion that it might not work. Nor could I think about the fact that the minutes were ticking away like a time bomb and there was no guarantee I could be at that bridge before the Camry reached it.

* * *

Zoe Marshall's fingers had never flown so fast across the keys of a PC keyboard as they were at that moment. Gabriel Vaughn had constructed his firewall to repel an external attack, not one coming from someone sitting at his PC. He hadn't anticipated that. He clearly hadn't expected his identity to be uncovered and for someone to be in his apartment, seated at his computer.

Zoe clicked on the security icon, navigated to the firewall, found the on/off selector for it, and switched it off.

"Okay, now I can access his remote command portal," she told Zach and Marcia.

Seconds later, she realized with a groan that she'd spoken too soon. She still could not access the portal. There had to be another, hidden firewall protecting the system. It appeared the Artist hadn't been as cavalier about this as she'd hoped.

"What is it?" Marcia asked.

"He's configured more security than is apparent."

A second, specially built firewall that would have been concealed somewhere that wasn't obvious. Zoe navigated to the PC's control panel and searched through the applications for something that didn't appear to belong.

Think. What would the Artist have named the firewall so that he could locate it quickly if and when he ever needed to?

From the directory, she came upon a port, named with a random group of letters.

Kkvmaegm.

Letters that would not have meant anything to another hacker. But they meant something to her.

Kan kun vaere mallet af en gal Mand.

Could only have been painted by a madman.

"Got it," she said.

But as Zoe interrogated the portal, she realized that Vaughn had also concealed the on/off selector option somewhere else in the server's labyrinth. It would be much more difficult to locate the linking code to that selector.

But if I approach this as though I was hacking the system from an external point, it would be easier, not to disable the firewall, but to find a way to bypass it.

She couldn't help her eyes flashing on the computer's clock. Five minutes had passed and she knew that time was just about up.

By now, the Camry must be on the approach to the Deception Pass Bridge.

Chapter Forty-Nine

I drove east on SE South Pioneer Way and turned left, continuing straight ahead onto State Route 20E, with Contiff and one of his deputies following. I'd set the vehicle's GPS to show the route and the timing to Deception Pass. I contacted Zoe via my comms and gave her my location.

"Fifteen minutes out from the bridge. Can you pinpoint where the Camry is?"

"Checking the Camry's GPS," Zoe said. "Already on SR 20 but not that far ahead of you."

I floored the accelerator pedal, ramping my speed up past 80 mph and activating the vehicle's police siren. A plan was forming in my mind. The headlights illuminated the road ahead and almost immediately a dark blue sedan came into view. A Prius. Was this Gabriel Vaughn? On the night Vaughn had approached Vasquez, Will, and me outside Nadine's motel, he'd parked a couple of houses back, so I hadn't seen the make of his vehicle.

"Zoe, what kind of car does Vaughn drive?"

"Won't take a sec to check records," Zoe said.

I swerved across into the oncoming lane and raced by the other car, trying to glance across for a view of the driver but my speed and the darkness made it impossible. I pulled in front of the car and shifted back into the correct lane. Dark swathes of old-growth forest flashed by on either side.

"Vaughn owns a Prius, which has the necessary autopilot system, freeing him up to control the Camry," Zoe said.

"I've just passed him," I told her.

Up ahead I saw the Camry, and as I advanced, its speed increased, and it darted further ahead of me. "Vaughn's getting ready to crash it."

"I can see he's accelerated. The Camry's doing fifty… sixty…" A longer pause. "He's up past eighty."

I kept my accelerator against the floor, flying toward ninety. I had to reach it. I planned to position the Ford between the Camry and the side of the road, acting as a buffer to Vaughn's attempts to smash the Camry through the side barrier once on that bridge.

In the rear vision mirror, I saw that Sheriff Contiff's patrol car was directly behind the Prius, lights flashing, siren screaming, but Vaughn ignored it, revving up his speed, pulling away from his pursuer, and rapidly gaining on me. He was doing over 80 mph, controlling both the Prius he was driving and the Camry.

90 mph. I was coming up, directly behind the Camry. I cursed the fact that I couldn't communicate with Will but knew he would have spied the patrol car gaining on him and figured there was a rescue attempt underway.

"Zoe, any luck with wrestling control from Vaughn?"

Zoe's reply was terse. "Working on it."

I drew on every bit of knowledge and skill I'd learned in the precision driving course at Quantico.

I figured there was just enough space between the Camry and the edge of the road for me to skew left and then rocket forward, positioning the Ford where it needed to be to prevent the Camry from being swung off. I bumped against the sides of the Camry to edge it a little over the double white line in the middle of the road, to ensure I had more space.

But Vaughn's reaction was instantaneous as the Camry's speed shot up. 95 mph. I matched it, determined to keep the Ford alongside, praying now that Zoe could break through Vaughn's PC security and into his remote-control portal. But I feared that maintaining this buffer would be impossible, the sides of the two vehicles bumping and scraping against each other, a shrill metallic wail erupting from the high-speed contact. Both vehicles now were in danger of being bounced off one another; with all control lost, a cataclysmic crash would be unavoidable. On my driver's side, the Ford continually scraped against the freeway's log railing, and in some places, the rocky outcrop.

I adjusted my earpiece as I told Zoe what I was doing.

I glanced briefly across at the Camry, glimpsing Will's face at the driver-side window, staring back, eyes wide. I could only return the stare with an expression to indicate that I was doing all I could to avert the Artist from crashing the Camry.

I struggled with the steering wheel, my hands closed in a vice-like grip around it. I was relying on the Ford's powerful all-wheel drive and ABS traction to keep it steady and resistant to Vaughn's attempts to outrun or outmaneuver it. My abject fear now was that Vaughn would realize this and steer the Camry into the oncoming lane and across to the opposite side of the road.

Ahead of me, I saw the curve that immediately preceded the first part of the bridge.

We were less than a minute away.

Zoe's voice crackled through my earpiece. "Ilona, I'm looking at an aerial map of the bridge. There isn't enough space between the lane and the railing for two cars."

"I'm going to try something," I said, wiping my brow, suddenly aware that my hairline and my forehead were damp from sweat.

I floored the pedal again, the arrow on the dashboard's speed dial ticking over 100 mph, and as I shot forward, I swung the Ford in front of the Camry. Now, with the Camry right on my tail, I applied the brakes, just a fraction, so that the Camry wouldn't smash into the Ford's rear but just touch it. I had to maintain just the right speed so that the Camry was nosing up against the Ford's rear bumper without crashing it. The two cars banged and buffeted against one other. The Ford Interceptor was more powerful than the Camry so would be able to at least temporarily prevent it from going faster while at the same time not giving it enough space to turn. Wheels squealed as we rounded the curve onto the bridge. I was primed for what I believed would be Vaughn's next move and, as I anticipated, he braked, pulling back just far enough to allow space for him to turn toward the bridge railing. I did the same, braking harder, in just enough time to close the gap again.

We zoomed forward. The Camry braked again, pulling back, I did the same in an instant, maintaining the status quo. Vaughn slowed the Camry yet again, but this time, as though in anger, he immediately reaccelerated, smashing into the Ford, sending it skidding as I applied pressure to the brakes to regain traction while struggling to keep the steering straight.

And then I was steering to accommodate the curve at the far end of the bridge as we screamed onto the road, onto Canoe Pass Bridge, and then beyond that, thick forest flashing by on either side, the road ahead dark, subtly braking to keep the Camry in check.

What would Vaughn do now?

I had my answer the moment the question was in my mind. The Camry braked sharply, skidding, swerving into the oncoming lane, and then charging forward on the wrong side of the road and zipping past me at over 110 mph. A collision with any oncoming vehicle would be fatal but Vaughn didn't need an oncoming vehicle. Crashing the Camry into the trees that lined the route would be just as catastrophic. But up ahead, Vaughn did the opposite. He remotely applied the brakes. The Camry drifted into a 180-degree drag-style turn and then shot back in the direction from which we'd come.

He's determined to enact his painting and crash the Camry over the Deception Pass Bridge.

I braked hard, performed a hurried three-point turn, and gave chase. I saw that Vaughn, following in the Prius, had done the same. He'd unexpectedly pulled over to the side, and as the patrol car with Contiff and his deputy soared past him, he turned and sped off in the opposite direction, repositioning himself behind the Camry.

Deception Pass was seconds ahead of him and I screamed inside, realizing I wouldn't reach the Camry in time.

Chapter Fifty

Zoe was looking at a software-based firewall, configured to block specific types of network traffic.

Vaughn's secondary firewall used static filtering – analyzing small amounts of data against a series of filters. By simply using Vaughn's PC's IP address and protocols, the firewall around the remote access portal was bypassed. Once inside his specially constructed command center,

Zoe issued a series of commands to counter Vaughn's usage via his phone, returning the main control function to the PC.

Icons that portrayed the Camry's dashboard and motoring functions appeared on the screen. The corresponding GPS graphic showed Zoe the movement of the car on the road in real time.

"You've got it," Zach said, watching in awe over her shoulder.

"Yes, but once he loses control, he'll issue instructions to override my command." Zoe gasped when she saw that the Camry was reentering the Deception Pass Bridge. She whipped her head about.

"Marcia, phone Will and put him on speaker. The block on the phone transmission should also have been disabled."

Seconds later, a startled Will was on the line.

"Will, it's Zoe. I've given you control of the vehicle, but it may not be for long. You need to stop and get out. Gabriel Vaughn is right behind you in the Prius."

"Vaughn?"

"Yes, Gabriel Vaughn is the Artist," Marcia said.

* * *

I pressed down on the accelerator, flying over the speed limit with the Ford Interceptor's siren shrieking. I was approaching the bridge but there was no sign of either the Prius or the Camry.

"Zoe," I said into my comms but the only reply was a blast of distortion.

Eyes focused intently on the road ahead, I cleared the bridge and eased back on the speed as I entered a curve on the other side. That was when I caught sight of the Prius in the distance. I ramped up the speed and was advancing on the Prius when I saw the Camry ahead of it.

My eyes widened in disbelief and I almost lost control of the vehicle when I saw what happened next. The Camry veered off the road, smashing at what must have been 110 mph into the tree line that skirted the boundary.

Will! No…

The Prius raced past but I pulled over, looking across to the wreckage of the Camry, enmeshed with the gnarled trunk of an old-growth Douglas-fir. No one could have survived that.

The pressure that crushed my temples was so great that for a moment I thought I was going to pass out. I drew in deep breaths and steadied myself. Shards of moonlight took on the appearance of ethereal mist in the darkness of the woods as I raced across to the wreck. I peered into the ruin of the vehicle and was immediately relieved that I didn't see Will in the driver's seat. I looked around the car and my heart sank as I glimpsed Brett's mangled body, lifeless, in the back.

Zoe's voice, alarmed, broke through the distortion in my earpiece. "Ilona, the Camry–"

"I know. I'm here now. Will must have got clear when he had control but Brett Rochester was in the vehicle." I didn't have to say anything more.

I knew I had to control the rage I felt inside. I marched, furious, back to the patrol car. The Prius had a couple of minutes lead on me but I wasn't going to let that – *anything* – stop me.

Back on the road, I sped faster and faster, past 100 mph. 110, then rounding on 120. The darkness, flecked by glimmers and flickers of light, flashed by.

I saw the lights of the Prius in the distance. I pushed the speed to 130, rapidly closing the span between us, hoping Vaughn wouldn't immediately notice, and wouldn't further increase his own speed, until I was almost upon him.

Vaughn would have to be a madman to advance his speed any further. But then wasn't that what he was?

It was then that I saw the Prius, rounding another bend, begin to shake. It seemed Vaughn had lost control and the Prius skidded, spinning across to the wrong side of the road and into the glare of oncoming headlights. At first, I couldn't see what the oncoming vehicle was, and then, suddenly illuminated by the lights, it exploded into view, an 80,000-pound semi-trailer. It smashed into the wildly skidding Prius, which crumbled and folded under the force of the impact and then rolled to the side of the road as though it was a fly being swatted.

The eighteen-wheeler squealed to a stop and the driver leaped from the cabin, standing and staring in shock at the mangled wreck that lay across the road, moonlight bouncing off its misshapen metallic ruin.

No chance of anyone surviving that.

I pulled over to the side of the road, my gaze fixed on the tableau in front of me. But I wasn't just seeing the aftermath of that collision. In my mind, overlaying one another, I imagined the scenes of all the devastating events that had led to this.

There would be no more mysterious murals foretelling horrific disasters. And the Devil's Artist's final mural had failed to fulfill its prophecy. Except for one glaring image that was seared in my mind. My gaze fell on Vaughn's lifeless, outstretched hand, splayed out through a jagged opening in the shattered remains of the Prius.

Chapter Fifty-One

Aftermath

Paramedics covered Brett Rochester's body and they loaded the gurney into the ambulance.

Will was standing off to the side, his body stiff, as though he intended to remain frozen at this point. Sheriff

Ray Contiff and his deputy were conferring with the emergency workers and several more police vehicles had arrived and were parked along the edges of the road. The police officers were closing off access to the road at opposite ends while workers directed a tow truck removing the wreck of the Camry. A few miles back the way I'd come, the same action would be taking place at the scene of the Prius collision.

Will glanced at me as I approached. I had never seen his eyes as vacant as they were at that moment.

His voice was a croak. "Despite all my years of training, my experience, the resources of the Bureau... I couldn't do the single most important thing of all. I couldn't save my best friend..." Will stared off, his face like granite but his eyes shimmering now as he fought back tears. "Helpless to save him."

Will had pulled the car over to the side of the road and got out, but before he could get Brett out of the back seat, the Artist had regained control of the Camry and it had sped off again, wrenching Will's arm and leaving him in its wake.

I moved in close and embraced him. Words wouldn't come. How do you console someone so inconsolable? Beyond devastated.

Presently, I said, "He was a good man, a great friend, a great brother, always looking out for young Luke."

It was hardly a consolation. Nothing was. And Will wouldn't want to hear me say things like 'you did everything you could'. He wasn't a man who would find solace in thoughts like that. He didn't handle any kind of personal failure well and that, I knew, was exactly how he would view this. His failure.

And that was what worried me.

It was a large funeral, attended by many of the agents from the Bureau's Seattle building, along with Brett Rochester's family and friends. After the service, we walked from the chapel across the grounds to a cottage for the reception. I walked silently alongside Will and Nadine. Brett Rochester's wife, Carol, their children, his parents, and Luke, were just ahead of us. Zoe, Marcia, and Zach were a little way behind, chatting to other attendees. I'd seen and nodded to Detective Radner, Brooke Goodman, and Aiden Sharpe earlier as we'd entered the chapel. Agent Rochester's death, and the story of how the Artist had engineered the disasters that killed and injured dozens, had dominated the news cycle for several days, impacting all of them. But behind those headlines there was a small community of shattered, grieving people much closer to Brett, coming to grips with the crushing reality of their deep loss.

I did not doubt that during the service, there would have been moments when Will's mind flashed back to the time, as a young boy, he'd attended the funeral of his much-loved uncle. That uncle had been killed in his shop during a robbery gone wrong.

* * *

As the group neared the cottage, Ilona trailed a little behind Will and Nadine, giving them some space.

Will wasn't finding it easy to speak, the words catching in his throat, but he managed to say to Nadine, "We may not be more than just friends, but I am that – always your friend – and if you need to talk at any time, if you need help with anything, I'm here."

"I know." Her voice was small.

"I mean it." He reached out and closed his hand around hers. "Brett was your brother and one of my best friends. The three of us…" His words trailed off and he felt a great weight of despair.

"I don't know if I can get past this."

"Brett would want you to get past it, to live your life the best you can, for him, for the both of you. You know that, right?"

"Right." Her voice was strained, uncertain. She cleared her throat. "I keep forcing myself to face the fact that this has happened, that it's real."

Will said nothing but he nodded his understanding.

* * *

Walking a little closer to Will and Nadine, I caught Nadine's eye. "It's been a service Brett would have been proud of," I said.

Even as I did, I caught sight of someone who hadn't been at the service but was standing and watching us from the nearby grove of trees, and now he moved, approaching us with a tentative step. Leo Vasquez.

"I'm so sorry about your brother," he said to Nadine, his expression pained, as he reached us.

She stopped and stared at him as though she hadn't heard. And then she spoke, her voice faint but indignant. "Are you?"

Vasquez grimaced. "I never wanted this, never anything like this."

"Then what did you want?" her voice rose, challenging him. "Your sister's death was investigated and ruled an accident, a terrible accident. You were told this, over and over, but you wouldn't listen. So, what did you want? Your sister Olivia back again? We *all* wanted that."

"I know—"

Will reached out and took Nadine's hand in a gesture of support but she wasn't finished. "So, what *did* you want? Perfection. Well, you're in the wrong world for that."

"I'm very sorry," he repeated. "I had no idea, none of us did, that Gabriel could do... anything like this."

Will remained remarkably restrained. "This is not the time or the place, Leo," he said.

Leo lingered for a moment, as though there was so much more he wanted to say, but then, looking lost, he nodded his understanding, turned, and left without another word.

"Give me a moment," I said as an aside to Will. I walked quickly, catching up to Vasquez. "Leo," I said.

He slowed his pace, looking at me but saying nothing.

"You know what I think?" I said. "I believe you're telling the truth when you say that Brett Rochester came around to your house."

He stopped, glancing at me expectantly as though unsure how to respond.

"I believe Brett asked you to stop your harassment," I continued, "but I also believe you made up the part about Brett threatening you with his gun."

The shift that passed across his eyes confirmed my suspicion. "Maybe I was mistaken about that part," he offered.

"Then if you want to make amends in any way, if you're truly sorry for what's happened, tell the FBI so they can close the door on their internal investigation without darkening Brett's record. Simply tell them what you've just told me."

"Okay," he said.

I nodded, holding his gaze, and then I returned to the others. I would tell Will and Nadine what Leo had said as soon as I had a chance.

Nadine was in conversation with Will, sweeping her arm around. "We stand in protection of all of them, putting our lives on the line to uphold law and order so that people can live their lives in peace, and what do we get in return? Contempt. Accusations."

"Not everyone thinks that way," Will said.

"But too many do."

At that moment, I knew what she meant, and how she felt. I took hold of her hand, an expression of understanding on my face, no words needed, and walked with her up the short flight of steps into the cottage.

* * *

Will's arm was in a sling. It wasn't broken, but the blow his shoulder had received when he'd attempted to get Brett out of the Camry as it had taken off again, caused injury to the tendons around the shoulder joint. Together with the earlier trauma to the same arm, it meant that he needed to give the arm a chance for a full recovery. He'd spent one day in the hospital and had been resting at home since then, and I knew he was under instructions from the AD to take an extended leave. Normally, the Will McCord I knew would have railed against that, but Will had been quiet and distant, doing his stoic thing and keeping his emotions guarded, when I'd phoned him and when I'd called by his place to see how he was. Marcia and Zoe had found him the same when they'd made contact.

He chatted for a short while with Nadine, Carol, and Brett's children, before I noticed him wander alone out to the porch that extended from the rear of the cottage's reception room. I followed. I'd felt more concern for his well-being this past week than I had on many occasions when we'd faced precarious situations in the field.

He was leaning against the railing, and I stood alongside. "You okay?" I asked, nursing a cup of coffee.

"Yeah."

"And Nadine?"

"It's going to take her some time to learn to cope with this."

"You two had been getting close again," I observed.

"She wants to."

"And you?"

"I don't know." He was distracted. His eyes wandered. "We'll always be friends but we've all got a lot to digest."

I nodded. We were comfortable for a few minutes with silence between us as we looked out on the rustic surrounds of the cemetery. Morning sunlight dappled the needle-like leaves of the sequoias that dotted the area.

I'd come to the funeral with Will in his car, and later, when the gathering had thinned, and Nadine had left with Carol and Luke Rochester, I walked alongside Will back to his car. But I wasn't going to let him go home and mope. I needed to coax him to open up about his grief, and to talk. About Brett. About his uncle. About the FBI. About anything.

"I think maybe I need to take you to a bar and get you a drink," I said. Thankfully, he didn't offer any resistance.

"I'll pull over the first bar I see."

There was no humor in his voice, no smile on his face, just a grim set to his features and I knew it was going to take him a long time to deal with Brett's death, or with any idea of beginning or rekindling any relationship with anyone. And that was okay. Maybe it would give us both the time we needed to reset before we began to consider getting serious about each other again. We got into the car, and he started the motor.

"Let's go find that bar," I said.

THE END

If you enjoyed this book, please let others know by leaving a quick review on Amazon. Also, if you spot anything untoward in the paperback, get in touch. We strive for the best quality and appreciate reader feedback.

editor@thebookfolks.com

www.thebookfolks.com

Also in this series

THE PIPER'S CHILDREN (Book 1)

A boy is found wandering in the woods, dressed in medieval clothes and speaking a strange language. When another child turns up, it doesn't shed any more light on the mystery for FBI agent Ilona Farris. Only by digging into her own past will she begin to work out what is going on, and who these children are, seemingly lost in time.

THE WHISTLER'S OMEN (Book 2)

Special FBI agent Ilona Farris faces a problem when a man is murdered in Seattle: the victim was meant to have died in a plane crash twenty years previously. Worse, spotted by the scene is a man dressed in a straw hat and long coat who rumor claims is the legendary El Silbón, a lost soul who stalks the living. Finding out the truth will be tough and perilous.

THE STORM KILLINGS (Book 3)

As tornado season gets under way, the FBI's advanced computer system highlights an anomaly in the casualties. It looks like someone is using the chaos caused by the weather as cover to kill unsuspecting women in their homes. Special Agent Ilona Farris heads into the eye of the storm to catch them in the act.

FREE with Kindle Unlimited and available in paperback!

More fiction by Iain Henn

DEAD SET ON MURDER

Eighteen years after disappearing without a trace, Jennifer's husband's body turns up, yards from her home. Apparently without aging one bit. She knows something is seriously amiss. Fortunately homicide detective Neil Lachlan shares her concerns. But when the case overlaps with a manhunt for a serial killer, it will put Jennifer's life on the line.

THE GREATEST BETRAYAL

Liz Carter is the proud owner of a successful advertising business when she begins a whirlwind romance with handsome airline pilot Callan McKenzie. Yet after his estranged ex contacts him, he disappears without a trace. Liz resolves to move on with her life, but a chain of events has been set in motion that threatens all she holds dear.

FREE with Kindle Unlimited and available in paperback!

Other titles of interest

WHICH CHILD
by Shane Spyre

Sarah is the proud mother of four identical daughters. But one day a woman forces her at gunpoint to give one of them up. Fearing for her life, she complies, and convinces the other girls, aged just four, that their sister was just imaginary. Some years later, however, there is a murder, and it turns out their sibling was not forgotten at all.

FREE with Kindle Unlimited and available in paperback!

THE OTHER DETECTIVE
by James Davidson

Days before World War Two, Polish detective Johann Tal is called out to investigate a brutal murder. A couple have been discovered dead in Danzig's dockyards, and a policeman's bloodied uniform found next to them. Many years later, another detective is called out to a different murder. If the two cases are linked, it spells serious danger.

FREE with Kindle Unlimited and available in paperback!

Sign up to our mailing list to find out about new releases and special offers!

www.thebookfolks.com